HEARTLESS

Why was this happening? Why did no one believe her? When she'd seen Ali in the woods on Saturday night, her heart had filled with joy. Ali was *back*. They could resume their friendship. And then, in a blink, Ali was gone again, and now everyone thought Emily had made her up. What if Ali really was out there, hurt and scared? Was Emily honestly the only person out there who wanted to help her?

She ran cold water on her face, trying to catch her breath. Suddenly her phone beeped, echoing loudly off the hard bathroom walls. She jumped and unhooked the backpack from her shoulder. Her phone was in the front pocket. *One new text message*, said the screen.

Her heart went into free fall. She looked around swiftly, anticipating a pair of eyes watching her from the utility closet, a pair of feet under a stall. But the bathroom was empty.

Her breathing was shallow in her chest as she looked at the screen.

Poor little Emily—
You and I both know she's alive. The question is:
What would you do to find her? – A

Pretty Little Liars

HEARTLESS

SARA SHEPARD

www.atombooks.net

ATOM

First published in the United States in 2010 by HarperTeen,
an imprint of HarperCollins Publishers
This paperback edition published in 2011 by Atom
Reprinted 2011, 2012, 2013 (twice)

A CIP catalogue record for this book
is available from the British Library.

ISBN 978-1-907410-85-7

Typeset in Sabon by M Rules
Printed and bound in Great Britain by
Clays Ltd, St Ives plc

Papers used by Atom are from well-managed forests
and other responsible sources.

For Gloria Shepard and Tommy Shepard

'If I only had a heart.'
– Tin Man, *The Wizard of Oz*

Lost And Found

Ever have something really important just up and vanish without a trace? Like that vintage Pucci scarf you wore to the ninth-grade formal. It was around your neck the whole night, but when it was time to head home, *poof*. Gone. Or that gorgeous gold locket your grandmother gave you. Somehow it grew legs and just walked away. But lost things don't just disappear into thin air. They have to be *somewhere*.

Four pretty girls in Rosewood have lost very important things too. Things much bigger than a scarf or necklace. Like the trust of their parents. An Ivy League future. Purity. And they thought they lost their childhood best friend, too ... but maybe not. Maybe the universe returned her, safe and sound. But just remember, the world has a way of balancing out: When something is given back, something else must be taken away.

And in Rosewood, that could be anything. Credibility. Sanity. *Lives*.

*

1

Aria Montgomery was the first to arrive. She tipped her bike onto the crushed-gravel drive, plopped down under a lavender weeping willow, and ran her fingers through the soft, clipped lawn. Just yesterday, the grass had smelled like summer and freedom, but after all that had happened, the scent no longer filled Aria with liberated glee.

Emily Fields appeared next. She was wearing the same faded, nondescript jeans and lemon yellow Old Navy tee she'd had on the night before. The clothes were wrinkled now, as if she'd slept in them. 'Hey,' she said listlessly, lowering herself down next to Aria. At the exact same moment, Spencer Hastings emerged from her front door, a solemn look on her face, and Hanna Marin slammed the door to her mom's Mercedes.

'So.' Emily finally broke the silence when they were all together.

'So,' Aria echoed.

Simultaneously, they turned and looked at the barn at the back of Spencer's yard. The night before, Spencer, Aria, Emily, Hanna, and Alison DiLaurentis, their best friend and leader, were supposed to have had their long-awaited, end-of-seventh-grade sleepover there. But instead of the party lasting until dawn, it had ended abruptly before midnight. Far from being the perfect kickoff to summer, it had been an embarrassing disaster.

None of them could make eye contact. Nor could they look next door at the big Victorian house that belonged to Alison's family. They were due over there any minute, but it wasn't Alison who'd invited them over today – it was her mother, Jessica. She'd called each girl mid-morning, saying Alison hadn't turned up after breakfast – was she at one of their houses? Ali's mom hadn't seemed too alarmed when they said no, but when she called back a few hours later, reporting that Ali *still* hadn't checked in, her voice was thin and high-pitched with distress.

Aria tightened her ponytail. 'None of us saw where Ali went, right?'

They shook their heads. Spencer gently prodded at a purple bruise that had appeared on her wrist that morning. She had no idea when she'd hurt herself. There were a few scratches on her arms, too, as if she'd gotten tangled in a vine.

'And she didn't tell anyone where she was going?' Hanna asked.

Each girl shrugged. 'She's probably off somewhere fun,' Emily concluded in an Eeyore voice, hanging her head. The girls had nicknamed Emily 'Killer,' as in, Ali's personal pit bull. That Ali could have more fun with anyone else made her heart break.

'Nice of her to include us,' Aria said bitterly, kicking at a clump of grass with her motorcycle boots.

The hot June sun beat down relentlessly on their winter-pale skin. They heard a splash from a backyard pool and the groan of a lawn mower in the distance. It was typical suburban summer bliss in Rosewood, Pennsylvania, a luxurious and pristine suburb about twenty miles from Philadelphia. Right now, the girls were supposed to be poolside at the Rosewood Country Club, ogling cute guys who went to their elite private school, Rosewood Day. They still *could* do that, but it felt weird to have fun without Ali. They felt adrift without her, like

3

actresses without a director or marionettes without a puppeteer.

At last night's sleepover, Ali had seemed more aggravated with them than usual. Distracted, too – she'd wanted to hypnotize them, but when Spencer insisted that the blinds be left open, Ali argued that they needed to be closed; then Ali abruptly left without saying good-bye. All the girls had a sinking feeling they knew why she'd left – Ali had found something better to do, with friends older and way cooler than they were.

Even though none of them would admit it, they'd sensed this might be coming. Ali was the girl at Rosewood Day who set trends, topped every guy's Hottest Girl list, and decided who was popular and who was an undesirable Not It. She could charm *anyone*, from her sullen older brother, Jason, to the school's strictest history teacher. Last year, she'd plucked Spencer, Hanna, Aria, and Emily from obscurity and invited them into her inner sanctum. Things were perfect for the first few months, the five of them ruling the Rosewood Day hallways, holding court at sixth-grade parties, and always scoring the best booth at Rive Gauche at the King James Mall, kicking out less-popular girls who had been seated there first. But toward the end of seventh grade, Ali grew more and more distant. She didn't call them immediately when she got home from school. She didn't surreptitiously text them during class. When the girls talked to her, her eyes often looked glazed over, like her thoughts were elsewhere. The only things that interested Ali were their deepest, darkest secrets.

Aria glanced at Spencer. 'You ran out of the barn after

4

Ali last night. You seriously didn't see which way she went?' She had to yell over the sound of someone's weed whacker.

'No,' Spencer said quickly, staring at her white J. Crew flip-flops.

'You ran out of the barn?' Emily tugged on one of her blondish-red ponytails. 'I don't remember that.'

'It was right after Spencer told Ali to leave,' Aria informed them, a tinge of irritation in her voice.

'I didn't think she was *going* to,' Spencer mumbled, plucking a rogue, bright yellow dandelion that had sprouted beneath the willow.

Hanna and Emily picked at their cuticles. The wind shifted, and the sweet smell of lilac and honeysuckle filled the air. The last thing they remembered was Ali's weird hypnosis: She counted down from one hundred, touched their foreheads with her thumb, and announced that they were in her power. What seemed like hours later, they'd awakened from a deep, disorienting sleep and Ali was gone.

Emily pulled her T-shirt collar over her nose, something she did when she was worried. Her shirt smelled faintly of All-Temperature Cheer and deodorant. 'So what do we say to Ali's mom?'

'We cover,' Hanna said matter-of-factly. 'We say Ali's with her field hockey friends.'

Aria tipped up her head, absently following the path of an airplane high in the cloudless blue sky. 'I guess.' But deep down, she didn't want to cover for Ali. The night before, Ali dropped some obvious hints about Aria's dad's horrible secret. Did she really deserve Aria's help now?

Emily's eyes followed a bumblebee as it meandered from flower to flower in Spencer's front garden. She didn't want to cover for Ali either. More than likely Ali was with her older field hockey friends – worldly, intimidating girls who smoked Marlboros out the windows of their Range Rovers and attended house parties with kegs. Was Emily terrible for wishing that Ali would get in trouble for running off with them? Was she a bad friend for wanting Ali all to herself?

Spencer scowled too. It wasn't fair that Ali just assumed they'd lie for her. Last night, before Ali could touch Spencer's forehead and put her under hypnosis, Spencer jumped up in protest. She was sick of Ali controlling them. She was sick of things being exactly the way Ali wanted.

'Come on, guys,' Hanna urged, sensing everyone's reluctance. 'We have to cover for Ali.' The last thing Hanna wanted was to give Ali a reason to drop them – if that happened, Hanna would go back to being an ugly, chubby loser. And that wasn't the worst thing that could happen. 'If we don't protect her, she might tell everyone about the …' Hanna trailed off, glancing across the street at the house where Toby and Jenna Cavanaugh lived. It had fallen into disrepair over the past year, the grass in the front yard badly in need of a mow, and the bottom of the garage doors covered in a thin layer of green, speckled mold.

Last spring, they'd accidentally blinded Jenna Cavanaugh while she and her brother were in their tree house. No one knew they'd set off the firework, though, and Ali had made them promise never to tell what really happened, saying the secret would bond their friendship forever. But what if they *weren't* friends anymore? Ali could be ruthless to people she didn't like. After she'd dropped Naomi Zeigler and Riley Wolfe out of nowhere at the beginning of sixth grade, she'd banned them from parties, made boys prank call their houses, and even hacked into their MySpace pages, writing half-mean, half-funny posts about their embarrassing secrets. If Ali ditched her four new friends, what promises would she break? What secrets would she tell?

The front door to the DiLaurentises' house opened, and Ali's mom stuck her head out onto the porch. Though normally stylish and polished, Mrs DiLaurentis had thrown her pale blond hair into a sloppy ponytail. A pair of frayed shorts hung low on her hips, and her ragged T-shirt stretched across her midriff.

The girls stood and walked up the stone path to Ali's door. As usual, the foyer smelled like fabric softener, and photos of Alison and her brother, Jason, lined the halls. Aria's gaze went immediately to Jason's senior picture, his longish blond hair pushed off his face, the corners of his lips curled up into just a hint of a smile. Before the girls could perform their usual ritual of touching the bottom right-hand corner of their favorite photo from their trip to the Poconos last July, Mrs DiLaurentis swept them into the kitchen and gestured for them to sit at the big wood table. It felt weird to be in Ali's house without Ali here – almost like they were spying on her. There was evidence of her everywhere: a pair of turquoise Tory Burch wedges by the laundry room door, a travel-size bottle of Ali's favorite vanilla hand cream on the telephone table, and Ali's report card – all A's, of course – pinned to the stainless-steel refrigerator with a pizza-shaped magnet.

Mrs DiLaurentis sat down with them and cleared her throat. 'I know you girls were with Alison last night, and I need you to think really hard. Are you sure she didn't give you any hints about where she might have gone?'

The girls shook their heads, staring at the woven jute place mats. 'I think she's with her field hockey friends,' Hanna blurted out, when it seemed no one else was going to speak.

Mrs DiLaurentis shredded a grocery list into small squares. 'I already called all the girls on the team's telephone tree – and her friends from hockey camp. No one has seen her.'

The girls exchanged alarmed glances. Nerves streaked through their chests, and their hearts began to thump a little faster. If Ali wasn't with any of her other friends, then where was she?

Mrs DiLaurentis drummed her fingers on the table. Her nails looked uneven, as if she'd been biting them. 'Did she mention coming home last night? I thought I saw her in the kitchen doorway when I was talking to ...' She trailed off for a moment, casting her eyes to the back door. 'She looked upset.'

'We didn't know Ali came back into the house,' Aria mumbled.

'Oh.' Ali's mom's hands trembled as she reached for her coffee. 'Has Ali ever talked about someone teasing her?'

'No one would do that,' Emily said quickly. 'Everyone loves Ali.'

Mrs DiLaurentis opened her mouth to protest but then

changed her mind. 'I'm sure you're right. And she never said anything about running away?'

Spencer snorted. 'No way.' Only Emily ducked her head. She and Ali sometimes talked about running away together. One of their fantasies about flying to Paris and adopting brand-new identities had recently been in heavy rotation. But Emily was sure Ali had never been serious.

'Did she ever seem sad?' Mrs DiLaurentis went on.

Each of the girls' expressions grew more and more baffled. '*Sad?*' Hanna finally blurted. 'Like ... depressed?'

'Absolutely not,' Emily stated, thinking about how gleefully Ali had pirouetted across the lawn the day before, celebrating the end of seventh grade.

'She'd tell us if something was bothering her,' Aria added, although she wasn't quite sure if this was true. Ever since Ali and Aria had discovered a devastating secret about Aria's dad a few weeks ago, Aria had avoided being around Ali. She'd hoped that they could put it behind them at last night's sleepover.

The DiLaurentises' dishwasher grumbled, shifting into the next cycle. Mr DiLaurentis wandered into the kitchen, looking bleary-eyed and lost. When he glanced at his wife, an uncomfortable expression came over his face, and he quickly wheeled around and left, vigorously scratching his beakish, oversize nose.

'Are you sure you don't know anything?' Mrs DiLaurentis asked. Worry lines creased her forehead. 'I looked for her diary, thinking she might've written something in there about where she went, but I can't find it anywhere.'

Hanna brightened. 'I know what her diary looks like.

Do you want us to go upstairs and search?' They'd seen Ali writing in her diary a few days ago, when Mrs DiLaurentis sent them up to Ali's room without telling Ali first. Ali had been so absorbed in her diary that she'd seemed startled by her friends, as if she'd momentarily forgotten that she'd invited them over. Seconds later, Mrs DiLaurentis had sent the girls downstairs because she wanted to lecture Ali about something, and when Ali emerged on the patio, she'd seemed annoyed they were there, like they'd done something wrong by staying at her house while her mom yelled at her.

'No, no, that's all right,' Mrs DiLaurentis answered, setting down her coffee cup fast.

'Really.' Hanna scraped back her chair and started down the hall. 'It's no trouble.'

'Hanna,' Ali's mom barked, her voice suddenly razor-sharp. 'I said no.'

Hanna halted under the chandelier. Something impossible to read rumbled beneath Mrs DiLaurentis's skin. 'Okay,' Hanna said quietly, returning to the table. 'Sorry.'

After that, Mrs DiLaurentis thanked the girls for coming over. They filed out one by one, blinking in the startlingly bright sun. In the cul-de-sac, Mona Vanderwaal, a loser girl in their grade, was making big figure eights on her Razor scooter. When she saw the girls, she waved. None of them waved back.

Emily kicked a loose brick on the walkway. 'Mrs D is overreacting. Ali's fine.'

'She isn't *depressed*,' Hanna insisted. 'What a retarded thing to say.'

Aria stuffed her hands into her miniskirt's back pockets.

10

'What if Ali did run away? Maybe not because she was unhappy, but because there was somewhere cooler she wanted to be. She probably wouldn't even miss us.'

'Of course she'd miss us,' Emily snapped. And then she burst into tears.

Spencer looked over, rolling her eyes. '*God*, Emily. Do you have to do that right now?'

'Lay off her,' Aria snapped.

Spencer turned her gaze to Aria, canvassing her up and down. 'Your nose ring is crooked,' she pointed out, more than a tinge of nastiness in her voice.

Aria felt for the stick-on, bedazzled nose stud on her left nostril. Somehow, it had slipped almost to her cheek. She pushed it back into position and then, in a rush of self-consciousness, pulled it off altogether.

There was a rustling noise, and then a loud *crunch*. They turned and saw Hanna reaching into her purse for a handful of Cheez-Its. When Hanna noticed them watching warily, she froze. 'What?' she said, a halo of orange around her mouth.

Each girl stood silently for a moment. Emily blotted her tears. Hanna took another sneaky handful of Cheez-Its. Aria fiddled with the buckles of her motorcycle boots. And Spencer crossed her arms, looking bored with them. Without Ali there, the girls suddenly seemed so defective. Uncool, even.

A deafening roar sounded from Ali's backyard. The girls turned and saw a red cement truck positioned next to a large hole. The DiLaurentises were building a twenty-person gazebo. A scruffy, scrawny worker with a stubby blond ponytail raised his mirrored sunglasses at the girls.

11

He gave them a lascivious smile, revealing a gold front tooth. A bald, beefy, heavily tattooed worker in a skimpy wifebeater and torn jeans whistled. The girls shivered uneasily – Ali had told them stories about how the workers were constantly calling out lewd comments as she passed. Then one of the workers signaled to the guy at the wheel of the cement mixer, and the truck slowly backed up. Slate gray concrete oozed down a long chute into the hole.

Ali had been telling them about this gazebo project for weeks. It was going to have a hot tub on one side and a fire pit on the other. Big plants, bushes, and trees would surround the whole thing so the gazebo would feel tropical and serene.

'Ali's going to love that gazebo,' Emily said confidently. 'She'll have the best parties there.'

The others nodded cautiously. They hoped they'd be invited. They hoped this wasn't the end of an era.

And then they parted ways, each girl going home. Spencer wandered into her kitchen, gazing out the back windows at the barn where the dreadful sleepover had taken place. So what if Ali ditched them forever? Her friends might be devastated, but maybe it wouldn't be such a bad thing. Spencer was over Ali pushing her around.

When she heard a sniffle, she jumped. Her mother was sitting at the island counter, staring into space, her eyes glassy. 'Mom?' Spencer said softly, but her mother didn't answer.

Aria walked down the DiLaurentises' driveway. The family's trash cans sat on the curb, waiting for the

Saturday garbage collection. One of the lids had fallen off, and Aria saw an empty prescription bottle sitting on top of a black plastic bag. The label was mostly scratched off, but Ali's name was printed there in block letters. Aria wondered if they were antibiotics or spring allergy meds – the pollen in Rosewood was brutal this year.

Hanna waited on one of the boulders in Spencer's front yard for her mom to pick her up. Mona Vanderwaal was riding her scooter around the cul-de-sac. Could Mrs DiLaurentis be right? Had someone dared to tease Ali, just like Ali and the others taunted Mona?

Emily grabbed her bike and walked to Ali's backwoods for the shortcut back to her house. The gazebo workers were taking a break. That same scrawny guy with the gold tooth was horsing around with someone sporting a wispy mustache, inattentive to the concrete as it flowed from the cement mixer into the hole. Their cars – a dented Honda, two pickups, and a bumper sticker-slathered Jeep Cherokee – were parked along the curb. At the very end of the line was a vaguely familiar black vintage sedan. It was nicer than the others, and Emily could see her reflection in the shiny doors as she biked past. Her face looked pensive. What would she do if Ali didn't want to be her friend any-more?

As the sun rose higher in the sky, each girl wondered what would happen if Ali dropped them cold, like she had Naomi and Riley. But none of them paid any attention to Mrs DiLaurentis's frantic questions. She was Ali's mom – it was her *job* to worry.

None of them could have predicted that by the following day, the DiLaurentises' front lawn would be

13

filled with news vans and police cars. Nor could they have known where Ali truly was or whom she'd really planned on meeting when she'd run out of the barn that night. No, on that pretty June day, the first full day of summer vacation, they pushed Mrs DiLaurentis's concerns aside. Bad things didn't happen in places like Rosewood. And they certainly didn't happen to girls like Ali. *She's fine*, they thought. *She'll be back*.

And three years later, maybe, just maybe, they were finally right.

1
Don't Breathe In

Emily Fields opened her eyes and looked around. She was lying in the middle of Spencer Hastings's backyard, surrounded by a wall of smoke and flames. Gnarled tree branches snapped and dropped to the ground with deafening thuds. Heat radiated from the woods, making it feel like it was the middle of July, not the end of January.

Emily's other old best friends, Aria Montgomery and Hanna Marin, were nearby, dressed in soiled silk and sequined party dresses, coughing hysterically. Sirens roared behind them. Fire truck lights whirled in the distance. Four ambulances barreled onto the Hastingses' lawn, giving no heed to the perfectly shaped shrubs and flower beds.

A paramedic in a white uniform burst through the billowing smoke. 'Are you all right?' he cried, kneeling down at Emily's side.

Emily felt as if she'd awakened from a yearlong sleep. Something huge had just happened ... but *what*?

The paramedic caught her arm before she collapsed to

the ground again. 'You've inhaled a lot of smoke,' he yelled. 'Your brain isn't getting enough oxygen. You're lapsing in and out of consciousness.' He placed an oxygen mask over her face.

A second person swam into view. It was a Rosewood cop Emily didn't recognize, a man with silvery hair and kind green eyes. 'Is there anyone else in the woods besides the four of you?' he shouted over the din.

Emily's lips parted, scrambling for an answer that felt just beyond her reach. And then, like a light switching on, everything that had happened in the last few hours flooded back to her.

All those texts from A, the torturous new text messages insisting that Ian Thomas hadn't killed Alison DiLaurentis. The sign-in book Emily had found at the Radley hotel party with Jason DiLaurentis's name all through it, indicating he might have been a patient back when the Radley was a mental hospital. Ian confirming on IM that Jason and Darren Wilden, the cop working on Ali's murder case, had been the ones to kill Ali – and warning them that Jason and Wilden would stop at nothing to keep them quiet.

And then the flicker. The horrible sulfuric smell. The ten acres of woods bursting into flames.

They'd run blindly to Spencer's yard, catching up with Aria, who'd cut through the woods from her new house one street over. Aria had a girl with her, someone who'd been trapped in the fiery woods. Someone Emily thought she'd never see again.

Emily pulled the oxygen mask away from her face. '*Alison*,' she shouted. 'Don't forget Alison!'

The cop cocked his head. The paramedic cupped his hand to his ear. 'Who?'

Emily turned around, gesturing to where Ali had just been lying on the grass. She took a big step back. Ali was gone.

'*No*,' she whispered. She wheeled around. The paramedics were loading her friends into ambulances. 'Aria!' Emily screamed. 'Spencer! Hanna!'

Her friends turned. 'Ali!' Emily screeched, waving at the now-empty spot where Ali had been. 'Did you see where Ali went?'

Aria shook her head. Hanna held her oxygen mask to her face, her eyes darting back and forth. Spencer's skin paled with terror, but then a bunch of EMTs surrounded her, helping her into the back of an ambulance.

Emily turned desperately to the paramedic. His face was backlit by the Hastingses' burning windmill. 'Alison's *here*. We just saw her!'

The paramedic looked at her uncertainly. 'You mean Alison DiLaurentis, the girl who ... died?'

'She's not dead!' Emily wailed, nearly tripping over a tree root as she backed up. She gestured toward the flames. 'She's hurt! She said someone was trying to kill her!'

'Miss.' The cop placed a hand on her shoulder. 'You need to settle down.'

There was a snap a few feet away, and Emily pivoted. Four news reporters stood near the Hastingses' deck, gaping. 'Miss Fields?' a journalist called, running toward Emily and jabbing her microphone in Emily's face. A man with a camera and another guy holding a boom raced forward too. 'What did you say? *Who* did you just see?'

17

Emily's heart pounded. 'We've got to help Alison!' She looked around again. Spencer's yard was crawling with cops and EMTs. By contrast, Ali's old yard was dark and empty. When Emily saw a shape dart behind the wrought-iron fence that separated the Hastingses' yard from the DiLaurentises', her heart leapt. *Ali?* But it was only a shadow made by the flashing lights of a police car.

More journalists gathered, spilling from the Hastingses' front and side yards. A fire truck screamed up too, the firefighters leaping from the vehicle and pointing a huge hose at the woods. A bald, middle-aged reporter touched Emily's arm. 'What did Alison look like?' he demanded. 'Where has she been?'

'That's enough.' The cop brushed everyone away. 'Give her some space.'

The reporter shoved the microphone at him. 'Are you going to investigate her claim? Are you going to search for Alison?'

'Who set the fire? Did you see?' another voice screamed over the sound of the fire hoses.

The paramedic maneuvered Emily away from them. 'We need to get you out of here.'

Emily let out a fevered whimper, desperately staring at the empty patch of grass. The very same thing had happened when they saw Ian's dead body in the woods last week – one minute he was lying there, bloated and pale on the grass, and the next he was ... *gone*. But it couldn't be happening again. It *couldn't*. Emily had spent years pining over Ali, obsessing over every contour of her face, memorizing every hair on her head. And that girl from the woods looked *exactly* like Ali. She had Ali's raspy, sexy

18

voice, and when she wiped the soot from her face, it had been with Ali's small, delicate hands.

They were at the ambulance now. Another EMT clapped the oxygen mask back over Emily's mouth and nose and helped her onto a small cot inside. The paramedics buckled themselves in beside her. Sirens whooped, and the vehicle rolled slowly off the lawn. As they turned onto the street, Emily noticed a police car through the ambulance's back window, its sirens silenced, the headlights off. It wasn't driving toward the Hastingses' house, though.

She turned her attention back to Spencer's house, looking once more for Ali, but all she saw were curious bystanders. There was Mrs McClellan, a neighbor from down the street. Hovering by the mailbox were Mr and Mrs Vanderwaal, whose daughter, Mona, had been the original A. Emily hadn't seen them since Mona's funeral a few months ago. Even the Cavanaughs were there, gazing at the flames in horror. Mrs Cavanaugh had a hand resting protectively on her daughter Jenna's shoulder. Even though Jenna's sightless eyes were obscured by her dark Gucci sunglasses, it seemed like she was staring straight at Emily.

But Ali wasn't anywhere in the chaos. She'd vanished – again.

2
Up In Smoke

About six hours later, a perky nurse with a long brown ponytail pushed back the curtain to Aria's little cordoned-off nook in the Rosewood Memorial emergency room. She handed Aria's dad, Byron, a clipboard and told him to sign at the bottom. 'Besides the bruises on her legs and all the smoke she inhaled, I think she's going to be fine,' the nurse said.

'Thank God.' Byron sighed, penning his name with a flourish. He and Aria's brother, Mike, had shown up at the hospital shortly after the ambulance deposited Aria here. Aria's mom, Ella, was in Vermont for the night with her vile boyfriend, Xavier, and Byron had told her that there was no reason for her to rush home.

The nurse looked at Aria. 'Your friend Spencer wants to see you before you go. She's on the second floor. Room two-oh-six.'

'Okay,' Aria said shakily, shifting her legs underneath the scratchy, standard-issue hospital linens.

Byron rose from the white plastic chair beside the bed and met Aria's gaze. 'I'll wait for you in the lobby. Take your time.'

Aria slowly got up. She raked her hands through her blue-black hair, little flakes of soot and ash raining onto the sheets. When she leaned down to pull on her jeans and put on her shoes, her muscles ached like she'd climbed Mount Everest. She'd been up all night, freaking out over what had just happened in the woods. Even though her old friends had been brought to the ER, too, they'd all been taken to separate corners of the ward, so Aria hadn't been able to speak to any of them. Every time she'd tried to get up, the nurses had swept into her room and told her that she needed to relax and get some sleep. *Right*. Like that was going to happen again.

Aria had no idea what to think about the ordeal she'd just been through. One minute, she was sprinting through the forest to Spencer's barn, the piece of Time Capsule flag she'd stolen from Ali in sixth grade tucked in her back pocket. She hadn't looked at the shiny blue fabric in four long years, but Hanna was convinced the drawings on it contained a clue about Ali's killer. And then, just as Aria had slipped on a patch of wet leaves, the acrid smell of gas had filled her nostrils and she'd heard the papery rasp of a match igniting. All around her, the woods exploded into flames, burning hot and bright and searing her skin. Moments later, she came upon someone in the woods screaming desperately for help. Someone whose body they'd all thought was in that half-dug hole in the DiLaurentises' old backyard. *Ali.*

21

Or so Aria had thought at the time. But now ... well, now she didn't know. She looked at her reflection in the mirror hanging on the door. Her cheeks were gaunt, her eyes rimmed with red. The ER doctor who'd treated Aria explained that it was common to see crazy things after inhaling a bunch of noxious smoke – when deprived of oxygen, the brain went haywire. The forest *had* been really suffocating. And Ali had seemed so hazy and sur-real, definitely like a dream. Aria hadn't known that group hallucinations were possible, but they'd all had Ali on their minds last night. Maybe it was obvious why Ali was the first thing each of them thought of when their brains began to shut down.

After Aria finished changing into the jeans and sweater Byron had brought her from home, she made her way to Spencer's room on the second floor. Mr and Mrs Hastings were slumped on chairs in the waiting area across the hall, checking their BlackBerrys. Hanna and Emily were already inside the room, dressed in jeans and sweaters, but Spencer was still in bed in her hospital gown. IV tubes fed into her arms, her skin was sallow, and there were dark purple circles under her blue eyes and a bruise on her square jaw.

'Are you all right?' Aria exclaimed. No one had told her Spencer was hurt.

Spencer nodded weakly, using the little remote on the side of the bed to sit up straighter. 'I'm much better now. They say smoke inhalation can sometimes affect people really differently.'

Aria looked around. The room smelled of sickness and bleach. There was a monitor in the corner tracking

22

Spencer's vital signs, and a small chrome sink with stacks of boxes of surgical gloves in the corner. The walls were wasabi green, and next to the floral-curtained window was a big poster explaining how to self-administer the monthly breast exam. Predictably, some kid had drawn a penis next to the woman's boob.

Emily was perched on a child-size chair near the window, her reddish-blond hair tangled, her thin lips cracked. She shifted uncomfortably, her broad swimmer's body too big for the seat. Hanna was by the door, leaning against a sign proclaiming that all hospital employees must wear gloves. Her hazel eyes were glazed and vacant. She looked even frailer than usual, her skinny, dark-denim jeans hanging loosely on her hips.

Wordlessly, Aria pulled Ali's flag from her yak-fur bag and spread it on Spencer's bed. Everyone moved in and stared. Shiny silver doodles covered the fabric. There was a Chanel logo, a Louis Vuitton luggage pattern, and Ali's name in big bubble letters. A stone wishing well, complete with an A-frame roof and crank, was in the corner. Aria traced the outline of the well with her finger. She didn't see any glaring, vital clues here about what might have happened to Ali the night she was killed. This was the same kind of stuff everyone drew on their Time Capsule flags.

Spencer touched the edge of the fabric. 'I forgot Ali made bubble letters like that.'

Hanna shivered. 'Just seeing Ali's writing makes me think she's here with us.'

Everyone raised their heads, exchanging a spooked glance. It was obvious they were all thinking the same

23

thing. *Just like she was with us in the woods a few hours ago.*

At that, they all spoke at once. 'We've got to—' Aria blurted.

'What did we—' Hanna whispered.

'The doctor said—' Spencer hissed a half-second later. They all stopped and looked at one another, their cheeks as pale as the pillowcases behind Spencer's head.

It was Emily who spoke next. 'We've got to do something, guys. Ali is *out there*. We need to figure out where she went. Has anyone heard anything about people looking for her in the woods? I told the cops we saw her, but they just stood there!'

Aria's heart flipped. Spencer looked incredulous. 'You told the cops?' she repeated, pushing a strand of dirty blond hair out of her eyes.

'Of course I did!' Emily whispered.

'But ... Emily ...'

'What?' Emily snapped. She glared at Spencer crazily, as if there was a unicorn horn growing out of her forehead.

'Em, it was just a hallucination. The doctors said so. Ali's *dead*.'

Emily's eyes boggled. 'But we *all* saw her, didn't we? Are you saying we all had the exact same hallucination?'

Spencer stared unblinking at Emily. A few tense seconds passed. Outside the room, a beeper went off. A hospital bed with a squeaky wheel rolled down the hall.

Emily let out a whimper. Her cheeks had turned bright pink. She turned to Hanna and Aria. 'You guys think Ali was real, right?'

'It *could* have been Ali, I guess,' Aria said, sinking into

24

a spare wheelchair by the tiny bathroom. 'But, Em, the doctor told me it was smoke inhalation. It makes sense. How else could she have just vanished after the fire?'

'Yeah,' Hanna said weakly. 'And where would she have been hiding all this time?'

Emily slapped her arms to her sides violently. The IV pole next to her rattled. 'Hanna, you said you saw Ali standing over you in your hospital bed the last time you were here. Maybe it really *was* her!'

Hanna fiddled with the high heel of her suede boot, looking uncomfortable.

'Hanna was in a coma when she saw Ali,' Spencer jumped in. 'It was obviously a dream.'

Undaunted, Emily pointed at Aria. 'You pulled someone out of the woods last night. If it wasn't Ali, then who was it?'

Aria shrugged, running her hands along the spokes on one of the wheelchair's wheels. Out the big window, the sun was just coming up. There was a line of shiny BMWs, Mercedes, and Audis in the hospital parking lot. It was amazing how normal everything looked after such a crazy night. 'I don't know,' she admitted. 'The woods were so dark. And ... oh *shit*.' She dug in the inner pocket of her bag. 'I found this last night.'

She opened her palm and showed them the familiar-looking Rosewood Day class ring with a bright blue stone. The inscription on the inside of the band said IAN THOMAS. When they'd discovered Ian's supposedly dead body in the woods last week, the ring had been on Ian's finger. 'It was just lying there in the dirt,' she explained. 'I don't know how the cops didn't find it.'

25

Emily gasped. Spencer looked confused. Hanna snatched the ring from Aria's palm and held it to the light above Spencer's bed. 'Maybe it fell off Ian's finger when he escaped?'

'What should we do with it?' Emily asked. 'Turn it in to the cops?'

'Definitely not,' Spencer said. 'It seems a little convenient that we see Ian's body in the woods, make the cops search the place, they find nothing, and then *voilà*! We find a ring just like that. It makes us look suspicious. You probably shouldn't have picked it up at all. It's evidence.'

Aria crossed her arms over her Fair Isle sweater. 'How was *I* supposed to know that? So what should I do? Put it back where I found it?'

'No,' Spencer instructed. 'The cops will be mobbing those woods again because of the fire. They might notice you putting it back and ask questions. Just hold on to it for now, I guess.'

Emily shifted impatiently in the little chair. 'You saw Ali after you found the ring. Right, Aria?'

'I'm not sure,' Aria admitted. She tried to think about those frantic minutes in the woods. They were growing blurrier and blurrier. 'I never actually *touched* her ...'

Emily stood up. 'What is wrong with you guys? Why do you suddenly not believe what we saw?'

'Em,' Spencer said gently. 'You're getting really emotional.'

'I am not!' Emily cried. Her cheeks flushed bright pink, making her freckles stand out.

They were interrupted by a loud, squawking alarm in

26

an adjacent room. Nurses yelled. There were frantic foot-steps. A sick feeling welled in Aria's stomach. She wondered if it was the alarm warning that someone was dying.

A few moments later, the wing fell silent again. Spencer cleared her throat. 'The most important thing is figuring out who set that fire. *That's* what the cops need to concentrate on right now. Someone tried to kill us last night.'

'Not just someone,' Hanna whispered. '*Them.*'

Spencer looked at Aria. 'We got in touch with Ian in the barn. He told us everything. He's sure Jason and Wilden did it. Everything we talked about last night is true, and they're definitely out to keep us quiet.'

Aria's chest heaved, remembering something else. 'When I was in the woods, I saw someone set the fire.'

Spencer sat up even more, her eyes saucers. '*What?*'

'Did you see their face?' Hanna exclaimed.

'I don't know.' Aria shut her eyes, calling back the hor-rible memory. Moments after she'd found Ian's ring, she'd seen someone skulking through the woods only a few paces ahead of her, his hood pulled tight and his face in the shadows. Instantly, she felt in her bones that it was someone she knew. When she realized what he was doing, her limbs froze. She felt powerless to stop him. In seconds, the flames were speeding along the forest floor, making a hungry beeline for her feet.

She felt her friends' stares, waiting for her answer. 'Whoever it was had a hood on,' Aria admitted. 'But I'm pretty sure it was ...'

Then she trailed off at the sound of a loud, long creak.

27

Slowly, the door to Spencer's hospital room swung open. A figure emerged in the doorway, his body backlit in the bright hall. When Aria saw his face, her heart jumped to her throat. *Don't pass out*, she told herself, instantly feeling woozy. It was one of the people A had warned them about. The person Aria was almost certain she'd seen in the woods. One of Ali's killers.

Officer Darren Wilden.

'Hello, girls.' Wilden strutted through the door. His green eyes were bright, and his handsome, angular face was chapped from the cold. His Rosewood police uniform fit him snugly, showing off how in shape he was.

Then he paused at the edge of Spencer's bed, finally noticing the girls' unwelcoming expressions. 'What?'

They exchanged terrified glances. Finally, Spencer cleared her throat. 'We know what you did.'

Wilden leaned against the bed frame, careful not to bump into Spencer's IV fluids. 'Excuse me?'

'I just called for the nurse,' Spencer said in a louder, more projected voice, the one she often used when she was on stage for the Rosewood Day drama club. 'She'll call security before you can hurt us. We know you set that fire. And we know *why*.'

Deep creases etched Wilden's forehead. A vein bulged in his neck. Aria's heart beat so loudly it drowned out all the other sounds in the room. No one moved. The longer Wilden glared at them, the tenser Aria felt.

Finally, Wilden shifted his weight. 'The fire in the *woods*?' He let out a dubious sniff. 'Are you serious?'

'I saw you buying propane at Home Depot,' Hanna said shakily, her shoulders rigid. 'You were putting three jugs into the car, easily enough to burn those woods. And why weren't you on the scene after the fire? Every other Rosewood cop was.'

'I saw your car speeding *away* from Spencer's house,' Emily piped up, curling her knees into her chest. 'Like you were fleeing the scene of the crime.'

Aria sneaked a peek at Emily, uncertain. She hadn't noticed a cop car leaving Spencer's house last night.

Wilden leaned against the little metal sink in the corner. 'Girls. *Why* would I set fire to those woods?'

'You were covering up what you did to Ali,' Spencer said. 'You and Jason.'

Emily turned to Spencer. 'He didn't *do* anything to Ali. Ali's alive.'

Wilden jerked and glanced at Emily for a moment. Then he appraised the other girls, a look of betrayal on his face. 'You really believe *I* tried to hurt you?' he asked them. The girls nodded almost imperceptibly. Wilden shook his head. 'But I'm trying to *help* you!' When there was still no response, he sighed. 'Jesus. Fine. I was with my uncle last night when the fire broke out. I lived with him in high school, and he's really sick.' He shoved his hands into his jacket pockets and whipped out a piece of paper. 'Here.'

Aria and the others leaned over. It was a receipt from CVS. 'I was picking up a prescription for my uncle at nine fifty-seven, and I heard the fire started around ten,' Wilden said. 'I'm probably even on the drugstore's security camera. How could I be in two places at once?'

The room suddenly smelled pungently of Wilden's

29

musky cologne, making Aria woozy. Was it possible Wilden *wasn't* the guy she'd seen in the woods lighting the fire?

'And as for the propane,' Wilden went on, touching the large bouquet of flowers that sat on Spencer's nightstand, 'Jason DiLaurentis asked me to buy it for his lake house in the Poconos. He's been busy, and we're old friends, so I said I'd do it for him.'

Aria glanced at the others, taken aback by Wilden's nonchalance. Last night, finding out that Jason and Wilden were friends had seemed like a huge breakthrough, a secret busted open. Now, in the light of day, with his open admission, it didn't seem to matter very much at all.

'And as for what Jason and I did to Alison ...' Wilden trailed off, stopping by a little tray on wheels that held a small pitcher of water and two foam cups. He looked dumbstruck. 'It's crazy to think I'd hurt her. And Jason's her brother! You really think he's capable of that?'

Aria opened her mouth to protest. Last night, Emily had found a sign-in ledger from when the Radley was a mental hospital with Jason DiLaurentis's name all through it. New A had also teased Aria that Jason was hiding something – possibly about issues with Ali – and tipped off Emily that Jenna and Jason were fighting in Jenna's window. Aria hadn't wanted to believe that Jason was guilty – she'd gone on a few dates with him the week before, fulfilling a longtime crush – but Jason had flown off the handle when Aria had gone to his apartment in Yarmouth on Friday.

Wilden was shaking his head with utter disbelief. He seemed so blindsided by all this, which made Aria wonder if anything A had led them to believe was even remotely true. She gazed questioningly at her friends. Their faces were laced with doubt, too.

Wilden shut Spencer's door, then turned around and glared at them. 'Let me guess,' he said in a low voice. 'Did your New A plant these ideas in your heads?'

'A is *real*,' Emily insisted. Time and again, Wilden had insisted that New A was nothing more than a copycat. 'A took pictures of you, too,' she went on. She rifled through her pocket, pulled out her phone, and scrolled to the picture message of Wilden going to confession. Aria caught sight of A's accompanying note: *What's he so guilty about?* 'See?' Emily dangled it under his nose.

Wilden stared at the screen. His expression didn't change. 'I didn't know it was a crime to go to church.'

Scowling, Emily stuffed her phone back into her swim bag. A long pause followed. Wilden pinched the flap of skin at the bridge of his long, sloped nose. It seemed like all the air in the room had seeped out the windows. 'Look. I need to tell you what I *really* came in here for.' His irises were so dark they looked black. 'You girls have to stop saying you saw Alison.'

Everyone exchanged a startled glance. Spencer looked a bit vindicated, raising a perfectly arched eyebrow as if to say, *I told you so*. Predictably, Emily was the first to speak. 'You want us to *lie*?'

'You *didn't* see her.' Wilden's voice was gruff. 'If you keep saying you did, it's going to bring a lot of unwanted

31

attention on you. You think the backlash was bad when you said you saw Ian's body? This will be ten times worse.'

Aria shifted her weight, fiddling with the cuff of her hooded sweater. Wilden was speaking to them like he was a South Philly cop and they were meth dealers. But what had they done that was so wrong?

'This isn't fair,' Emily protested. 'She needs our help.'

Wilden raised his hands to the white popcorn ceiling in defeat. His sleeves were rolled to his elbows, revealing a tattoo of an eight-pointed star. Emily was glancing at the star too. From her narrowed eyes and wrinkled nose, Aria guessed she wasn't a fan.

'I'm going to tell you something that's supposed to be top secret,' Wilden said, lowering his voice. 'The DNA results for the body the workers found in the hole are at the station. It's a perfect match for Alison, girls. She's dead. So do what I say, okay? I really *am* looking out for your best interest.'

At that, he flipped open his phone, strode out of the room, and slammed the door hard. The foam cups on the food tray wobbled precariously. Aria turned back to her friends. Spencer's lips were pressed together fretfully. Hanna chewed anxiously on a thumbnail. Emily blinked her round, green eyes, stunned into speechlessness.

'So now what?' Aria whispered.

Emily whimpered, Spencer fiddled with her IV, and Hanna looked like she was going to keel over. All their perfectly crafted theories had gone up in smoke – literally. Maybe Wilden hadn't set the fire – but Aria had seen *someone* out there in the woods. Which unfortunately meant only one thing.

Whoever had lit that match was still out there. Whoever had tried to kill them was still on the loose, maybe waiting for a chance to try it again.

3

If Only Someone Had Scammed
Spencer Years Ago ...

As the dim, midwinter Sunday sun disappeared over the horizon, Spencer stood in her family's backyard, surveying the fire's destruction. Her mother stood next to her; her eye makeup was smudged, her foundation blotchy, and her hair limp – she hadn't gotten her daily blowout from Uri, her hairdresser, this morning. Spencer's dad was there too, for once without his Bluetooth headset fastened to his ear. His mouth wobbled slightly, as if he was trying to hold in a sob.

Everything around them was ruined. The towering, old-growth trees were blackened and battered, and a stinky gray haze hung over the treetops. The family's windmill was now not much more than a carcass, the blades charred, the latticework splintered and crumbled. The Hastingses' lawn was crisscrossed with tire treads from the emergency vehicles that had rushed to the fire. Cigarette butts, empty Starbucks cups, and even a drained can of beer were strewn across the grass, remnants of the rubberneckers who had

34

swarmed the scene and lingered long after Spencer and the others had been taken to the ER.

But the worst, most heartbreaking result of the fire was what it had done to the family's barn apartment, which had been standing since 1756. Half the structure was still intact, though the wood siding, once cherry red, was now a charred, toxic gray. Most of the roof was missing, all of the leaded glass in the windows had blown out, and the front door was a pile of ash. Spencer could see straight through the empty shell into the barn's great room. There was a huge puddle of water on the Brazilian cherrywood floor, left over from the gallons of water the firemen had pumped into the barn. The four-poster bed, plush leather couch, and mahogany coffee table were ruined. So was the desk where Spencer, Emily, and Hanna had gathered just the night before, IMing Ian about who really killed Ali.

Only, it looked like Jason and Wilden *weren't* Ali's murderers. Which meant Spencer was back to knowing absolutely nothing.

She turned away from the barn, her eyes tearing up from the gas fumes. Closer to the house was the spot where she and her friends had collapsed on the lawn after running from the flames. Like the rest of the yard, it was littered with trash and soot, and the grass was scrubby and dead. There was nothing special about it at all, no magical indication that Ali had been there. Then again, Ali *hadn't* been there – they'd hallucinated her. It had been nothing more than a side effect of inhaling too much smoke. Workers had found her decomposed body in the DiLaurentises' old backyard months ago.

'I'm so sorry,' Spencer whispered as a piece of red

roofing dislodged itself from the barn and tumbled to the ground with a thud.

Slowly, Mrs Hastings reached out and grabbed Spencer's hand. Mr Hastings touched her shoulder. Before Spencer knew it, both her parents were wrapping their arms around her, engulfing her in a shaking, blubbering hug. 'I don't know what we would have done if something had happened to you,' Mrs Hastings cried.

'When we saw the fire, and then when we heard you might be hurt ...' Mr Hastings trailed off.

'None of this matters,' Mrs Hastings went on, her voice thick with sobs. 'All of this could've burned down. At least we still have you.'

Spencer clung to her parents, her breath catching in her bruised throat.

In the past twenty-four hours, her parents had been beyond wonderful to her. They'd sat by her hospital bed all night, hyper-vigilantly watching Spencer's chest rise and fall with every ragged breath. They'd bugged the nurses about getting Spencer water as soon as she wanted it, pain pills as soon as she needed them, and warmer blankets when she felt cold. When the doctor discharged her this afternoon, they'd taken her to the Creamery, her favorite ice cream parlor in Old Hollis, and bought her a double scoop of maple chip. It was a big change – for years, they'd treated her like the unwanted kid they begrudgingly let live in their home. And when she'd recently come clean about plagiarizing her award-winning Golden Orchid essay from her perfect sister, Melissa, they'd basically excommunicated her.

Only now there really *was* a reason for them to hate

36

her, and the minute Spencer told them, their concern, their rare show of love, would vanish. Spencer squeezed them hard, savoring the very last moment they'd probably ever speak to her again. She'd put this off for as long as she possibly could, but she had to tell them sometime.

She stepped back and squared her shoulders. 'There's something you need to know,' she admitted, her voice hoarse from the smoky air.

'Is it about Alison?' Mrs Hastings's voice swooped. 'Because, Spence—'

Spencer shook her head, cutting her off. 'No. Something else.'

She gazed at the blackened branches high in the sky. Then the truth spilled out in rapid succession. How, after Spencer's grandmother, Nana Hastings, didn't leave Spencer any money in her will, Melissa suggested Spencer might have been adopted. How Spencer registered with an online adoption site and just days later received a message that her birth mother had been found. How her visit with Olivia Caldwell in New York had been so wonderful that Spencer decided she wanted to move to the city permanently. Spencer just kept talking, afraid that if she stopped, she'd burst into tears. She didn't dare look at her parents, either, for fear their devastated expressions would break her heart.

'She had left behind her real estate agent's card, so I called and gave him my college savings account number to cover the security deposit and first month's rent,' Spencer went on, curling her toes inside her gray suede slouch boots. She could barely get the words out.

A squirrel scuttled in the grimy underbrush. Her father

groaned. Her mother squeezed her eyes shut and pressed her hand to her forehead. Spencer's heart sank. *Here we go.* Commence Operation: You're Not Our Daughter Anymore. 'You can guess what happened next.' She sighed, gazing at a tall birdhouse near the deck. Not a single bird had approached it since they'd been out here. 'The broker was obviously working with Olivia, and they cleaned out the account and disappeared.' She swallowed hard.

The backyard was silent and still. Now that the sunlight was almost gone, the barn looked like a ghost town relic, the dark windows like hollow eye sockets in a skull. Spencer sneaked a peek at her parents. Her dad was pale. Her mom sucked in her cheeks, as if she'd swallowed something sour. They exchanged a nervous look, then checked the front yard, perhaps scanning for press vans. Reporters had been pulling up to the house all day, grilling Spencer about whether she'd *really* seen Ali.

Her dad took a deep breath. 'Spencer, the money doesn't matter.'

Spencer blinked, startled.

'We can trace what happened to it,' Mr Hastings explained, wringing his hands. 'It's possible we'll be able to get it back.' He gazed off at the weather vane on top of the roof. 'But ... well, we should have seen it coming too.'

Spencer frowned, wondering if her brain was screwed up from inhaling residual fumes from the fire. 'W-what?'

Her dad shifted his weight and glanced at his wife. 'I knew we should've told her years ago, Veronica,' he mumbled.

'I didn't know this was going to happen,' Spencer's

38

mom squeaked, raising her hands. The air was so chilly, her breath came out in visible puffs.

'Tell me what?' Spencer pressed. Her heart started to thud. When she breathed in, all she could smell was ash.

'We should go inside,' Mrs Hastings said distractedly. 'It's awfully cold out here.'

'Tell me *what*?' Spencer repeated, planting her feet. She wasn't going anywhere.

Her mother paused for a long time. A creaking noise sounded from inside the barn. Finally, Mrs Hastings sat down on one of the enormous boulders that peppered the big backyard. 'Honey, Olivia did give birth to you.'

Spencer's eyes widened. 'What?'

'*Kind of* gave birth to you,' Mr Hastings corrected.

Spencer took a step back, a brittle twig snapping under her boot. 'So I was really adopted? Olivia was telling the truth?' *Is this why I feel so different from you guys? Is this why you've always preferred Melissa – because I'm not really your daughter?*

Mrs Hastings spun the three-carat diamond on her finger. Somewhere deep in the woods, a tree branch fell to the ground with an earsplitting crack. 'This certainly isn't something I thought we'd discuss today.' She took a Zen-centering breath, shook out her hands, and raised her head. Mr Hastings rubbed his gloved hands together fast. Suddenly, they both looked so clueless. Not like the always-poised, absolutely-in-control parents Spencer knew so well.

'Melissa's delivery was complicated.' Mrs Hastings drummed her hands on the slick, heavy boulder. Her eyes flickered to the front of the house for a moment, watching as a battered Honda slowed at their driveway. Curious neighbors had been circling the cul-de-sac all afternoon. 'The doctors told me that giving birth to another child could endanger my health. But we wanted another baby, so we ended up using a surrogate. Basically ... we used my egg and your dad's ... you know.' She lowered her eyes, too demure and proper to say *sperm* aloud. 'But we needed a woman to carry the baby – you – for us. So we found Olivia.'

'We screened her thoroughly to make sure she was healthy.' Mr Hastings sat down next to his wife on the rock, barely noticing that his handmade A. Testoni loafers had sunk into the sooty mud. 'She seemed to fit what we wanted, and she seemed to want us to have you. Only, toward the end of her pregnancy, she started to get ... demanding. She wanted more money from us. She threatened to escape to Canada and keep you for herself.'

'So we paid her more,' Mrs Hastings blurted. She put her blond head in her hands. 'And in the end, she did give you up, obviously. It's just ... after how possessive she became, we didn't want you to have any contact with her. We decided that the best thing we could do was keep it a secret from you – because, really, you *are* ours.'

'But some people didn't get that,' Mr Hastings said, rubbing his salt-and-pepper hair. His cell phone rang in his pocket, playing the first few bars of Beethoven's Fifth. He ignored it. 'Like Nana. She thought it was unnatural, and she never forgave us for doing it. When Nana's will said she was only giving money to her "natural-born grandchildren," we should have come clean. It seems

40

like Olivia has been waiting for a moment like this all along.'

The wind calmed down, coming to an eerie standstill. The Hastingses' dogs, Rufus and Beatrice, clawed at the back door, eager to get out and see what the family was doing. Spencer gaped at her parents. Mr and Mrs Hastings looked ragged and exhausted, like admitting this had taken everything out of them. It was obvious this was something they hadn't talked about in a long time. Spencer looked back and forth at them, trying to process it all. Their words made sense individually, but not as a whole. 'So Olivia *carried* me,' she repeated slowly. A shiver went up her spine that had nothing to do with the wind.

'Yes,' Mrs Hastings said. 'But *we're* your family, Spencer. You're *ours*.'

'We wanted you so badly, and Olivia was our only option,' Mr Hastings said, gazing up at the purplish clouds. 'Lately we seem to have lost sight of how important we all are to one another. And after everything you've gone through with Ian and Alison and this fire ...' He shook his head, staring again at the barn and then at the ruined woods beyond. A crow screeched and circled overhead. 'We should have been there for you. We never wanted you to think you weren't loved.'

Her mother tentatively took Spencer's hand and squeezed. 'What if we ... start fresh? Could we try that? Could you forgive us?'

The wind gusted again and the smell of smoke intensified. A couple of black leaves blew across the lawn into Ali's yard, coming to a stop near the half-dug hole where Ali's body had been found. Spencer fiddled with the plastic hospital bracelet that still circled her wrist, oscillating from shock to compassion to anger. In the past six months, her parents had taken away Spencer's barn apartment living privileges and let Melissa stay there instead, cut off her credit cards, sold her car, and told her on more than one occasion that she was dead to them. *Damn right I haven't felt like I had a real family*, she wanted to scream. *Damn right you haven't been there for me!* And now they wanted to just wipe the slate clean?

Her mother chewed on her lip, twisting a twig she'd picked up off the ground in her hands. Her father seemed to be holding his breath. This was Spencer's decision to make. She could choose to never forgive them, to stamp her foot and stay angry ... but then she saw the pain and regret in their faces. They really meant it. They wanted her to forgive them more than anything. Wasn't this what she wanted most in the world – parents who loved and wanted her?

'Yes,' Spencer said. 'I forgive you.'

Her parents let out an audible sigh and wrapped their arms around her. Her dad kissed the top of Spencer's head, his skin smelling like his favorite Kiehl's aftershave.

Spencer felt like she was floating outside her body. Just yesterday, when she'd discovered her college savings were gone, she'd assumed her life was over. She'd actually thought A was behind it all and had punished Spencer for not trying hard enough to track down Ali's true killer. But losing that money might have been the best thing that could have happened.

As her parents stood back and appraised their younger daughter, Spencer attempted a wobbly smile. They wanted her. They really *wanted* her. Then, a slow, roiling wind blew through the yard and another familiar scent tickled her nose. It smelled like ... *vanilla soap*, the kind Ali always used to use. Spencer flinched and the horrifying image of Ali covered in soot, choking on flames, sped back.

She shut her eyes, willing the vision out of her head. *No.* Ali was dead. She had hallucinated her. And that was that.

4

Does Prada Make Straitjackets?

As the smell of fresh-brewed Starbucks French roast wafted up the stairs, Hanna Marin lay on her bed, soaking up the last few minutes before she had to get ready for school. MTV2 blared in the background; her miniature Doberman, Dot, snoozed fitfully on his back in his Burberry doggie bed; and Hanna had just finished polishing her toenails Dior pink. Now she was talking on the phone to her new boyfriend, Mike Montgomery.

'Thanks again for the Aveda stuff.' She gazed again at the new products sitting on her nightstand. Yesterday, when Hanna had been leaving the hospital, Mike presented her with the deluxe destressing gift basket, which included a cooling eye mask, cucumber-mint body butter, and a handheld massager. Hanna had used all of them already, desperate to find a panacea that would wipe the fire – and the bizarre Ali sighting – from her mind. The doctors had chalked up the Ali vision to smoke inhalation, but it still seemed *so* real.

In some ways, Hanna was crushed that it wasn't. After

all these years, she still had a burning wish for Ali to see with her own eyes how much Hanna had changed. The last time Hanna saw Ali, Hanna had been a chubby ugly duckling – definitely the dorkiest of the group – and Ali always made countless cracks about Hanna's weight, frizzy hair, and bad skin. She'd probably never have guessed that Hanna would transform into a thin, gorgeous, popular swan. Sometimes Hanna wondered if the only way she'd truly know for sure that her transformation was complete was if Ali gave Hanna her blessing. Of course, now that could never happen.

'My pleasure,' Mike answered, snapping Hanna out of her reverie. 'And be forewarned – I sent some very juicy Twitters to some of the press people who were waiting outside the ER. Just to get them focused on something other than the fire.'

'Like what?' Hanna asked, instantly on alert. Mike sounded up to something.

'*Hanna Marin in talks with MTV about reality show*,' Mike recited. '*Multimillion-dollar deal*.'

'Awesome.' Hanna let out a breath and started waving her hands around to dry her nails.

'I wrote one about myself, too. *Mike Montgomery turns down date with Croatian supermodel*.'

'You turned *down* a date?' Hanna giggled flirtatiously. 'That doesn't seem like the Mike Montgomery *I* know.'

'Who needs Croatian supermodels when you have Hanna Marin?' Mike said.

Hanna wriggled with giddy delight. If someone had told her a few weeks ago that she'd be dating Crest Montgomery, she would have swall

Whitestrip in surprise – she'd only pursued Mike because her soon-to-be stepsister, Kate, wanted him too. But somehow in the process, she'd actually started to like him. With his ice blue eyes, pink, kissable lips, and raunchy sense of humor, he was becoming more than just Aria Montgomery's popularity-obsessed younger brother to her.

She stood up, crossed the room to her closet, and ran her fingers along Ali's piece of the Time Capsule flag, which she'd taken at the hospital when Aria wasn't looking. She didn't feel guilty about it, either – it wasn't like the flag *belonged* to Aria. 'So I heard that you guys were getting notes from a new A,' Mike said. His voice was suddenly serious.

'I haven't gotten any notes from A,' Hanna said truthfully. Since she'd gotten her new iPhone and changed her number, A had left her alone. It was certainly a welcome change from the old A, who had horribly turned out to be Hanna's former bestie, Mona Vanderwaal – something she tried very hard never to think about. 'Let's hope it stays that way.'

'Well, let me know if there's anything I can do,' Mike assured her. 'Kick someone's ass, whatever.'

'Aw.' Hanna flushed with pleasure. No other boyfriend had ever offered to defend her honor. She made a kissing sound, promised she and Mike would meet for lattes at Steam, Rosewood's coffee bar, this afternoon, and hung up.

pu... she padded down to the kitchen for breakfast, smelled like ... through her long auburn hair. The kitchen ...nd fresh fruit. Her soon-to-be step-mother, Isabel, and Kate were already at the table, eating bowls of cut-up melon and cottage cheese. Hanna couldn't think of a more vomit-inspiring food combination.

When they saw Hanna in the doorway, they both leapt to their feet. 'How are you feeling?' they gushed at the same time.

'Fine,' Hanna answered tightly, scraping the brush against her scalp. Predictably, Isabel began to wince – she was a germaphobe, and had a thing against hair-brushing near food.

Hanna plopped down in an empty chair and reached for the carafe of coffee. Isabel and Kate sat back down, and there was a long, pregnant pause, like Hanna had interrupted something. They'd probably been gossiping about her. She wouldn't put it past either of them.

Hanna's father had been dating Isabel for years – even Ali had met both Isabel and Kate a few months before she disappeared – but they'd only begun living in Rosewood after Hanna's mother was transferred to Singapore and Hanna's father took a job in Philly. It was bad enough that her dad had decided to marry a fake-tan-obsessed ER nurse named Isabel – *such* a trade down from Hanna's glamorous, successful mother – but throwing a tall, skinny stepsister Hanna's exact same age into the mix was just unbearable. In the two weeks since Kate had moved in, Hanna had had to endure her daily medley of *American Idol* songs in the shower, the foul-smelling raw-egg conditioner Kate concocted to keep her hair shiny, and her father's bottomless praise for every tiny thing Kate did well, as if *she* were his real daughter. Not to mention that Kate had won over

Hanna's new underlings Naomi Zeigler and Riley Wolfe and then told Mike that Hanna had asked him out on a bet. Then again, at a party a couple of weeks ago, Hanna had blurted out that Kate had herpes, so maybe they were even now.

'Melon?' Kate asked sweetly, pushing the bowl toward Hanna with her annoyingly thin arms.

'No thanks,' Hanna said in the same saccharine tone. It seemed like they'd called a cease-fire at the Radley party – Kate had even smiled when Hanna and Mike got together – but Hanna wasn't about to push it.

Then Kate gasped. 'Oops,' she whispered, pulling the Opinions section of this morning's *Philadelphia Sentinel* toward her plate. She tried to fold it before Hanna saw the headline, but it was too late. There was a large picture of Hanna, Spencer, Emily, and Aria standing in front of the burning woods. *How Many Lies Can We Allow?* screamed one of the essays. *According to Best Friends, Alison DiLaurentis Rises from the Dead.*

'I'm so sorry, Hanna.' Kate covered the story with her bowl of cottage cheese.

'It's fine,' Hanna snapped, trying to swallow her embarrassment. What was wrong with these reporters? Weren't there more important things in the world to obsess over? And hello, it was smoke inhalation!

Kate took a dainty bite of melon. 'I want to help, Han. If you need me to, like, be your advocate with the press – go on camera and stuff like that – I'd be happy to.'

'Thanks,' Hanna said sarcastically. Kate was *such* an attention whore. Then she noticed a photo of Wilden on the part of the Opinions page that was still visible.

Rosewood PD, said the headline under his photo. *Are They* Really *Doing Everything They Can?*

Now *that* was an op-ed worth reading. Wilden might not have killed Ali, but he'd certainly been acting bizarrely over the past few weeks. Like how he'd given Hanna a ride home from her jog one morning, driving at twice the speed limit and playing chicken with an oncoming car. Or how he'd vehemently demanded that they stop saying Ali was alive ... or else. Was Wilden really trying to protect them, or did he have his own reasons for keeping them quiet about Ali? And if Wilden was innocent, who the hell set that fire ... and why?

'Hanna. Good. You're up.'

Hanna turned around. Her father stood in the doorway, dressed in a button-down and pin-striped pants. His hair was still wet from the shower. 'Can we talk to you for a minute?' he asked, pouring himself a cup of coffee.

Hanna lowered the paper. *We?*

Mr Marin walked to the table and pulled back a chair. It scraped noisily against the tile. 'A few days ago I received an e-mail from Dr Atkinson.'

He was staring at Hanna as if she should understand. 'Who's that?' she finally asked.

'The school's psychologist,' Isabel piped up in a know-it-all voice. 'He's very nice. Kate met him when she was touring the school. He insists that students call him Dave.'

Hanna fought the urge to snort. What, had goody-goody Kate sucked up to the entire Rosewood Day staff during her tour of the school?

'Dr Atkinson said he's been keeping an eye on you at school,' her father went on. 'He's very concerned, Hanna.

49

He thinks you may have post-traumatic stress disorder from Alison's death and your car accident.'

Hanna swirled the remaining coffee in her cup. 'Isn't PTSD the thing soldiers get?'

Mr Marin spun the thin platinum ring he wore on his right hand. The ring had been a gift from Isabel, and when they got married, he was going to switch it over to his left. *Barf.* 'Well, apparently it can happen to anyone who's gone through something really terrible,' he explained. 'Usually people get cold sweats, heart palpitations, stuff like that. They also relive what happened over and over.'

Hanna traced the wood grain pattern on the kitchen table. All right, she *had* been experiencing symptoms like that, usually experiencing the moment when Mona mowed her down with her SUV. But c'mon – anyone would freak about that. 'I've been feeling great,' she chirped.

'I didn't think much of the letter at first,' Mr Marin went on, ignoring her, 'but I pulled a psychiatrist aside at the hospital yesterday before you were discharged. Sweats and palpitations aren't the only symptoms of PTSD. It can manifest itself in lots of other ways, too. Like self-destructive eating patterns, for example.'

'I don't have eating problems,' Hanna snapped, horrified. 'You guys see me eat all the time!'

Isabel cleared her throat, glancing pointedly at Kate. Kate wound a piece of chestnut hair around her finger. 'It's just, Hanna ...' She gazed at Hanna with her enormous blue eyes. 'You kind of told me you do.'

Hanna's jaw dropped. 'You *told* them?' A few weeks ago, in a moment of insanity, Hanna had spilled to Kate that she used to have an eensy-weensy binge-purge problem.

'I thought it was for your own good,' Kate whispered. 'I swear.'

'The psychiatrist said lying could also be a symptom,' Mr Marin went on. 'First telling everyone you saw Ian Thomas's dead body in the woods, and now with you girls saying you saw Alison. And that got me thinking about the lies you've told *us* – sneaking out of our dinner last fall to go to that dance at school, stealing Percocet from the burn clinic, shoplifting from Tiffany, crashing your boyfriend's car, even telling your whole class that Kate had ...' He trailed off, clearly not wanting to say *herpes* aloud. 'Dr Atkinson suggests that it might be best if you took a few weeks off from all this craziness. Go somewhere where you can relax and focus on your problems.'

Hanna brightened. 'Like Hawaii?'

Her father bit his lip. 'No ... like a facility.'

'A *what*?' Hanna slammed her mug down. Hot coffee sloshed over the side, burning the side of her index finger.

Mr Marin reached into his pocket and pulled out a pamphlet. Two blond girls were strolling down a grassy lane, the sun setting in the background. They both had bad dye jobs and fat legs. *The Preserve at Addison-Stevens* said swirly writing at the bottom. 'It's the best in the country,' her father said. 'It treats all kinds of things – learning disabilities, eating disorders, OCD, depression. And it's not too far from here, just over the border in Delaware. There's an entire ward dedicated to young patients, like you.'

Hanna stared blankly at a wreath of dried flowers

Isabel had hung up when she took ownership of the house, replacing Hanna's mother's far more preferable stainless-steel wall clock. 'I don't have problems,' she squeaked. 'I don't need to go to a mental institution.'

'It's not a mental institution,' Isabel chirped. 'Think of it as more like … a spa. People call it the Canyon Ranch of Delaware.'

Hanna wanted to wring Isabel's scrawny, faux-orange neck. Hadn't she ever heard of *euphemisms*? People also called the Berlitz Apartment Town, a dumpy, dilapidated housing complex on the outskirts of Rosewood, the Berlitz-Carlton, but no one took *that* literally.

'Maybe it's a good time to escape from Rosewood,' Kate simpered, in an equally *I know what's best* voice. 'Especially the reporters.'

Hanna's dad nodded. 'I had to chase one guy off the property yesterday – he was trying to use a telescopic lens to get a picture of you in your bedroom, Hanna.'

'And someone called here last night, wanting to know if you'd give a statement on *Nancy Grace*,' Isabel added.

'It's only going to get worse,' Mr Marin concluded.

'And don't worry,' Kate said, taking another bite of melon. 'Naomi, Riley, and I will still be here when you get back.'

'But …' Hanna trailed off. How could her dad believe this bullshit? So she'd lied a few times. It had always been for a good reason – she'd ditched out on their dinner at Le Bec-Fin last fall because A had warned that her then recently ex-boyfriend, Sean Ackard, was at the Foxy benefit with another girl. She'd told everyone Kate had herpes because she was sure Kate was going to tell everyone

52

about Hanna's eating issues. Who cared? That didn't mean she had post-traumatic stress whatever.

It was another painful reminder of how far apart Hanna and her dad had grown. When Hanna's parents were still married, she and her father had been two peas in a pod, but after Isabel and Kate came along, Hanna was suddenly as obsolete as shoulder pads. Why did her dad hate her so much now?

And then, her blood pressure plummeted. Of *course*. A had finally found her. She stood up from the table, jostling the ceramic pot of mint tea near her plate. 'That letter isn't from Dr Atkinson. Someone else wrote it to hurt me.'

Isabel folded her hands on the table. 'Who would do that?'

Hanna swallowed hard. 'A.'

Kate covered her mouth with her hand. Hanna's father laid his cup on the table. 'Hanna,' he said in a kindergarten-slow voice. '*Mona* was A. And she died, remember?'

'No,' Hanna protested. 'There's a new A.'

Kate, Isabel, and Hanna's father exchanged nervous looks, as if Hanna was an unpredictable animal that needed a tranquilizer dart in her butt. 'Honey ...' Mr Marin said. 'You're not really making sense.'

'This is just what A wants,' Hanna cried. 'Why don't you believe me?'

Suddenly, she felt overwhelmingly dizzy. Her legs went numb and a faint buzzing sounded in her ears. The walls closed in, and the minty aroma of tea turned her stomach. In a blink, Hanna was standing in the dark Rosewood Day parking lot. Mona's SUV was barreling down on her, its headlights two angry homing beacons. Her palms began to sweat. Her throat burned. She saw Mona's face behind the wheel, her lips pulled back in a diabolical grin. Hanna covered her face, bracing for impact. She heard someone scream. After a few seconds, she realized it was her.

It was over as quickly as it had begun. When Hanna opened her eyes, she was lying on the floor, clutching her chest. Her face felt hot and wet. Kate, Isabel, and Hanna's father loomed over her, their brows furrowed with concern. Hanna's miniature Doberman, Dot, was frantically licking Hanna's bare ankles.

Her father helped her up and back into a chair. 'I really think this is for the best,' he said gently. Hanna wanted to protest, but she knew it wasn't any use.

She rested her head on the table, addled and shaky. All the sounds around her grew sharp and acute in her ears. The fridge hummed softly. A garbage truck rumbled down the hill. And then, underneath that, she heard something else.

The hair on the back of her neck rose. Maybe she *was* crazy, but she swore she heard ... a *laugh*. It sounded like someone snickering gleefully, delighted that things were going precisely according to plan.

5

A Spiritual Awakening

Monday morning, Byron offered to drive Aria to school in his ancient Honda Civic since Aria's Subaru was still on the fritz. She moved a pile of slides, battered textbooks, and papers off the passenger seat to the back. The area below her feet was littered with empty coffee cups, SoyJoy wrappers, and a bunch of receipts from Sunshine, the eco-friendly baby store that Byron and his girlfriend, Meredith, shopped at.

Byron turned the ignition, and the old diesel engine grumbled to life. One of his acid jazz tapes blared through the speakers. Aria stared at the blackened and twisted trees in her backyard. Little curls of smoke rose from the woods, the fire still smoldering in places. An entire roll of yellow DO NOT CROSS tape had been strung up along the tree line, as the woods were now too brittle and danger-ous to enter. Aria had heard on the news this morning that cops were combing through the woods in search of an answer as to who might have set the fire, and last night she'd received a call from the Rosewood PD, wanting to know about the person she'd seen in the woods with the can of gasoline. Now that the person definitely *wasn't* Wilden, Aria didn't have much to tell them. It could have been anyone under that enormous hood.

Aria held her breath as they rolled past the large colonial that belonged to Ian Thomas's family. The lawn was covered with morning frost, the red mailbox flag was up, and a couple of coupon circulars were scattered on the Thomases' driveway. There was fresh graffiti on the garage door that said *Murderer*, the paint an exact match to the *KILLER* graffiti someone had painted on Spencer's garage door. On instinct, Aria reached into her yak-fur bag and felt for Ian's class ring in the inside pocket. She'd been tempted just to give it to Wilden yesterday – she didn't want to be responsible for it – but Spencer had a point. The Rosewood PD had missed the ring entirely during their massive search through the woods; they might assume Aria had planted it there. But why *hadn't* they found the ring? Maybe they hadn't searched the woods at all.

And where *was* Ian, anyway? Why had he given them the wrong information in his IMs? And how had he not noticed that his ring was gone? Aria doubted that it had just slipped off his finger – the only time that had happened to her was when she washed out brushes after painting, and she always noticed her rings falling off right away. Was it possible that Ian *was* dead, and that the ring had fallen off him as someone roughly dragged his body away when Aria and the others had run back to find Wilden? But if that was the case, then who was speaking with them on IM?

She sighed loudly, and Byron gave her a surreptitious look. He was extra disheveled today, his dark hair standing up in thinning tufts. Despite the cold, he wasn't wearing a coat, and there was a big hole in the elbow of his heavy wool sweater. Aria recognized it as one he'd bought when the family had been living in Iceland. She wished her family had never left Reykjavík.

'So how are you doing?' Byron asked gently.

Aria shrugged. At the corner, they passed a bunch of public school kids waiting for the bus. They pointed at Aria, instantly recognizing her from the news. Aria pulled her faux-fur hood around her head. Then they passed Spencer's street. A big tree service vehicle was parked at the curb, a police car behind it. Across the street, Jenna Cavanaugh and her German shepherd service dog walked daintily to Mrs Cavanaugh's Lexus, avoiding patches of ice. Aria shivered. Jenna knew more about Ali than she'd let on. Aria even wondered if Jenna was keeping a burgeoning secret – on the day of Meredith's baby shower, Jenna had been standing in the middle of Aria's yard as if she needed to tell Aria something. But when Aria asked Jenna what was wrong, Jenna turned and fled. She seemed to know Jason DiLaurentis pretty well, too – but why would Jason have barged into her house last week and started arguing with her? And why did A want them to know it, if Jason truly had nothing to do with Ali's death?

'Officer Wilden said you guys were trying to figure out who really killed Ali,' Byron said, his gravelly voice so loud and booming that Aria jumped. 'But, honey, if Ian didn't kill her, the cops will figure out who did.' He scratched the back of his neck, something he only did when he was stressed. 'I'm worried about you. Ella is, too.'

Aria winced at Byron's reference to her mother. Aria's parents had separated this fall, and both had moved on to new relationships. Ever since Ella began dating Xavier, a lecherous artist who'd hit on Aria, Aria had been avoiding her. And while her dad certainly had a point, Aria was in too deep to unwind herself from the Ali investigation now.

'Talking about it might help,' Byron tried when Aria still didn't answer, turning down the jazz CD. 'You can even tell me about ... you know. Seeing Alison.'

They passed a farm that had six stout white alpacas, then a Wawa. *Stop saying you saw Ali*, Wilden's voice reverberated in Aria's mind. Something about it continued to bother her. He sounded so ... *aggressive*. 'I don't know what we saw,' she admitted weakly. 'I want to believe that we just inhaled a lot of smoke and that's the end of it. But what are the odds of us all seeing Ali at the exact same time, doing the exact same thing? Isn't that kind of strange?'

Byron put his blinker on and shifted to the right lane. 'It is strange.' He sipped from his Hollis College coffee mug. 'Remember how a few months ago you asked me if ghosts could send text messages?'

The conversation was blurry in Aria's mind, but she remembered talking to Byron after receiving the first message from Old A. Before Ali's body was found in her old backyard, Aria had wondered if Ali's ghost had been sending those messages from beyond the grave.

'Some people believe that the dead can't rest until they impart an important message.' Byron braked at a stoplight behind a Toyota Prius that had a VISUALIZE WHIRLED PEAS bumper sticker.

'What do you mean?' Aria sat up straighter.

They swept past Clocktower, a million-dollar housing development with its own golf club, and then the little township park. A few brave souls were out in heavy down parkas, walking their dogs. Byron breathed out through his nose. 'I just mean ... Alison's death was a mystery. They've arrested the killer, but no one really knows for sure what happened. And you girls *were* right where Alison died. Her body had been there for years.'

Aria reached over and took a sip from her dad's mug. 'So you're saying ... it could've been Ali's ghost?'

Byron shrugged, making a right. They pulled into the drive at Rosewood Day and slowed to a crawl behind a line of buses. 'Maybe.'

'And you think she wants to tell us something?' Aria asked incredulously. 'So you don't think Ian did it either?'

Byron shook his head vehemently. 'I'm not saying that. I'm just saying that sometimes, certain things can't be explained rationally.'

A ghost. It sounded like he was channeling hippy-dippy Meredith. But as Aria glanced at her dad's profile, there were taut lines around his mouth. His eyebrows were knitted together, and he was doing that neck-scratching thing again. He was serious.

She turned to Byron, suddenly filled with questions. Why would Ali's ghost be here? What was her unfinished business? And what was Aria supposed to do now?

But before she could say a word, there was a sharp knock on the passenger door. Aria hadn't realized they'd already pulled to the curb of Rosewood Day. Three reporters swarmed around the car, snapping photos and pressing their faces against the window. 'Miss Montgomery?' a woman called, her voice loud through the glass.

Aria gaped at them and then looked desperately at her dad. 'Ignore them,' Byron urged. 'Run.'

Taking a deep breath, Aria pushed the door open and barreled her way through the throng. Cameras flashed. Reporters babbled. Behind them, Aria saw students gaping, perversely fascinated by the commotion. 'Did you really see Alison?' the reporters called. 'Do you know who set the fire?' 'Did someone set that fire in the woods to cover up a vital clue?'

Aria swiveled around at the last question but kept her mouth shut.

'Did *you* set the fire?' a dark-haired thirty-something man shouted. The reporters moved in closer.

'Of course not!' Aria shouted, alarmed. Then she elbowed past them, scampering up the walk and bursting through the first available door, which led to the back stage of the auditorium.

The doors banged shut, and Aria let out a held breath and looked around. The big, high-ceilinged theater was empty. Boat sets from *South Pacific*, the school's recent musical, were stacked in a corner. Sheet music was strewn haphazardly on the floor. The red velvet auditorium chairs spread out before her, every single seat folded up and unoccupied. It was too quiet in here. Eerily quiet.

When the wood floor squeaked, Aria stiffened. A shadow disappeared behind the curtain. She whipped around, a horrible possibility darting through her mind. *It's the person who set the fire. The person who tried to kill us. They're here.* But when she moved closer, there was no one there.

Or maybe, just maybe, it was Ali's spirit, lurking close, desperate. If what Byron said was true – if a dead person couldn't rest until her message had been heard – then maybe Aria needed to figure out how to communicate with her. Maybe it was time to hear what Ali had to say.

6
Down The Rabbit Hole

Emily slammed her locker door Monday afternoon and hefted her biology, trig, and history books into her arms. A piece of paper slid out from inside one of her notebooks, HOLY TRINITY YOUTH GROUP BOSTON TRIP said big, curly letters.

She scowled. This paper had been lodged in her notebook since the week before when her then-boyfriend, Isaac, had asked her to come. Emily had even gotten permission from her parents – she'd thought it would be the perfect way to spend time with Isaac alone.

Not anymore.

Her chest tightened. It was hard to believe that just a few days ago, Emily had really and truly thought she and Isaac were in love – enough, in fact, to sleep with him, for her very first time. But then everything had gone horribly, dreadfully wrong. When Emily tried to tell Isaac about his mom's evil glares and hurtful remarks, he'd broken up with her on the spot, more or less telling Emily she was psycho.

A few sophomores passed behind her, giggling and comparing lip glosses. How could Emily have thought he loved her? How could she have slept with him? By the time Isaac had found her at the Radley party on Saturday night and apologized, she wasn't sure if she wanted him back anymore. Since the fire, he'd texted and called her several times, wanting to know if she was okay, but Emily hadn't replied to those messages either. Things felt ruined between them. Isaac hadn't even listened to her side of the story. Now, whenever she thought about what they'd done that day after school in Isaac's bedroom, she wished she could grab a big bar of soap and scrub the deed off her skin.

Balling up the flyer in her hands, she tossed it in the nearest trash can and continued down the hall. The classical between-classes music lilted through the overhead speakers. Red-and-pink posters for the upcoming Rosewood Day Valentine's Ball wallpapered the halls. There was the usual traffic jam on the stairs, and someone had farted in the stairwell. It was a status quo Monday at school ... except for one thing: Everyone was staring at her.

Literally *everyone*. Two senior boys on the baseball team mouthed *freak* as she passed. Mrs Booth, Emily's creative writing teacher from the year before, poked her head out of her classroom door, widened her eyes at Emily, and then scuttled back inside, like a mouse darting back into a hole. The only person who didn't stare was Spencer. Instead, Spencer pointedly turned her head in the opposite direction, obviously still annoyed that Emily had told the police they'd seen Ali in her backyard.

63

Whatever. Her friends might be convinced they'd collectively hallucinated, the DNA report might allegedly say the body in the hole was Ali's, and all of Rosewood might think Emily was delusional, but she knew what she saw. Last night while she slept, she'd endured dream after dream about Ali, like Ali was begging Emily's subconscious to come find her. In the first one, Emily had walked into her church and found Ali and Isaac sitting together in the back pew, giggling and whispering. In the dream after that, Emily and Isaac had been naked under the covers in Isaac's bed, just like they'd been the week before. They heard footsteps on the stairs. Emily thought it was Isaac's mother, but Ali had walked into the room instead. Her face was covered with soot, and her eyes were huge and frightened. 'Someone's trying to kill me,' she said. And then she disintegrated into a pile of ash.

Ali was out there. But … whose body was in the hole then? And why was Wilden insisting it was Ali's DNA if it really wasn't? Someone had obviously set that fire to cover something up. Sure, Wilden had an alibi for when the fire started, but who was to say that receipt from CVS was even his? And wasn't it a little convenient that he had the receipt at the ready? Emily thought of the lone police car she'd seen sneaking away from the Hastingses' house the night of the fire, almost like whoever was driving didn't want to be noticed. Wilden wasn't on the scene that night … or *was* he?

She entered her biology classroom. It smelled of its usual jumble of leaky Bunsen burner gas, formaldehyde, and marker-board bleach. The teacher, Mr Heinz, wasn't there yet, and the students were gathered around one desk in the middle of the room, looking at something on a silver MacBook Air. When Sean Ackard noticed Emily, he paled and broke from the crowd. Lanie Iler, one of Emily's friends from swimming, saw Emily next and opened and closed her mouth like a fish.

'Lanie?' Emily tried, her heart starting to thud. 'What is it?'

Lanie had a conflicted expression on her face. After a moment, she pointed at the laptop.

Emily took a few steps toward the computer. A hush fell over the room and the crowd parted. The local news web page glowed on the screen, POOR, POOR PRETTY LITTLE LIARS read the headline under Emily, Aria, Spencer, and Hanna's school pictures. Farther down on the page was a blurry picture of the girls in Spencer's hospital room. They were all gathered over Spencer's bed, talking worriedly.

Emily's pulse raced. Spencer's hospital room had been on the second floor, so how had the paparazzi gotten this photo?

Her eyes returned to their new nickname. *Pretty Little Liars*. A couple of kids behind her tittered. They thought this was *funny*. They thought Emily was a joke. She took a big step back, almost bumping into Ben, her old boyfriend from swimming. 'I guess I should watch out for you, Little Liar,' he teased, smirking.

That was *it*. Without another glance at her classmates, she rushed out of the room and headed straight for the bathroom, her rubber Vans squeaking on the polished floor. Luckily, there was no one inside. The air smelled like freshly smoked cigarettes, and water dripped from one of the faucets into a pale blue basin. Leaning against the wall, Emily took heaving breaths.

Why was this happening? Why did no one believe her? When she'd seen Ali in the woods on Saturday night, her heart had filled with joy. Ali was *back*. They could resume their friendship. And then, in a blink, Ali was gone again, and now everyone thought Emily had made her up. What if Ali really was out there, hurt and scared? Was Emily honestly the only person who wanted to help her?

She ran cold water on her face, trying to catch her breath. Suddenly, her phone beeped, echoing loudly off the hard bathroom walls. She jumped and unhooked the backpack from her shoulder. Her phone was in the front pocket. *One new text message*, said the screen.

Her heart went into free fall. She looked around swiftly, anticipating a pair of eyes watching her from the utility closet, a pair of feet under a stall. But the bathroom was empty.

Her breathing was shallow in her chest as she looked at the screen.

Poor little Emily—
You and I both know she's alive. The question is:
What would you do to find her? – A

Gasping, Emily opened the keyboard to her phone and started to type. *I'll do anything*.

There was a return message almost immediately. *Do exactly as I say. Tell your parents you're going on that church trip to Boston. But instead, you'll go to Lancaster. For more, go to your locker. I've left you something there.*

Emily squinted. Lancaster … Pennsylvania? And how

66

did A know about the Boston trip? She envisioned the crumpled-up flyer sitting at the bottom of the hall trash can. Had A seen her throw it away? Was A here at school? And more specifically, could she actually trust A?

She looked down at her phone. *What would you do to find her?*

Quickly, she sprinted up the stairs back to her locker, which was in the Foreign Languages wing. As French students sang along to 'La Marseillaise,' Emily spun the dial and opened her locker door. At the bottom, next to a spare pair of swim fins, was a small grocery bag. *Wear me*, said messy Magic Marker scrawl on the front.

Emily's hand fluttered to her mouth. How had this gotten here? Taking a deep breath, she picked up the bag and pulled out a long, plain dress. Underneath that was a simple wool coat, stockings, and odd-looking shoes with little eyelet buttons. It looked like the *Little House on the Prairie* Halloween costume Emily had worn in fifth grade.

Her hand touched a piece of paper at the bottom of the grocery bag. It was another note, seemingly banged out on an old typewriter.

Tomorrow, take a bus to Lancaster, go north for about a mile from the depot, and turn at the big sign of the horse and buggy. Ask for Lucy Zook. Don't dare take a cab to get there – no one will trust you. – A

Emily devoured the note three more times. Was A suggesting what Emily *thought* she was suggesting? Then she noticed typing on the other side of the note. She flipped the paper over.

Your name is Emily Stoltzfus. You're from Ohio, but you've come to Lancaster for a visit. If you want to see your old BFF again, you'll do exactly what I say. And . . . oh, did I forget to mention? You're Amish. Everyone else there is, too. Viel Glück! (That's German for 'good luck'!) – A

7

An Old Friend Is Back

When the final bell of the day rang, Spencer plodded gratefully to her locker. Her limbs ached. Her head felt like it weighed a million pounds. She was ready for this day to be over. Her parents had told her she could take a few days off school to recuperate after the fire, but Spencer wanted to get back into the swing of things as soon as possible. She vowed to get straight A's this semester, whatever it took. And maybe by spring, Rosewood Day would take her off academic probation and let her keep her spot on the lacrosse team – she needed it for college applications. There was still time to get into an Ivy League summer program, and she could sign up for Habitat for Humanity to round out her community service.

As she pulled her English books from her locker, she felt a tug on her jacket sleeve. When she turned around, Andrew Campbell was standing there, his hands shoved in his pockets, his longish blond hair pushed off his face.

'Hi,' he said.

'H-hi,' Spencer stammered. She and Andrew had started dating a few weeks ago, but Spencer hadn't spoken to him since she told him she was moving to New York to be with Olivia. Andrew had tried to warn her not to trust Olivia, but Spencer hadn't listened. In fact, she'd kind of called him a clingy loser. Since then, he'd ignored her at school – which was a nearly impossible feat, since they had every class together.

'Are you okay?' he asked.

'I guess,' she answered shyly.

Andrew fiddled with the ANDREW FOR PREZ! pin on his messenger bag. It was from the previous semester's campaign for class president, which he'd won over Spencer. 'I was at the hospital when you were still unconscious,' he admitted. 'I talked to your parents, but I ...' He looked down at his lace-up Merrells. 'I wasn't sure if you'd want to see me.'

'Oh.' Spencer's heart did a flip. 'I – I would have wanted to see you. And ... I'm sorry. For ... you know.'

Andrew nodded, and Spencer wondered if he'd found out what happened with Olivia. 'Maybe I can call you later?' he asked.

'Sure,' Spencer said, feeling a flutter of excitement. Andrew raised a hand awkwardly, doing a little bow in good-bye. She watched him disappear down the hall, skirting around a bunch of orchestra girls holding violin and cello cases. She'd come close to crying twice today, overstressed and tired of kids staring at her like she'd come to school in only a thong. Finally, something pleasant had happened.

The front walk was crowded with yellow buses, a

traffic guard in a bright orange vest, and, of course, the ubiquitous news vans. A CNN cameraman noticed Spencer and nudged his reporter. 'Miss Hastings?' They sprinted over. 'What do you think about the people who doubt that you saw Alison Saturday night? Did you really see her?'

Spencer gritted her teeth. Damn Emily for blurting out that they'd seen Ali. 'No,' she said into the lens. 'We didn't see Ali. It was a misunderstanding.'

'So you *lied*?' The reporters were practically frothing at the mouth. A bunch of students had stopped just behind Spencer too. A couple of kids were waving at the cameras, but most were staring at her, agog. A freshman boy snapped a photo with his camera phone. Even Spencer's AP econ teacher, Mr McAdam, had paused in the lobby and was gaping at her through the big front windows.

'The brain conjures up all kinds of strange things when deprived of oxygen,' Spencer said, parroting what the ER doctor had told her. 'It's the same phenomenon that happens to people right before they die.' Then she extended her palm toward the screen. 'No more questions.'

'Spencer!' called a familiar voice. Spencer whirled around. Her sister, Melissa, was in her silver Mercedes SUV, parked in one of the visitors' spots. She waved her arm. 'Come on!'

Saved. Spencer ducked the reporters and darted past the buses. Melissa smiled as Spencer climbed into the SUV, as if it wasn't completely out of the ordinary that she was picking Spencer up from school.

'What are you doing back?' Spencer blurted. She hadn't

seen Melissa in almost a week, not since she swiftly bolted from the house after coming home from Nana's funeral. That was right around the time Spencer had begun talking to Ian Thomas on IM. Spencer had looked for him on IM last night, hoping to talk to him about the fire, but he hadn't logged on.

Spencer suspected Melissa thought Ian was innocent too – after Ian had been arrested and thrown in jail, Melissa insisted that he didn't deserve a life sentence. She even admitted she'd talked to Ian on the phone when he was in prison. Her sister had packed up her things so hastily last week that Spencer wondered if Melissa felt she needed to get out of Rosewood for the same reasons Ian did – because she knew too much about what had really happened to Ali.

Melissa started the car. NPR blared, and she quickly turned it down. 'I'm back because I heard about your brush with death. Obviously. And I wanted to see the destruction from the fire. It's terrible, huh? The woods ... the windmill ... even the barn. So much of my stuff, too.'

Spencer hung her head. The barn had been Melissa's apartment all through high school. She had stashed tons of yearbooks, journals, memorabilia, and clothes there.

'Mom told me about you, too.' Melissa backed out of the space, almost hitting a CNN cameraman filming the front of the school. 'About ... the surrogate thing. How are you doing?'

Spencer shrugged. 'It was a shock. But for the best. It's good that I know.'

'Yeah, well.' They passed the journalism barn and then

the teachers' parking area. It was filled with cars that were considerably older and humbler than the ones in the student lot. 'I wish you wouldn't have said *I* put the idea in your head. Mom really whaled on me for that. She was ruthless.'

Spencer felt a hot twinge of anger. *Poor you*, she wanted to snap. Like that really compared to what Spencer had been through.

They came to a stop at the light behind a Jeep Cherokee full of meaty-shouldered boys in baseball caps. Spencer took a long look at her sister. Melissa's skin looked papery and tired, there was a zit on her forehead, and ligaments stood out in her neck, as if she was clenching her jaw tight. Last week, Spencer had noticed someone who looked suspiciously like Melissa searching through the woods behind their house, not far from where they'd discovered Ian's body. Aria had found Ian's ring in the woods just before the fire started – was that what Melissa had been looking for?

But before Spencer could ask, her cell phone bleated. She unclasped her purse and pulled it out. *Take tomorrow off from school*, a text said. *Let's have a spa day. My treat. Mom.*

Spencer let out an involuntary squeal of delight. 'Mom and I are having a spa day tomorrow!'

Melissa paled. Several emotions washed over her face at once. 'You are?' She sounded incredulous.

'Uh-huh.' Spencer hit reply and typed *Yes! Definitely.*

Melissa smirked. 'Is she trying to buy your love now?'

'No.' Spencer bristled. 'It's not like that.'

The light turned green, and Melissa hit the gas. 'I guess

our roles are reversed,' she said breezily, taking a corner too fast. 'Now you're Mom's favorite and I'm the outcast.'

'What do you mean?' Spencer asked, trying to ignore the fact that Melissa had referred to her as an outcast. 'Aren't you getting along?'

Melissa rolled her jaw until the joint cracked. 'Forget it.'

Spencer debated just letting it drop – Melissa was always overly theatrical. But curiosity got the best of her. 'What happened?'

They whizzed past Wawa, Ferra's Cheesesteaks, and the Rosewood Historical District, a string of old buildings that had been converted into candle shops, day spas, and real estate offices. Melissa let out a long sigh. 'Before Ian was arrested, Wilden came over and questioned us about the night Ali went missing. He asked if we'd been together the whole time, if we saw anything strange, whatever.'

'Yeah?' Spencer had never told Melissa that she'd spied on her and Ian from the stairs that day, worried her sister was going to mention the fight Spencer and Ali had had outside the barn right before Ali disappeared. It was a memory Spencer had suppressed for years, but she'd let it slip to Melissa, even mentioning that Ali had admitted that she and Ian were secretly together and teased Spencer for wanting Ian too. Spencer had shoved Ali out of frustration, and Ali had slipped and hit her head on the rocky path. Luckily, Ali had been okay – until a few minutes later, anyway, when someone else shoved her in that half-dug hole in her backyard.

'I told Wilden that we hadn't seen anything strange and that we'd been together the whole time,' Melissa went on.

Spencer nodded. 'But after that, Mom asked if I would've given Wilden the same story if Ian hadn't been in the room with me. I told her it was the truth. But after she kept pushing, I slipped up and said we'd been drinking. Mom pounced on me. "You need to be really, really sure about what you tell the police," she kept saying. "The truth really matters." She kept grilling me about it until I suddenly wasn't really *sure* what happened. I mean, there might have been a couple minutes when I woke up and Ian wasn't there. I was pretty wasted that night. And I mean, I don't even know if I was in my room the whole time or . . .'

She stopped abruptly, a muscle in her eye twitching. 'My point is, I finally buckled. I said that maybe Ian *had* gotten up . . . even though I really didn't know if he had or not. And she was like, "Okay then. You have to tell the cops that." Which is why we called Wilden back in to talk to me again. It was the day after you had that memory of Ian being in our yard when Ali died. My account was just the final nail in the coffin.'

Spencer's jaw dropped. 'But that's the thing,' she whispered. 'I'm not sure I remember Ian in the yard anymore. I saw *someone* . . . but I have no idea if it was him.'

Melissa made a left onto Weavertown Road, which was narrow and filled with apple orchards and farm co-ops. 'Then I guess we both were wrong. And Ian paid the price.'

Spencer sat back, thinking about that second time Wilden had come to their house. The night before, they'd discovered that Mona Vanderwaal was A, and she had almost pushed Spencer over the edge of Floating Man Quarry. The next morning, Melissa had slumped guiltily on the couch. Their parents stood at the back of the room, their arms crossed impassively at their chests, the disappointment obvious on both their faces.

'I was a mess that day,' Melissa said, as if reading Spencer's thoughts. She turned onto the Hastingses' street, sweeping past the cop cars and landscaping trucks that were parked at the curb. Across the street, a plumber's truck sat in the Cavanaughs' driveway. During the latest freeze, one of the family's main water pipes had burst. 'I acted like I was really ashamed for not coming forward with the information sooner,' Melissa said. 'But really, I was upset because I felt like I was selling out Ian for something I wasn't sure he'd done.'

So that was why Melissa had seemed so sympathetic to Ian when he was in prison. 'We should go to the cops,' she said. 'Maybe they'll drop the case against Ian.'

'There's nothing we can do now.' Melissa gave her a wary sidelong glance, and Spencer wanted to ask if she was in contact with Ian, too. She had to be, didn't she? But there was something closed-off about Melissa's expression as she pulled up the driveway and into the garage. Her fingers gripped the steering wheel tightly, even after they'd come to a complete stop.

'Why do you think Mom pushed you to say Ian was guilty?' she asked instead.

Melissa turned, reaching for her Foley + Corinna purse from the backseat. 'Maybe she sensed something was wrong with my story and was just trying to get the truth out of me. Or maybe ...' An uncomfortable look crossed her face.

'Maybe ... what?' Spencer pressed.

Melissa shrugged, pressing her thumb on the Mercedes logo in the middle of the steering wheel. 'Who knows? Maybe she just felt guilty because she wasn't exactly Ali's biggest fan.'

Spencer squinted, feeling more lost than before. As far as she knew, her mom had liked Ali as much as she'd liked Spencer's other friends. If anyone hadn't liked Ali, it was Melissa. Ali had stolen Ian from her.

Melissa gave Spencer a taut smile. 'I don't even know why I brought any of this up,' she said breezily, patting Spencer's shoulder. Then she stepped out of the car.

Spencer watched numbly as Melissa navigated around her dad's line of power tools and into the house. Her head felt like an upended suitcase, the contents of her brain like jumbled clothes all over the floor. Everything her sister just said was crazy. Melissa had been wrong about Spencer's adoption, and she was wrong about this, too.

The interior lights in the Mercedes snapped off. Spencer unbuckled her seat belt and climbed out of the car. The garage smelled like a dizzying combination of motor oil and fumes from the fire. In the Mercedes side mirror she caught a glimpse of a flash of dark hair across the street. It felt, like someone's eyes were on her back. When she turned, there was no one there.

She reached for her phone, about to call Emily or Hanna or Aria and tell them what Melissa just said about Ian. But then she noticed an alert on her screen. *One new text message*.

As she pressed read, an ache of dread wormed its way through her abdomen.

All those clues I've given you are right, Little Liar – just not in the way you think. But since I'm such a nice person, here's another hint. There's a major cover-up taking place right under your nose ... and someone close to you has all the answers. – A

8
Hanna, Interrupted

Bright and early on Tuesday morning, Hanna's father navigated a narrow, woodsy back road somewhere in Bumblefuck, Delaware. Isabel, who was sitting in the front passenger seat, suddenly leaned forward and pointed. 'There it is!'

Mr Marin cut the wheel sharply. They veered onto a blacktopped road and stopped at a security gate. The plaque on the bars said THE PRESERVE AT ADDISON-STEVENS.

Hanna slumped in the backseat. Mike, who was sitting next to her, squeezed her hand. They'd been driving around lost for a half hour. Even the GPS didn't know where they were – it kept bleating 'Recalculating route!' without actually recalculating anywhere for them to go. Hanna had hoped with all her heart that this place didn't exist. All she wanted was to go home, snuggle with Dot, and forget about this whole train wreck of a day.

'Hanna Marin, checking in,' Hanna's father said to a khaki-clad man in the security hut. The guard consulted his clipboard and nodded. The gate behind him slowly lifted.

The past twenty-four hours had galloped by, everyone rushing around and making decisions about Hanna's life without bothering to ask her opinion. It was as if she were a helpless baby or a troublesome pet. After her panic attack at breakfast, Mr Marin called the hospital Hanna was sure A had recommended. And wouldn't you know it, the Preserve at Addison-Stevens was able to accommodate Hanna the very next day. Next, Mr Marin called up Rosewood Day and told Hanna's guidance counselor that Hanna would be missing two weeks of school, and if anyone asked, she was visiting her mom in Singapore. Then he rang Officer Wilden and told him that if the press showed up at the hospital, he would sue the entire police force. And finally, in a move that further complicated how Hanna felt about her dad, he looked squarely at Kate, who was still lingering in the kitchen, no doubt loving every minute of this, and said that if Hanna's visit to the hospital got out to *anyone* at school, he'd immediately blame her. Hanna was so thrilled that she didn't bother to point out that even if Kate kept quiet about Hanna's disappearance, it didn't mean A would.

Hanna's father continued up the drive. Isabel shifted in her seat. Hanna stroked the two pieces of Time Capsule flag that were carefully nestled in her purse, one of them Ali's, the other the piece she'd found at the Rosewood Day coffee bar last week. She didn't want to let either flag out of her sight. Mike craned his neck, trying to get a view of the facility. Unlike Kate, Hanna didn't have to worry about Mike uttering a word about this – she'd threatened to make her boobs off-limits if he did.

They pulled into a circular roundabout. A stately white building with Grecian columns and small terraces on the second and third floors loomed in front of them, looking more like a railroad baron's mansion than a hospital. Mr Marin killed the ignition, and both he and Isabel turned around. Hanna's dad attempted a smile. Isabel still had that pitying, puckered-lips face she'd been making all morning.

'It looks really nice,' Isabel tried, gesturing at the bronze sculptures and carefully maintained topiaries in the doorway. 'Like a palace!'

'It does,' Mr Marin agreed quickly, releasing his seat belt. 'I'll get your stuff out of the trunk.'

'No,' Hanna snapped. 'I don't want you to come in, Dad. And I especially don't want *her*.' She nodded at Isabel.

Mr Marin's eyes narrowed. He was probably about to say that Hanna needed to show Isabel some respect, she was going to be her stepmom soon, *blah, blah, blah*. But Isabel laid an orangey, cronelike hand on his arm. 'It's okay, Tom. I understand.' Which made Hanna's scowl even deeper.

She shot out of the car and began to haul her suitcases out of the trunk. A full wardrobe had come along – just because she was being committed didn't mean she was going to walk around in a hospital gown and Crocs. Mike climbed out too and loaded the suitcases onto a large, unwieldy cart and pushed them into the facility. The lobby was a wide, marble-floored expanse that smelled like the clementine soap she kept on her dressing table. There were large, modern oil paintings on the walls, a bubbling fountain in the center, and a wide stone desk at the back. The receptionists wore white lab coats, just like skin care specialists at Kiehl's, and youngish, attractive people sat on wheat-colored sofas, laughing and talking.

'This doesn't look like Alcatraz,' Mike said, scratching his head.

Hanna's eyes darted back and forth. Okay, the lobby was nice, but it had to be a front. These people were probably actors rented out for the day, like the Shakespearean troupe Spencer's parents had hired to perform *A Midsummer Night's Dream* for her thirteenth birthday party. Hanna was sure the *real* patients were hidden in the back of the building, probably in wire-mesh dog kennels.

A blond woman wearing a wireless headset and a sage sheath dress rushed over. 'Hanna Marin?' She stuck out her hand. 'I'm Denise, your concierge. We're looking forward to having you stay with us.'

'Uh, good for you,' Hanna deadpanned. There was no way she was going to kiss this woman's ass and say she was looking forward to it, too.

Denise turned to Mike and smiled apologetically. 'We can't have visitors past this point. You'll have to say your good-byes here, if that's okay.'

Hanna gripped Mike's hand, wishing he were a teddy bear she could drag inside with her. Mike pulled Hanna out of earshot. 'Now listen.' His voice dropped an octave. 'I snuck a Pepperidge Farm cheese Danish into your red suitcase. Inside it is a file. You can saw through the bars of

82

your room and slip out when the guards aren't looking. It's the oldest trick in the book.'

Hanna laughed nervously. 'I don't really think there are going to be *bars* on the doors.'

Mike put a finger to his lips. 'You never know.'

Denise reappeared and placed her arm on Hanna's shoulder, telling her it was time to go. Mike gave her a long kiss, gestured suggestively at her red suitcase, and then walked backward toward the entrance. One of his shoes was untied; the lace flapped against the marble floor. His Rosewood Day lacrosse bracelet flopped around his wrist. Tears blurred Hanna's eyes. They'd only been an official couple for three days. This wasn't fair.

When he was gone, Denise shot Hanna a crisp, rehearsed smile, swiped a card through a reader at a door at the far end of the lobby, and ushered Hanna into a corridor. 'Your room is just through here.'

A strong scent of mint wafted through the air. Surprisingly, the corridor was as nice as the lobby, with lush, potted plants, black-and-white photographs, and carpeting that didn't appear to be speckled with blood or tufts of hair torn straight from crazy people's scalps. Denise stopped at a door marked 31. 'Your home away from home.'

The door opened into a dark room. It had two queen-size beds, two desks, two walk-in closets, and a big picture window that overlooked the front drive.

Denise looked around. 'Your roommate isn't here right now, but you'll meet her soon enough.' Then she explained the protocol at the facility – Hanna would be assigned to a therapist, and they would meet anywhere from a few times a week to once a day. Breakfast was at nine, lunch noon, and dinner six. Hanna was free to do what she wished for the rest of the day, and Denise encouraged Hanna to meet and mingle with the other residents – they were all very nice. *Right*, Hanna thought wryly. Did she *look* like the kind of girl who made friends with schitzos?

'Privacy is of the utmost importance to us, so your door has a lock and only you, your roommate, and the security guards have the key. And there's one more thing we need to take care of before I leave,' Denise added. 'I need you to surrender your cell phone.'

Hanna flinched. 'W-what?'

Denise's lips were candy pink. 'Our mantra here is "no outside influences." We only allow phone calls between four and five P.M. on Sundays. We don't allow you to surf the Internet or read the paper, and we don't allow live TV. We do have an extensive selection of DVDs for you to choose from. *And* lots of books and board games!'

Hanna opened her mouth, but only a small, squeaky *ohh* sound came out. No TV? No Internet? No phone calls? How the hell was she supposed to talk to Mike? Denise held out her palm, waiting. Helplessly, Hanna handed over the iPhone and watched as Denise wound the little earbuds around the device and dropped it in her lab coat pocket.

'Your schedule is on your nightstand,' Denise said. 'You have an evaluation with Dr Foster at three today. I really think you'll enjoy it here, Hanna.' She squeezed Hanna's hand and left. The door swished shut.

Hanna collapsed on her bed, feeling like Denise had

84

just beaten her up. What the hell was she going to do here? Peering out the window, she saw Mike climbing back into her dad's car. The Acura slowly pulled away. Hanna was suddenly gripped with the same panic she used to experience when her parents dropped her off at Rosewood Happyland Day Camp every summer morning. *It's only for a couple hours*, her dad always used to say when Hanna tried to convince him that she'd be happier accompanying him to work instead. And now, he'd shipped her off to the Preserve at the slightest provocation, falling for A's fake guidance counselor note. As if counselors at Rosewood Day even *noticed* the students! But her dad seemed thrilled to get rid of her. Now he could live his perfect life with perfect Isabel and perfect Kate in *Hanna's* house.

Hanna twisted the blinds shut. *Nice job, A.* So much for A being their BFF and wanting them to hunt down Ali's true killer – there wasn't much Hanna could do locked up in the nuthouse. But maybe what A really wanted was for Hanna to be crazy, miserable, and isolated from Rosewood forever.

If that was the case, A had most definitely succeeded.

9

Aria Crosses Over

Tuesday after school, Aria stood on the sidewalk in downtown Yarmouth, a town a few miles from Rosewood. Dirty piles of slush from last week's snow lined the sidewalks, making the stores look dingy. There was a chalkboard in front of the Yee-Haw Saloon, advertising that it was Drink Three Beers, Get Two Free night. The neon sign in the window of the salon next door was half burnt out so that only *lon* was illuminated.

Aria took a deep breath and faced the store in front of her, the reason she'd come. YE OLDE MYSTICK SPIRIT SHOPPE, said the calligraphy on the awning. There was a neon pentacle in the window and a green sign on the door that read TAROT CARDS, PALM READINGS, PAGAN, WICCAN, CURIOS. And underneath that, SEANCES AND OTHER PSYCHIC SERVICES OFFERED HERE. INQUIRE INSIDE.

After Aria's talk with Byron yesterday, she'd become more and more convinced that they'd seen Ali's ghost.

It made so much sense – for months, Aria had sworn someone had been watching her, looming near her old

86

bedroom window, peeking out of the thick woods, ducking out of sight around a corner at Rosewood Day. In some of those instances, the girl might've been Mona Vanderwaal, collecting secrets as A … but maybe not always. What if Ali had something to tell Aria and the others about the night she died? Wasn't it their duty to listen?

Bells tinkled as she entered. The shop smelled like patchouli, probably from the sticks of incense that smoldered in every corner. Crystal amulets, apothecary bottles, and dragon-inscribed chalices lined the shelves.

A radio was perched on a shelf behind the register, tuned to the news. 'The Rosewood police are investigating the cause of the fire that decimated ten acres of suburban woods and almost killed Rosewood's Pretty Little Liars,' the WKYW reporter squawked, the sound of typing in the background.

Aria let out a low growl. She hated their new nickname. It made them sound like deranged Barbie dolls.

'In related news,' the reporter added, 'the police are teaming up with the FBI to broaden the search for Miss DiLaurentis's alleged killer, Ian Thomas. There's also some discussion over whether Mr Thomas had accomplices. More to come after this short break.'

Someone cleared his throat, and Aria looked up. A balding guy in his twenties in a vest made out of what looked like horsehair was slumped by the register, HI, I'M BRUCE, said his name tag. RESIDENT WITCH. There was a musty, ornately bound book in his lap, and he was studying her as if he thought she might shoplift. Aria backed away from the table of ritual oils and gave him a sweet smile.

'Uh, hi.' Aria's voice cracked. 'I'm here for the séance. It starts in fifteen minutes, right?' She'd found a séance schedule on the store's website.

The shopkeeper flipped a page, looking bored. He slid a clipboard across the table. 'Put your name on the list. It's twenty bucks.'

Aria rifled through her yak-fur bag and scraped together a couple of limp bills. Then she leaned over and wrote her name on the sign-in sheet. Three other people had registered for today's event.

'*Aria?*'

She jumped and looked up. Standing next to a wall of voodoo talismans was a boy in a Rosewood Day blazer, a yellow rubber Rosewood Day lacrosse bracelet circling his wrist, and a huge, pleased smile on his face.

'Noel?' Aria sputtered. Noel Kahn was her brother's best friend, the typicalest Typical Rosewood Boy she'd ever met, and just about the last person she'd ever expect to see in a place like this. Back in sixth and seventh grade, when being popular mattered, Aria had had a huge crush on Noel – but of course he was crazy for Ali instead. *Everyone* loved Ali. Irony of ironies, the moment she'd stepped off the plane from Iceland at the beginning of this year, Noel had been all over her, suddenly finding her exotic instead of kooky. Or maybe he finally noticed she had boobs.

'Fancy meeting you here,' Noel drawled. He strolled up to the counter and scrawled his name below hers on the séance sign-in sheet.

'*You're* going to a séance?' Aria squeaked incredulously. Noel nodded, examining a set of tarot cards with a half-naked sorceress on the front. 'Séances rock. Have you listened to any Led Zeppelin? They were obsessed with the dead. I heard they got their song lyrics from Satan worshippers.'

Aria stared at him. Led Zeppelin was Noel and Mike's latest craze. The other day, Mike had asked Byron if he had an old copy of *Led Zeppelin IV* on vinyl – he wanted to play 'Stairway to Heaven' backward and listen for secret messages.

'Anyway, now that *you're* here, it's getting me closer to a hot girl, isn't it?' Noel snickered lasciviously. 'And hey, maybe if this works, you'll come to my hot tub party Thursday night.'

Aria's skin felt like it was crawling with leeches. The various skull talismans lined up on a nearby shelf were leering at her. Behind the counter, the shopkeeper smiled mysteriously, like he was keeping a secret. What was Noel really doing here? Had someone from the Rosewood press put him up to this, asking him to follow Aria around and report her every move? Or maybe this was a prank thought up by some of the lacrosse boys. In sixth grade, before Ali had welcomed Aria into her exclusive clique, kooky Aria had been relentlessly teased by girls and guys alike.

Noel picked up a phallic purple candle, then put it down again. 'So I guess you're here because of Ali?'

The patchouli incense was beginning to clog Aria's sinuses. She gave a noncommittal shrug.

Noel looked at Aria carefully. 'So *did* you see her in the woods?'

'It's none of your business,' Aria snapped, looking

89

around for hidden cameras or recorders nestled among the boxes of clove cigarettes. That seemed like just the kind of question a Rosewood reporter would encourage him to ask.

'Okay, okay,' Noel said defensively. 'I didn't mean to upset you.'

The shopkeeper slammed his book shut with a *whump*. 'The medium says you can go in now,' he proclaimed, parting a bead curtain at the back of the store.

Aria looked at the curtain, then at Noel. What if a bunch of Typical Rosewood Boys were waiting to jump out from behind the boxes in the back room, take pictures of her, and post them online? But the shopkeeper was glaring at her, so Aria gritted her teeth, pushed through the curtain, and slumped down on one of the folding chairs that had been set up in the center of the room. Although she wasn't sure if she wanted him to, Noel sat next to her and shrugged off his coat. Aria peeked at him. It was obvious why so many girls wanted to date Noel – he had dark, wavy hair, heavy-lidded eyes, and a tall, athletic body. His breath smelled like Altoids. But whatever. Even if he was here for legitimate reasons, he was so not her type. His perfectly broken-in dark denim jeans clearly came from a high-end boutique, and he was too groomed for Aria's taste; he didn't have a millimeter of stubble on his face.

Aria looked around the back of the occult shop, frowning. The only lights in here were a naked bulb hanging from the ceiling and a foul-smelling candle in the corner. Unidentified boxes were piled high on shelves, and toward the emergency exit was an enormous, oblong wooden thing that looked suspiciously like a coffin. Noel followed her gaze. 'Yep, that's a coffin,' he said. 'People buy those for, like, personal use. They get off on pretending they're dead.'

'How do you know that?' she whispered, flabbergasted.

'I know more than you think.'

Noel's ultra-white teeth gleamed in the darkness and Aria shivered.

The beads parted again, and two more people shuffled in and found seats. One was an old man with a handlebar moustache, and the other was a woman who looked like she was in her thirties, but it was hard to tell. She had a kerchief over her hair and wore big sunglasses. A young man came in last. He wore a velvet cloak and had a scarf wrapped around his head. Pendants and strings of beads dripped from around his neck, and he carried a dry ice contraption that spilled smoke around the already hazy room.

'Greetings,' he boomed. 'My name is Equinox.'

Aria stifled a laugh. *Equinox?* Come *on*. But next to her, Noel tipped his chair forward in rapt attention.

Equinox spread his palms toward the ceiling. 'To conjure up the spirits you're looking for, I need everyone to close their eyes and concentrate as one.' He began to om.

A few people – including Noel – joined in. The cold metal of the chair penetrated Aria's wool skirt. She cracked one eye open and peeked around. Everyone was leaning forward expectantly and a few people had joined hands. Suddenly Equinox teetered backward, as if an invisible force had just shoved him. A shiver ran through Aria's body and the air felt heavy around her. Taking a leap of faith, she omed too.

There was a long silence. The heating ducts rattled. There were soft patterns from the floor above. Incense wafted in from the front room, sweet and pungent. Something soft and featherlike brushed very faintly across Aria's cheek, and she jumped. When she opened her eyes, there was nothing there.

'Goooood,' Equinox said. 'Okay, we can open our eyes now. I'm feeling someone with us. Someone very close to one of you. Has anyone lost a friend?'

Aria stiffened. Ali couldn't be here, just like that ... could she?

Horrifyingly, the medium walked right to Aria and crouched down. His goatee ended in a sharp point, and he smelled faintly of pot. His eyes were wide and unblinking. 'It's you,' he said in a low voice, his lips close to her ear.

'Um,' Aria whispered, the hairs on the back of her neck standing on end.

'You've lost a special friend, haven't you?' he asked hauntingly.

The room was still. Aria's heart started to pound. 'Is she ... *here*?' She looked around the room, expecting to see the girl she'd rescued from the fire, dressed in a sweatshirt, her face tinged with soot.

'She's close,' the medium assured her. He tented his fingers and clenched his jaw, as if deep in concentration. A few more seconds ticked by. The room seemed to darken. The only lights were the glow-in-the-dark digits on Noel's IWC Aquatimer diving watch. Aria's pulse swished in her ears. Her fingers began to tremble, almost like they were picking up a vibration. *Ali's* vibration.

'She's telling me she knew everything about you,' Equinox said, almost teasingly.

Aria prickled with fear – and hope. That certainly sounded like Ali. 'We were best friends.'

'But you hated that she knew everything about you,' Equinox corrected. 'She knew this, too.'

Aria gasped. Now her legs trembled in sync with her fingers. Noel shifted in his seat. 'She ... did?'

'She knew a lot of things,' Equinox whispered. 'She knew you wanted her gone. It made her very sad. Many things made her very sad.'

Aria fluttered her hand to her mouth. All the other audience members were staring at her. She could see the whites of their wide eyes. 'I didn't want her gone,' she squeaked.

Equinox tilted his head to the ceiling, as if it gave him a better view of Ali. 'She forgives you, though. She knows she wasn't fair to you either.'

'Really?' Aria stammered. She pressed her palms against her knees to settle them. It was true, of course. Sometimes Ali *wasn't* fair to her. Lots of times, actually.

Equinox nodded. 'She knows it wasn't nice to steal your boyfriend. Especially since you two had been a couple for such a long time.'

Aria cocked her head, wondering if she'd heard him wrong. A chair squeaked and an audience member coughed. 'My ... boyfriend?' she repeated. A gnawing feeling roiled in her stomach. She hadn't had a boyfriend in seventh grade.

Which meant this quack wasn't talking to Ali at all.

Aria leapt up, almost banging her head on a low-hanging lantern. She fumbled her way through the haze of incense smoke and dry ice vapor toward the exit. 'Hey!' Equinox called.

'Aria, wait!' Noel said, but she ignored them.

A cardboard cutout of a warlock pointed the way to the store's bathroom. Aria ran for it, slammed the door, and collapsed against the sink, not caring that she'd knocked a cake of hand-milled dragon's blood soap to the floor. *Idiot*, she told herself. Of course Ali wasn't here. Of *course* séances were scams. This guy had probably approached her about Ali because he'd recognized Aria from the news. What had she been thinking?

Aria stared at her reflection in the round, streaky mirror above the sink. Her skin was milk-pale. But even though Equinox was a quack, he'd pointed out something awful – and something that was kind of true. Aria *had* wanted Ali gone.

Ali had been with Aria when Aria saw her dad making out with Meredith in the Hollis parking lot in seventh grade. In the weeks after, she just wouldn't let it drop. She cornered Aria between classes to ask her if there had been any updates. She invited herself over to Aria's house for dinner, giving Byron damning looks and Ella sympathetic ones. Whenever the five best friends were together, Ali dropped hints that she would tell Aria's secret *any minute* unless Aria did exactly what Ali wanted. Aria had reached a boiling point and, in the weeks before Ali's death, had started to avoid her as much as possible.

It made her very sad, the medium said. Could Ali have known how much Aria wanted her gone? A memory had popped into Aria's mind, suddenly: The day after Ali went missing, Mrs DiLaurentis had invited Aria and her friends over and grilled them about where Ali might have gone. At one point, Mrs DiLaurentis leaned forward on her elbows and asked, 'Did Ali ever seem ... sad?' The girls immediately protested – Ali was beautiful and smart and irresistible. Everyone adored her. *Sad* wasn't in Ali's emotional vocabulary.

Aria had always thought of herself as the victim and Ali the predator, but what if Ali had been going through stuff of her own? What if Ali needed someone to talk to – and Aria just pushed her away?

'I'm sorry,' she whispered, starting to weep. Clumps of mascara skidded down her cheeks. 'Ali, I'm so sorry. I never wanted you to die.'

There was a sharp *sfft* sound, like steam escaping from a radiator. Then the bulb over the mirror flicked off, bathing the room in darkness. Aria froze, her heart in her throat. Then, her nose twitched. There was a sudden fragrance in the air, chokingly pungent. *Vanilla soap.*

Aria grabbed the sides of the sink to steady herself. Then, without warning, the light snapped back on with a sizzle. Aria's frightened eyes stared back at her in the mirror. But her face wasn't the only one reflected there.

In the space behind her own ice blue eyes was a girl with a heart-shaped face, two wide, blue eyes, and a dazzling smile. Aria gasped and whirled around. Tacked to a corkboard on the back of the bathroom door, layered on top of other posters for upcoming poetry slams, futons for sale, and available rooms for rent, was a color photo of Ali.

Aria leaned closer, Ali's eyes drawing her in. Her breath caught in her throat. It was the Missing Persons flyer from when Ali vanished, the same picture that was splashed across milk cartons and local public service announcement commercials. MISSING, 72-point font said. ALISON DILAURENTIS. BLUE EYES, BLOND HAIR, 5'0", 90 POUNDS. LAST SEEN JUNE 20. Aria hadn't seen it in years. She searched frantically along every inch of the poster, even turning it over, for a clue as to why it was here – and who had put it up. But there was nothing.

10
The Simplest Life

Later that same day, Emily stood in front of a black-and-white clapboard farmhouse in Lancaster, Pennsylvania. Instead of a car in the driveway, there was a black buggy with giant wheels and a red triangular SLOW-MOVING VEHICLE sign on the back. She fingered the cuffs of the gray cotton dress A had given her and adjusted the white cloth cap on her head. Next to her was a hand-painted wooden sign that said ZOOK FARM.

Emily bit her lip. *This is crazy*. A few hours earlier, she'd told her parents she was going on the youth group trip to Boston. Then she'd boarded a Greyhound for Lancaster, changing into the dress, cap, and boots in the tiny, chemical-scented bathroom at the back of the bus. She sent her old friends short texts to let them know she'd be in Boston until Friday – if she told them the truth, they'd think she was nuts. And just in case her parents became suspicious, she'd turned off her cell phone so they couldn't activate its GPS child-tracking function and discover she was in Lancaster pretending to be Amish.

Emily had been idly curious about Amish people her whole life, but she knew nothing about what it was like to really *be* Amish. From what she understood, the Amish just wanted to be left alone. They didn't like tourists to take their pictures, they didn't take kindly to non-Amish trespassing on their land, and the few Amish people Emily had seen up close looked humorless and stern. So why was A sending her to an Amish community? Did Lucy Zook know Ali? Had Ali run away from Rosewood and secretly become Amish? That seemed impossible, but hope fluttered at the edge of Emily's thoughts. Was it possible that Lucy ... *was* Ali?

With each passing moment, Emily thought of more reasons why – and how – Ali might still be out there. There was the time when Emily and her friends met with Mrs DiLaurentis the day after Ali vanished, and Mrs DiLaurentis asked if Ali had run away. Emily had dismissed the notion, but the truth was she and Ali *did* used to talk about leaving Rosewood forever. They made all kinds of wistful plans – they'd go to the airport and pick the first flight that was leaving. They'd take Amtrak to California and find roommates in L.A. Emily couldn't imagine why Ali would want to leave Rosewood; she always secretly hoped that it was because Ali wanted Emily all to herself.

Then the summer between sixth and seventh grade, Ali had dropped off the face of the earth for two weeks. Every time Emily called Ali's cell phone it went to voice mail. Whenever she rang Ali's house, the answering machine picked up. And yet, the DiLaurentises were definitely home – Emily biked by their house and saw Mr

DiLaurentis washing his car in the driveway and Ali's mom pulling weeds in the front yard. She became convinced Ali was angry at her, though she had no idea why. And she couldn't talk to her other best friends about it. Spencer and Hanna were vacationing with their families, and Aria was at an art camp in Philly.

Then, two weeks later, Ali called out of the blue. 'Where *were* you?' Emily demanded.

'I ran away!' Ali chirped. When Emily didn't answer, she laughed. 'I'm kidding. I went to the Poconos with my aunt Giada. There's no cell service up there.'

Emily glanced at the handwritten sign again. As much as she didn't trust A's cryptic instructions about going to Lancaster – after all, A had misled them into believing that Wilden and Jason were Ali's killers, when Ali was in fact still alive – one tiny sentence fragment kept swirling in her head: *What would you do to find her?* She'd do anything, of course.

Taking a deep breath, Emily climbed the steps to the front porch of the farmhouse. A bunch of shirts hung from the laundry line, though it was so cold out that they looked half-frozen. Smoke poured from the chimney, and a big windmill in the back of the property churned. The yeasty smell of freshly baked bread wafted through the frigid air.

Emily looked over her shoulder, squinting at the far-off rows of dead cornstalks. Was A watching right now? She raised her hand and knocked three times, her nerves jangling. *Please let Ali be there*, she chanted to herself.

There was a creak and then a bang. A figure disappeared out the back door, slipping through the cornfield.

It looked like a guy about Emily's age, wearing a puffy down jacket, jeans, and bright red-and-blue sneakers. He ran at top speed without looking back.

Emily's heart banged in her chest. Moments later, the front door opened. A teenage girl stood on the other side. She wore a dress like Emily's, and her brown hair was pulled into a bun. Her lips were very red, as if they'd been recently kissed. She searched Emily's face wordlessly, her eyes narrowed with disdain. Emily's stomach swooped with disappointment.

'Uh, my name is Emily Stoltzfus,' she blurted, reciting the name from A's note. 'I'm from Ohio. Are you Lucy?'

The girl looked startled. 'Yes,' she said slowly. 'Are you here for Mary's wedding this weekend?'

Emily blinked. A hadn't told her about a wedding. Was it possible Ali's new Amish name was Mary? Maybe she was being forced to be a child bride, and A had sent Emily here to save her. But Emily's return bus ticket was for Friday afternoon, the very same time the church group returned from Boston. She couldn't possibly stay for what was probably a Saturday wedding without raising her parents' suspicions. 'Um, I came to help with the preparations,' she said, hoping she didn't sound incredibly foolish.

Lucy glanced at something behind Emily. 'There's Mary now. Do you want to go say hi?'

Emily followed her gaze. But Mary was much smaller and dumpier than the girl Emily had seen in the woods just days ago. Her black hair was pulled back in a tight bun, showing off her chubby cheeks. 'Um, that's okay,' Emily said glumly, her heart yo-yoing. She turned back to

Lucy, inspecting her face. Lucy's lips were pressed tightly together, like she was biting back a secret.

Lucy opened the door wider, letting Emily in. They walked into the parlor. It was a big square room, lit only by a gas-powered lantern in the corner. Handcrafted wooden chairs and tables crowded the walls. A bookshelf in the corner housed a jar full of celery and a large, well-worn copy of the Bible. Lucy walked into the center of the room and gazed at Emily carefully. 'Where are you from in Ohio?'

'Um, near Columbus,' Emily said, blurting out the first Ohio town she could think of.

'Oh.' Lucy scratched her head. This must have been an acceptable answer. 'Did Pastor Adam send you to me?'

Emily swallowed hard. 'Yes?' she guessed. She felt like she was an actress in a play, but no one had bothered to give her the script.

Lucy *tsk*ed and glanced over her shoulder toward the back door. 'He always thinks things like this will make me feel better,' she muttered acidly.

'I'm sorry?' Emily was surprised at how annoyed Lucy seemed. She'd thought the Amish were eternally temperate and calm.

Lucy waved her thin, pale hand. 'No, *I'm* sorry.' She turned and started down a long hall. 'You'll take my sister's bed,' she said matter-of-factly, leading Emily into a small bedroom. Inside were two twin beds covered by lively colored homemade quilts. 'It's the one on the left.'

'What's your sister's name?' Emily asked, glancing at the bare white walls.

'Leah.' Lucy punched a pillow.

'Where is she now?'

Lucy smacked the pillow harder. Her throat bobbed, and then she turned away toward the corner of the bedroom, as if she'd done something shameful. 'I was just going to start the milking. Come on.'

At that, she marched out of the bedroom. After a moment, Emily followed Lucy, snaking through a rabbit warren of hallways and rooms. She poked her head into each room, aching to see Ali in one of them, sitting in a rocker, her finger to her lips, or crouching behind a bureau, her knees pulled into her chest. Finally they crossed the big, bright kitchen, which smelled overpoweringly like wet wool, and Lucy led her out the back door to an enormous, drafty barn. A long line of cows stood in stalls, their tails swishing. Upon seeing the girls, a few of them let out loud moos.

Lucy handed Emily a metal bucket. 'You start on the left. I'll do the right.'

Emily shifted her feet in the scratchy hay. She'd never milked a cow before, not even when she had been shipped to her aunt and uncle's farm in Iowa the fall before. Lucy had already turned away, tending to her own line of cows. Not knowing what else to do, Emily approached the cow closest to the door, slid the bucket under her udder, and crouched. How hard could it be? But the cow was enormous, with strong legs and a broad, trucklike butt. Did cows kick, like horses? Did cows *bite*?

She cracked her knuckles, eyeing the other stalls. *If a cow moos in the next ten seconds, everything will be okay*, she thought, relying on the superstitious game she'd created for tense situations like this one. She silently counted to ten in her head. There weren't any moos, although there was a noise that sounded suspiciously like a fart.

'*Ahem.*'

Emily shot up. Lucy was glaring at her.

'Haven't you ever milked a cow before?' Lucy demanded.

'Uh.' Emily grappled for a response. 'Well, no. We have really specific jobs where I'm from. Milking isn't my responsibility.'

Lucy looked at her as if she'd never heard of such a thing. 'You'll have to do it as long as you're here. It's not hard. Just pull and squeeze.'

'Um, okay,' Emily stammered. She turned to the cow. Her teats dangled. She touched one; it felt rubbery and full. When she squeezed, milk squirted into the bucket. It was a strange dusty color, nothing like the milk her mother brought home from Fresh Fields grocery store.

'That's good,' Lucy said, standing over her. She had that funny look on her face again. 'Why are you speaking English, by the way?'

The sharp scent of hay tickled Emily's eyes. Did Amish people not speak English? She'd read various Wikipedia articles about Amish people last night in an attempt to absorb as much information as possible – how had she not stumbled upon that? And why hadn't A said anything?

'Did your community not speak Pennsylvania Dutch?' Lucy prompted incredulously.

Emily adjusted her woolen cap nervously. Her fingers smelled like sour milk. 'Um … no. We're pretty progressive.'

Lucy shook her head in wonderment. 'Wow. You're so lucky. We should switch places. You stay here, and I'll go there.'

Emily laughed nervously, relaxing a teensy bit. Maybe Lucy wasn't so bad. And maybe even Amish country wasn't so bad either – at least it was quiet and drama-free. But disappointment welled in her chest all the same. Ali didn't seem to be hiding out in this community, so why had A sent her here? To make her look stupid? To distract her for a while? To send her on a wild-goose chase?

As if on cue, one of the Holsteins let out a loud, lowing moo and dropped fresh cow pies on the hay-strewn floor. Emily gritted her teeth. Perhaps a wild *cow* chase was more like it.

11
Not Your Typical
Mother–Daughter Outing

As soon as Spencer stepped into the lobby of the Fermata spa, a smile flitted over her lips. The room smelled like honey, and the soft, burbling sounds of the fountain in the corner were soothing and tranquil.

'I booked you for a deep tissue massage, a carrot body buff, and an oxygen facial,' Spencer's mother said, taking out her wallet. 'And then after that, I made us reservations for a late lunch at Feast.'

'Wow,' Spencer gushed. Feast, the bistro next door, was Mrs Hastings and Melissa's regular lunch spot.

Mrs Hastings squeezed Spencer's shoulder, the smell of her liberally applied Chanel No. 5 perfume tickling Spencer's nose. An aesthetician showed Spencer the locker where she could stash her clothes and change into a robe and slippers. Before she knew it, she was lying on a massage table, melting into a puddle of goo.

Spencer hadn't felt this close to her parents in a long, long time. Last night, she and her dad had watched *The*

Godfather in the den, her dad quoting every line by heart, and later, she and her mother began planning the Rosewood Day Hunt Club benefit that would take place in two months. Plus, when she checked her grades online this morning, she'd seen that she had aced the last AP econ test. Good news like that called for an appreciative text to Andrew – he'd been her tutor – and he wrote back saying he knew she could do it. He also asked if she wanted to go with him to the Valentine's Day dance in a few weeks. Spencer said yes.

Her conversation with Melissa still nagged at her, though, as did A's note about a cover-up. Spencer couldn't believe her mother would make Melissa blame Ian for Ali's murder. Melissa must have misinterpreted their mother's concern. And as for A ... well, Spencer certainly didn't trust anything A had to say.

'Honey?' The masseuse's voice floated down from above. 'You've suddenly turned to stone. Let go.'

Spencer forced her muscles to relax. Crashing ocean waves and cawing seagulls swelled from the sound machine. She shut her eyes, huffing three short yoga fire breaths. She would *not* overreact. That was probably just what A wanted.

After the massage, the carrot buff, and the oxygen facial, Spencer felt loose, soft, and glowing. Her mother was waiting for her at Feast, drinking a glass of lemon water and reading a copy of *MainLine* magazine. 'That was wonderful,' Spencer said, flopping down. 'Thank you so much.'

'It's my pleasure,' Mrs Hastings answered, unfolding her napkin and placing it neatly on her lap. 'Anything to help you relax after everything you've gone through.'

They fell silent. Spencer stared at the hand-thrown ceramic plate in front of her. Her mother ran her pointer finger around the lip of her glass. After sixteen years of playing second fiddle, Spencer had no idea what to say to her mom. She couldn't even remember the last time they'd been alone together.

Mrs Hastings sighed and stared absently at the oak bar in the corner. A couple of customers were sitting on high stools, nursing lunchtime martinis and glasses of chardonnay. 'I didn't mean for it to get like this between us, you know,' she said, as if reading Spencer's mind. 'I don't really know what happened.'

Melissa happened, Spencer thought. But she just shrugged and tapped her toes to the beat of 'Für Elise,' one of the last pieces of music she'd learned during her piano lessons.

'I pushed you too hard in school, and that pushed you away,' her mother lamented, lowering her voice as four coiffed women carrying yoga mats and Tory Burch purses followed the hostess to a back booth. 'With Melissa, it was easier. There were fewer standouts in her grade.' She paused to sip her water. 'But with you ... well, your class was different. I saw how you were satisfied with being number two. I wanted you to be a leader, not a follower.'

Spencer's heart sped up, yesterday's conversation with Melissa fresh in her mind. *Mom wasn't exactly Ali's biggest fan*, Melissa had said. 'Do you mean ... Alison?' she asked.

Mrs Hastings took a measured sip of her sparkling water. 'She's one example, yes. Alison definitely liked to be the center of attention.'

Spencer chose her words carefully. 'And ... you thought *I* should have been?'

Mrs Hastings pursed her lips. 'Well, I thought you could have asserted yourself more. Like that time Alison got the spot on the JV field hockey team and you didn't. You just ... *accepted* it. You usually had a little more fight in you. And you certainly deserved that spot.'

The restaurant suddenly smelled like sweet potato fries. Three waiters paraded out of the kitchen with a slice of cake for a stately, graying woman a few tables over. They serenaded her with 'Happy Birthday.' Spencer ran her hand over the back of her neck, which was a little sweaty. For years, she'd hoped someone would say out loud that Ali wasn't all that, but now, she only felt guilty and slightly defensive. Was Melissa right? *Had* her mom disliked Ali? It felt like a personal criticism. After all, Ali had been *her* best friend, and Mrs Hastings always liked all of Melissa's friends.

'Anyway,' Mrs Hastings said after the waiters had stopped singing, lacing her long fingers together, 'I worried that you were settling for being second best, so I started pushing you harder. I realize now it was more about me than it was about you.' She tucked a strand of pale hair behind her ear.

'What do you mean?' Spencer asked, gripping the edge of the table.

Mrs Hastings's gaze fixed on a large Magritte *Ceci n'est pas une pipe* print across the room. 'I don't know, Spence. Maybe it's not worth getting into right now. It's something I haven't even told your sister.'

A waitress passed, carrying a tray of Waldorf salads and

focaccia sandwiches. Out the window, two women with Maclaren baby carriages were chatting and laughing. Spencer leaned forward, her mouth dry as paper. So there *was* a secret, just like A said. Spencer hoped it had nothing to do with Ali. 'It's okay,' she said bravely. 'You can tell me.'

Mrs Hastings pulled out a tube of Chanel lipstick, coated her lips, and then shook out her shoulders. 'You know how your dad went to Yale Law?' she began.

Spencer nodded. Her dad dutifully donated to the law school every year and drank coffee out of his Handsome Dan the Yale Bulldog mug. At the family's annual Christmas party, he always drank too much eggnog and sang that 'Boola Boola' Yale fight song with his old school buddies.

'Well, I was at Yale Law too,' Mrs Hastings said. 'It's where I met your father.'

Spencer pressed her hand to her mouth, wondering if she'd heard her mother wrong. 'I thought you guys met at a party on Martha's Vineyard,' she squeaked.

Her mother gave her a wistful smile. 'One of our first dates was to that party. But we met the first week of school.'

Spencer unfolded then refolded her linen napkin on her lap. 'How come I never knew?'

A waitress arrived, handing Spencer and her mom their menus. When she flounced away, Mrs Hastings continued. 'Because I didn't *finish* law school. After my first year I got pregnant with your sister. Nana Hastings found out and demanded that your dad and I marry. We decided that I'd defer Yale for a few years and raise the baby. I planned to go back ...'

An expression Spencer couldn't gauge flickered across

her mom's face. 'We fudged the date on our marriage certificate because we didn't want to make it seem like it was a shotgun marriage.' She pushed a pale blond strand of hair out of her eyes. A BlackBerry beeped two tables over. A man at the bar let out a loud guffaw. 'It was what I wanted. But I'd also always wanted to be a lawyer. I know that I can't control how your life turns out, Spence, but I want to make sure you have every opportunity in the world. It's why I've been so tough on you about everything ... grades, Golden Orchid, sports. But I'm sorry. I haven't been fair.'

Spencer stared at her mother for a long beat, speechless. Someone dropped a tray of plates in the kitchen, but she didn't flinch.

Mrs Hastings reached across the table and touched Spencer's hand. 'I hope it's not a burden to hear this. I just wanted you to know the truth.'

'No,' Spencer croaked. 'It explains a lot. I'm glad you told me. But why didn't you go back to school after Melissa was old enough?'

'I just ...' Mrs Hastings shrugged. 'We wanted you ... and that time had passed.' She leaned forward. 'Please don't tell Melissa,' she urged. 'You know how sensitive she is. She'd worry I resent her.'

Inside, Spencer felt a tiny thrill. So *she* was the daughter they'd planned for ... and Melissa was the one they hadn't.

And maybe this was even the cover-up A had been talking about, although it didn't have anything to do with Ali, or Mrs Hastings not liking her. But as Spencer reached for a piece of flatbread, a tiny, buried memory from the night Ali vanished twinkled in her mind.

After Ali ditched them in the barn, Spencer and the others decided to go home. Emily, Hanna, and Aria called their parents for rides, and Spencer went back into her house and up into her bedroom. The television had been on downstairs – Melissa and Ian were in the den – but her parents weren't anywhere to be seen. That was odd, because they typically didn't allow Spencer or Melissa to be alone with boys in the house.

Spencer had slid under her duvet, miserable at how badly the night had gone. Something woke her much later. When she stepped into the hall and peered over the railing, she saw two figures in the foyer. One was Melissa, still wearing the gray flutter-sleeve top and black silk headband she'd had on earlier. She was whispering heatedly with Mr Hastings. Spencer couldn't hear much of what they were saying, only that Melissa sounded angry and her father sounded defensive. At one point, Melissa let out a frenzied cry. 'I can't believe you,' she said. And then her father said something Spencer couldn't discern. 'Where's Mom?' Melissa asked, her voice rising with hysterics. 'We need to find her!' Then they hurried toward the kitchen, and Spencer shut the door quickly and scuttled back into her room.

'Spence?'

Spencer jumped. Her mother was staring at her with large, round eyes across the table. When Spencer looked down at her hands, cupped around her water glass, she realized they were trembling uncontrollably.

'Are you okay?' Mrs Hastings asked.

Spencer opened her mouth, then shut it fast. Was that a real memory, or a dream? Had her mother been missing

111

that night too? But it was implausible that she'd seen Ali's true killer. If she had, she would've gone to the cops immediately. She wasn't that heartless – or lawless. And what would be the point of covering up something like that?

'Where did you go just now?' Mrs Hastings asked, her head tilted.

Spencer squeezed her softened, paraffin-soaked palms together. Since they were being honest with each other, maybe she could talk about this. 'I ... I was just thinking about the night Ali went missing,' she blurted.

Mrs Hastings twirled the two-carat diamond stud in her right ear, letting this sink in. Then her forehead wrinkled. The lines around her mouth looked etched as though with a chisel. Her eyes darted down to her plate.

'Are *you* okay?' Spencer asked quickly, her heart rocketing to her throat.

Mrs Hastings's mouth snapped into a tight smile. 'That was a terrible night, honey.' Her voice dropped an octave. 'Let's not talk about it ever again.'

And then she turned away, flagging down the waitress to take their orders. She seemed nonchalant enough as she asked for the Asian chicken salad with sesame dressing on the side, but Spencer couldn't help but notice that her hand was clenched tightly around her knife, and her finger was slowly tracing the sharpened edge of the blade.

12
Even A Nuthouse Needs An In Crowd

Hanna stood in the cafeteria at the Preserve at Addison-Stevens, a tray of baked chicken and steamed veggies in her arms. The cafeteria was a large, square room with honey-colored wood floors, small farm tables, a glossy black Steinway grand piano off to one side, and a wall of windows that looked out onto the shimmering meadow. There were textured, abstract paintings on the walls and gray velvet curtains on the windows. On a table near the back were two shiny, expensive-looking cappuccino makers, a long, stainless-steel cooler full of every kind of soda imaginable, and platters upon platters of divine-looking chocolate cakes, lemon meringue pies, and toffee-fudge brownies. Not that Hanna would be partaking in the desserts, of course. This place might have a James Beard Award-winning pastry chef, but the last thing she needed was to pack on ten pounds of fat.

Admittedly, her first day in the loony bin hadn't been that bad. She'd spent the first hour or so staring at the plaster swirls in the ceiling of her room, ruminating on

113

how badly her life sucked. Then a nurse had come into her room, handing out a pill like it was a Tic Tac. Turned out, it had been a Valium, which she was *allowed* to take whenever she wanted here.

Then she'd had an appointment with her therapist, Dr Foster, who promised she would contact Mike and tell him that Hanna wasn't allowed to use the phone or send e-mails except for Sunday afternoons, so he wouldn't think she was ignoring him. Dr Foster also said Hanna didn't have to talk about Ali, A, or Mona in session if she didn't want to. And finally, the therapist reiterated over and over again that none of the girls on Hanna's floor knew who she was – most of them had been at the Preserve for so long that they'd never heard of A or Ali to begin with. 'So you won't have to think about it while you're here,' Dr Foster said, patting Hanna's hand. And all that took up the entire therapy hour. *Score*.

Now it was mealtime. Everyone else in the girls' wing was gathered at tables of three and four. Most patients were wearing hospital scrubs or flannel jammies, their hair mussed, their faces without makeup, their fingernails without polish. There were, however, a few tables of pretty girls in skinny jeans, long tunics, and soft cashmere sweaters, their hair shiny, their bodies toned. But no one had noticed Hanna or welcomed her to sit with them. They all seemed to look through her, as if she were just a two-dimensional image drawn on tracing paper.

As Hanna stood in the doorway, shifting from foot to foot, she felt transported back to the Rosewood Day cafeteria on the first day of sixth grade. Sixth graders were officially part of the middle school, which meant they ate lunch with kids in seventh and eighth. Hanna had stood at the edge of the room just like this, wishing she were pretty and thin and popular enough to sit with Naomi Zeigler and Alison DiLaurentis. Then Riley Wolfe bumped Hanna's elbow, and Hanna's spaghetti-and-meatballs lunch splattered all over her shoes and the floor. Even today, she could still hear Naomi's high-pitched laugh, Ali's demure chuckle, and Riley's apathetic and insincere 'Sorry.' Hanna had run out of the cafeteria in tears.

'Excuse me?'

Hanna turned around and saw a short, dumpy girl with dull brown hair and braces. She would've mistaken her for a twelve-year-old except that the girl had enormous boobs. Her melon-colored hoodie stretched tight across them, making them look rather like melons themselves. With a sad twinge, Hanna thought of Mike. He'd probably make the same boobalicious remark.

'Are you new?' the girl asked. 'You look kind of lost.'

'Uh, yeah.' Hanna wrinkled her nose at the sudden, grandmotherly smell of Vicks VapoRub. It seemed to be wafting from this girl's skin.

'I'm Tara.' The girl spat a little as she spoke.

'Hanna,' Hanna murmured apathetically, moving aside to let an aide in pink scrubs pass.

'You want to eat with us? It sucks to eat alone. We've all been there.'

Hanna lowered her eyes to the polished wood floor, considering her options. Tara didn't seem crazy – just dorky. And beggars couldn't be choosers. 'Uh, sure,' she said, struggling to be polite.

'Great!' Tara – and her boobs – jiggled up and down. She wove through the tables, leading Hanna to a four-top at the back. A rail-thin girl with a long, hangdog face and goth-pale skin was picking at a plate of plain penne noodles, and a pudgy redhead with a noticeable bald patch above her right ear was nibbling furiously on an ear of corn. 'This is Alexis and Ruby,' Tara announced. 'And this is Hanna. She's new!'

Alexis and Ruby shyly said hi. Hanna said hi back, feeling more and more unsettled. She was dying to ask these girls why they were here, but Dr Foster had emphasized that diagnoses were not to be discussed except in private sessions or group therapy. Instead, patients were supposed to pretend that they were here by choice, like this was some kind of freaky camp.

Tara plopped down next to Hanna and immediately started cutting up the impressive pile of food on her plate – she had a hamburger, a square of lasagna, green beans bathed in butter and almonds, and a giant hunk of bread as big as Hanna's palm.

'So this was your first day, right?' Tara asked cheerfully. 'How was it?'

Hanna shrugged, wondering if Tara had overeating issues. 'Kind of boring.'

Tara nodded, chewing with her mouth open. 'I know. The no-Internet thing sucks. You can't Twitter or blog or anything. Do you have a blog?'

'No,' Hanna answered, trying not to scoff. Blogs were for people who didn't have lives.

Tara shoved another forkful of food into her mouth. She had a tiny cold sore at the corner of her lip. 'You'll get

116

used to it. Most people here are really nice. There are only a couple girls to stay away from.'

'They're bitches,' Alexis said, her voice surprisingly husky for someone so thin.

The other girls giggled naughtily at the word *bitches*. 'They spend all their time at the spa,' Ruby said, rolling her eyes. 'They can't go one day without getting a manicure.'

Hanna almost choked on a broccoli stalk, certain she'd heard Ruby wrong. 'Did you just say this place has a spa?'

'Yeah, but it costs extra.' Tara wrinkled her nose.

Hanna ran her tongue over her teeth. How had she not heard about the spa? And who cared if it cost extra? She was totally charging treatments to her dad's tab. It served him right.

'So who's your roomie?' Tara asked.

Hanna tucked her pebbled leather Marc Jacobs bag under her seat. 'I haven't met her yet.' Her roommate hadn't returned to their shared room all day. She'd probably been sent to a padded isolation room or something.

Tara smiled. 'Well, you should hang with us. We're awesome.' She pointed her fork at Alexis and Ruby. 'We make up plays about the hospital staff and perform them in our rooms. Ruby's usually the lead.'

'Ruby is destined for the Broadway stage,' Alexis added. 'She's *really* good.'

Ruby blushed and ducked her head. Little corn kernels were stuck to her left cheek. Hanna had a feeling the closest Ruby would get to a Broadway stage would be as a cashier in the lobby snack bar.

'We play *America's Next Top Model*, too,' Tara went on, stabbing at the lasagna.

This instantly sent Alexis and Ruby into hysterics. They slapped hands and belted out the show's theme song, very off-key. '*I wanna be on top! Na na na na NA na!*'

Hanna slumped in her seat. It seemed like all the overhead lights in the cafeteria had dimmed except for the one directly over their table. A couple of girls at nearby tables turned and stared. 'You guys pretend you're models?' she asked weakly.

Ruby took a swig of Coke. 'Not really. Mostly we just put together outfits from our closets and strut down the hall like it's a runway. Tara has awesome clothes. And she's got a Burberry bag!'

Tara dabbed her mouth with a napkin. 'It's fake,' she confessed. 'My mom got it for me in Chinatown in New York. But it totally looks like the real thing.'

Hanna felt her will to live slowly drain out the soles of her feet. She eyed two chatting nurses near the dessert tray and wished she could hit them up for a double dose of Valium right then. 'I'm sure it does,' she lied.

Suddenly, a blond girl watching them by the soup tureens caught Hanna's eye. She had corn-silk blond hair, pale, gorgeous skin, and an alluring, indefinable presence about her. A shiver snaked through Hanna's body. *Ali?*

She did a double take and realized this girl's face was rounder, her eyes were green, not blue, and all her features were a little pointy. Hanna slowly let out a breath.

But the girl was now making a beeline for Hanna, Tara, Alexis, and Ruby, winding quickly around the tables. She had the exact same smirk on her face that Ali used to get

118

when she was about to tease someone. Hanna gazed despondently at her dinner companions. Then she ran her hands along her thighs, stiffening with alarm. Did her legs feel chunkier than usual? And why did her hair feel so brittle and frizzy? Her heart began to pound. What if, just by sitting here with these dorks, Hanna had instantly reverted to her lame, loserish, pre-Ali self? What if she'd sprouted a double chin and back fat, and what if her teeth had gone instantly crooked? Nervous, Hanna reached for a piece of bread from the basket in the middle of the table. Just as she was about to shove the whole thing into her mouth, she recoiled in horror. What was she *doing*? Fabulous Hanna *never* ate bread.

Tara noticed the girl walking toward them and nudged Ruby. Alexis sat up straighter. Everyone held their breath as the girl approached the table. When she touched Hanna's arm, Hanna bristled, bracing for the worst. She'd probably morphed into a hideous troll by now.

'Are you Hanna?' the girl said in a clear, mellifluous voice.

Hanna tried to speak, but her words got caught in her throat. She made a sound that was a cross between a hiccup and a burp. 'Yeah,' she finally managed, her cheeks flaming.

The girl stuck out her hand. Her long nails were painted Chanel black. 'I'm Iris,' she said. 'Your roommate.'

'H-hi,' Hanna said cautiously, staring into Iris's pale green, almond-shaped eyes.

Iris stepped away, looking Hanna up and down appraisingly. Then she offered her hand. 'Come with me,' she said airily. 'We don't hang out with losers.'

Everyone at the table let out an outraged gasp. Alexis's face was as long as a horse's. Ruby pulled nervously at her hair. Tara shook her head vehemently, as if Hanna was about to eat something poisonous. She mouthed the word *bitch*.

But Iris smelled like lilacs, not Vick's VapoRub. She was wearing the same long Joie cashmere cardigan Hanna had bought two weeks ago at Otter, and she didn't have bald patches on her scalp. Long ago, Hanna vowed to never be a dork again. Those rules even applied inside a mental hospital.

Shrugging, she stood up and plucked her purse from the ground. 'Sorry, ladies,' she said sweetly, blowing them a kiss. And then she looped her arm around Iris's waiting elbow and walked away, not once looking back.

As they strutted through the cafeteria, Iris leaned down to Hanna's ear. 'You totally lucked out by getting a room with me instead of with some of the other freaks. I'm the only normal one here.'

'Thank God,' Hanna said under her breath, rolling her eyes.

Iris stopped and gave Hanna a long, hard look. A smile washed over her face, one that seemed to say, *Yeah, you're cool.* And Hanna realized that Iris might be cool too. More than cool. The two of them exchanged a smug, knowing look that only pretty, popular girls understood.

Iris twisted a long strand of pale blond hair around her finger. 'So, mud masks after dinner? I'm assuming you know about the spa.'

'Done.' Hanna nodded. Hope swelled in her chest. Maybe this place wouldn't be so bad after all.

13
Someone's Not As Typical As You Think

Wednesday afternoon, Aria sat at the kitchen table at Byron and Meredith's new house, staring gloomily into a bag of organic honey-wheat pretzels. The house had been built in the 1950s, with ornate crown molding, a three-tier deck, and beautiful French doors leading from room to room. Unfortunately, the kitchen was small and cramped, and the appliances hadn't been updated since the Cold War era. To make up for its old-fashionedness, Meredith had stripped the plaid wallpaper and painted the walls neon green. Like *that* would be soothing for the baby.

Mike sat next to Aria, grumbling that the only beverage in the house was nonfat Rice Dream soy milk. Byron had invited Mike over after school so he could get to know Meredith better, although the only thing Mike had said to Meredith so far was that her boobs had really grown since she'd gotten knocked up. She'd smiled tightly then clomped upstairs to prepare the baby's nursery.

Mike turned the little kitchen TV to the news. *Public Calls for Pretty Little Liars to Take Polygraphs* said a block-letter headline on the screen. Aria gasped and leaned forward.

'Some people suspect the four Rosewood girls who claimed they saw Alison DiLaurentis may be keeping vital information from the police,' a smug, blond reporter said into the camera. Downtown Rosewood, with its quaint village square, French cafe, and Danish furniture store, was in the shot behind her. 'They've been at the center of many scandals involving Alison DiLaurentis's case. Then on Saturday they were found at the site of a fire that ravaged the woods where Mr Thomas was last seen, destroying any possible clues as to his whereabouts. According to several reports, the police are ready to take action against the Liars should any evidence of conspiracy emerge.'

'Conspiracy?' Aria repeated, dumbfounded. Did they honestly think Aria and the others had helped Ian escape? It seemed Wilden's warning had been right. They'd lost any remaining shred of credibility when Emily claimed they saw Ali. The entire town had turned against them.

She gazed vacantly out the bay window to the backyard. Workers and cops were scattered around the woods behind her house, poking through the ashes and searching for clues as to who had set the fire. They looked like busy ants in a colony. A woman cop stood near a big telephone pole, two panting German shepherds wearing K-9 Unit vests at her side. Aria wanted to run outside in her hemp slippers and drop Ian's ring back where she'd found it, but guards and dogs were patrolling the perimeter 24/7.

Sighing, she pulled out her phone and started a new text to Spencer. *Did u just see the news about polygraphs?*

122

Yes, Spencer texted back immediately.

Aria paused, considering how to word her next question. *Do you think it's possible that Ali's spirit is trying to tell us something? Maybe that's what we saw the night of the fire?*

Seconds after she fired off the text, Spencer wrote back. *Like her ghost?*

Yes.

No way.

Aria turned her phone facedown on the table. It wasn't surprising that Spencer didn't believe her. Back when they used to go swimming in Peck's Pond, Ali made them chant a rhyme that would keep the spirit of the dead man who'd drowned there from harming them. Spencer was the only one who rolled her eyes and refused to play along.

'Dude,' Mike said excitedly, and Aria looked up. 'You *have* to tell me what a polygraph is like. I bet it's awesome.' When he saw Aria's sick expression, he scoffed. 'I'm *kidding*. The cops won't make you take a test. You haven't done anything wrong. Hanna would tell me if you had.'

'Are you and Hanna really dating?' Aria asked, desperate to change the subject.

Mike squared his shoulders. 'Is that really such a surprise? I'm hot.' He popped a pretzel into his mouth. Crumbs fell to the tile floor. 'And speaking of Hanna, if you've been looking for her, she went to Singapore to be with her mom. She's not, like, locked away somewhere or anything. She's not, like, I don't know, in Vegas training to be a stripper.'

Aria stared at him crazily. She really had no idea how

123

Hanna put up with him. She didn't blame Hanna for taking off to Singapore either – Aria would do anything to get out of Rosewood too. Even Emily had gotten out of town, off on some church trip to Boston.

'I heard something about *you*.' Mike pointed at her accusingly, wiggling his dark eyebrows. 'A reliable source told me that you and Noel Kahn hung out yesterday.'

Aria groaned. 'Would that reliable source be Noel himself?'

'Well, yeah.' Mike shrugged. He leaned forward and asked in a gossipy voice, 'So what did you guys do?'

Aria licked pretzel salt off her fingers. Huh. So Noel hadn't told Mike that they'd gone to a séance. It appeared that he hadn't told the press, either. 'We just ran into each other somewhere.'

'He totally likes you.' Mike propped his dirty sneakers on the kitchen table.

Aria ducked her head, staring at what looked like a morsel of Kashi on the tile floor. 'No, he doesn't.'

'He's having a hot tub party on Thursday,' Mike added. 'You heard about that, right? The Kahns are going away and Noel and his brothers are going all out.'

'Why is the party on a Thursday?'

'Thursday is the new Saturday,' Mike quipped, rolling his eyes as if *everyone* should know that. 'It's going to be sick. You should go.'

'No, thanks,' Aria said quickly. The last thing she wanted to do was go to another Noel Kahn party – they were full of Typical Rosewood Boys doing keg stands, Typical Rosewood Girls puking up their chocolate martinis and Jell-O shots, and Typical Rosewood

Couples making out on the Kahn family's Louis XV-style sofas.

The doorbell rang, and they both sat up straighter. 'You get it,' Aria insisted. 'If it's the press, I'm not home.' Reporters had become so brazen, walking right up to the porch and ringing the doorbell several times a day, as nonchalant as the UPS man; Aria half-expected that one of these days they were going to barge right in.

'No problem.' Mike peeked at his reflection in the hall mirror and smoothed back his hair.

Just as Mike was about to open the door, Aria realized that she was plainly visible from the front porch. If it was the press, they'd push past Mike and never leave her alone. Feeling panicked and trapped, Aria looked around, darted into the pantry, wedged herself awkwardly under a shelf that contained sacks of brown rice, and slid the door shut.

The pantry smelled like pepper. One of Meredith's brandings – words burned onto big slabs of wood – was propped over a box of couscous. WOMEN UNITE, it said.

Aria heard the front door creak open. 'Waaaasssuuup?' Mike yelled. Palms smacked together, and sneakers thudded back down the hall. *Two* sets of sneakers. Aria peered between the slats of the pantry door, wondering what was happening. To her horror, she saw Mike leading Noel Kahn into the kitchen. What was *he* doing here?

Mike swiveled around the big kitchen, looking confused. When he faced the pantry, he raised one eyebrow and opened the little door. 'Found her!' he crowed. 'She's hanging out with the Rice-A-Roni!'

'Whoa.' Noel appeared behind Mike. 'I wish there was Aria in *my* pantry!'

125

'Mike!' Aria stepped out of the pantry quickly, as if she hadn't been hiding. 'I told you to say I wasn't home!'

Mike shrugged. 'You told me to say that only if it was someone from the press. Not *Noel*.'

Aria gave both of them a sharp look. She still didn't trust Noel. And she felt ashamed after her behavior at the séance, too. She'd spent several minutes in the occult shop's little bathroom, staring crazily at the Missing Person flyer. Noel had finally knocked on the door, telling her that the power had gone out and everyone needed to leave.

Noel turned and snickered at the pregnancy exercises Meredith had hung on the fridge. Many were about strengthening the vaginal muscles. 'I wanted to talk to you, Aria.' He glanced at Mike. 'Alone, if that's cool.'

'Of course!' Mike boomed loudly. He shot Aria a look that said *Don't screw this up*, then headed for the den.

Aria looked in every direction but at Noel's face. 'Um, want a drink?' she asked, feeling awkward.

'Sure,' Noel said. 'Water's fine.'

Aria held the glass to the refrigerator dispenser, her back straight and tense. She could still smell the prenatal kelp-and-pumpkin shake Meredith had made fifteen minutes earlier. After she returned to the table with Noel's drink, Noel reached into his backpack, produced a gray plastic bag, and thrust it at her. 'For you!'

Aria reached inside and pulled out a large packet of what looked like dirt. SUCCESS INCENSE said the label. When Aria pressed it to her nose, her eyes crossed. It smelled like her cat's litter box. 'Oh,' she mumbled, uncertain.

126

'I bought it from that freaky store,' Noel explained. 'It's supposed to bring you good luck. That warlock dude told me you have to burn it in a magick circle, whatever the hell that is.'

Aria snorted. 'Uh, thanks.' She laid the incense on the table and plunged her hand into the pretzel bag. Noel was reaching into the bag at the same time. Their fingers bumped together.

'Oops,' Noel said.

'Sorry,' Aria said, yanking her hand away. Her cheeks blazed.

Noel leaned his elbows on the table. 'So, you bolted from the séance yesterday. Everything cool?'

Aria shoved the pretzel in her mouth fast so she wouldn't have to answer.

'That medium guy was bogus,' Noel added. 'A total waste of twenty bucks.'

'Uh-huh,' Aria mumbled, crunching pensively. *She was very sad*, Equinox the medium had said. Maybe he was bogus, but what if that part was true? Mrs DiLaurentis had insinuated as much the day after Ali went missing. A few unsettling memories about Ali had popped into Aria's mind over the past twenty-four hours, too. Like the time that, not long after they'd become friends, Ali had invited Aria to go with her and her mom to the family's new vacation home in the Poconos; her dad and Jason were staying in Rosewood. The house was a big, rambling Cape Cod with a patio, a game room, and a hidden staircase that led from one of the back bedrooms to the kitchen. One morning, when Aria was playing on the secret stairs by herself, she'd heard whispering through the grates.

'I just feel so *guilty*,' Ali was saying.

'You shouldn't,' her mother replied sternly. 'This isn't your fault. You know this is the best thing for our family.'

'But ... that place.' Ali sounded repulsed. 'It's so ... *sad*.'

At least that was what Aria *thought* Ali had said. Ali's voice got very low after that, and Aria couldn't hear anything else.

According to the logbook Emily found at the Radley, Jason began visiting the hospital right around the time Aria, Ali, and the others became friends. Maybe the *place* Ali was referring to in that conversation with her mom was the Radley. Perhaps Ali felt guilty that Jason was there. Maybe it had been Ali's final decision that he go. As much as Aria didn't want to believe that Ali and Jason had issues, maybe they did.

She felt Noel's eyes on her, waiting for an answer. This wasn't worth thinking about now, especially with Noel sitting here. 'There's no such thing as ghosts speaking to us from the afterlife,' she mustered, parroting Spencer's sentiment.

Noel stared at her indignantly, like Aria had just told him there was no such thing as lacrosse. As he shifted his weight, Aria could smell his spicy, woodsy deodorant. It was surprisingly pleasant. 'What if Ali really *does* have something to tell you? Are you sure you want to give up now?'

Suspicion boiled in Aria's stomach. Fed up, she slammed her palm on the table. 'Why do you care? Did someone put you up to this? Is this some weird lacrosse prank to embarrass me?'

'No!' Noel's mouth drooped. 'Of course not!'

'Then why were you at a séance? Guys like you aren't into this stuff.'

Noel lowered his chin. 'What do you mean, *guys like me*?'

Meredith slammed an upstairs door shut, making the whole house shiver. Aria had never actually told anyone that she'd dubbed guys like Noel Typical Rosewood Boys – not her parents, not her friends, and certainly not a Typical Rosewood Boy himself. 'You seem so, well, preppy,' she fudged. 'Well adjusted.'

Noel rested his elbow on a stack of baby catalogues, his dark hair falling into his face. He breathed in a couple of times, as if he was ramping up to say something, and finally looked up. 'Okay, it's true – I don't go to séances because I like Led Zeppelin.' He shot her a look out of the corner of his eye, then stared into his glass, as if the ice cubes were tea leaves that contained his future. 'Ten years ago, when I was six, my brother killed himself.'

Aria blinked, caught off guard. She thought of Noel's two brothers, Erik and Preston. They were constant fixtures at the Kahns' house parties, even though they were both in college. 'I don't understand.'

'My brother Jared.' Noel rolled the top catalogue tightly in his hands. 'He was a lot older. My parents don't talk about him much anymore.'

Aria clutched the edge of the worn table. Noel had had another brother? 'How did it happen?'

'Well, my parents were out,' Noel explained. 'Jared was babysitting me. We were playing *Myst*, this computer game, but then it got late and I started dozing off. Jared seemed reluctant to put me to bed, but he finally did.

129

When I woke up a while later, something just felt … *weird*. The house was too quiet or something. So I got up and walked to the end of the hall. Jared's door was closed, and I knocked, but he didn't answer. So I just went in. And …' Noel shrugged and unfurled the catalogue. It flopped open to a page showing a blond, smiling baby in a red bouncy chair. 'There he was.'

Having no idea what to say, she touched Noel's hand. He didn't pull away.

'He'd … you know. Hung himself.' Noel closed his eyes. 'I didn't really understand what I was seeing at first. I thought he was just playing or whatever, maybe punishing me because I hadn't stayed up to play *Myst* with him longer. My parents came home then and I don't remember anything after that.'

'God,' Aria whispered.

'He was going to Cornell the following year.' Noel's voice cracked. 'He was an all-star basketball player. His life seemed … *awesome*. My parents didn't see it coming either. Neither did my brothers or his girlfriend. No one did.'

'I'm so sorry,' Aria whispered. She felt like an insensitive, sanctimonious ass. Who knew Noel had such an awful secret? And here she thought he'd been just pulling a stupid prank on her. 'Have you ever been able to talk to him at séances?'

Noel fiddled with the frog-shaped saltshaker in the middle of the table. 'Not really. But I keep trying. And I talk to him at the cemetery a lot. That seems to help.'

Aria made a face. 'I've tried to do that with Ali, but I always feel so weird. Like I'm talking to myself.'

'I don't think so,' Noel said. 'I think she's listening.'

The vacuum cleaner groaned to life, vibrating the ceiling above them. Aria and Noel sat still for a moment, listening. Noel's piercing green eyes met hers. 'Can you keep this to yourself? You're kind of the only person who knows.'

'Of course,' Aria said quickly, studying Noel. He didn't seem mad that she'd forced this out of him at all.

When she looked down, she realized that her hand was still touching his. She pulled it away fast, suddenly feeling very flustered. Noel was still staring at her. Aria's heart began to pound. She fidgeted nervously with the antique silver chain around her neck. Noel moved closer and closer until she could feel his breath on her neck. It smelled like black licorice, one of Aria's favorite candies. She held her breath, waiting.

But then, as if awakening from a dream, Noel jerked back, grabbed his glass from the table, and stood. 'I guess I'll go find Mike now. See ya.'

Giving her a little wave, he ducked through the archway and into the hall. Aria pressed her cool glass of water to her forehead. For a moment there, she'd thought Noel was going to kiss her. And in a very *un*typical Aria moment, she kind of wished he had.

14
Even Good Girls Have Secrets

Early that same Wednesday evening, Emily crunched across the fields behind Lucy's house, carrying a bucket of water to the animals in the barn. The wind whipped across her face, making her eyes water. A couple of houses in the distance already had their lanterns lit, and a horse and buggy clopped up the dirt path toward the road, the reflective, triangular sign on its back glowing.

'Thanks,' Lucy called, catching up to Emily. She carried a bucket of water too. 'After this, all we have to do is clean the floors of Mary's house for her wedding ceremony on Saturday.'

'Okay,' Emily said. She didn't dare ask why Mary was having her wedding in her house instead of the church. It was probably just some Amish thing she was supposed to know.

Their day had been jam-packed with early-morning farm chores, hours at the one-room schoolhouse reading Bible passages and helping the younger kids learn the alphabet, and then helping Lucy's mom prepare dinner.

Mr and Mrs Zook, Lucy's parents, looked classic *National Geographic* Amish – Lucy's father had a big, bushy, gray, moustacheless beard and wore a black hat, and her mother had a stern, makeupless face and rarely smiled. Still, they seemed gentle and kind enough – and they didn't suspect Emily was faking. Or if they did, they didn't say anything. But amid all that activity, Emily had still looked for clues about Ali everywhere they went. But no one had uttered a name even close to one that sounded like *Alison* or talked of the missing girl from Rosewood.

Most likely, A had just taken out a map of the U.S. and blindly picked any old place to ship Emily off to, eager to get her out of Rosewood. And Emily had fallen for it. Emily had tried to turn her phone back on this morning to see if A had written her again, but the battery had died. Her return bus ticket was for Friday afternoon, but she was considering leaving early. What was the point in staying here if she wasn't going to find any answers?

But a big part of Emily didn't want to believe that A was truly evil. A had given them all kinds of clues – maybe they'd just put the puzzle together incorrectly. What else had A told them that pointed to where Ali might be now ... or where she'd been all along? As Emily stood on the porch, the chilly wind sneaking down her collar, she saw a dark-haired girl carrying a bucket of water into a barn across the field. From this distance, the girl looked a lot like Jenna Cavanaugh.

Jenna. Could she be the answer? A had sent Emily an old photo of Jenna, Ali, and the back of an anonymous blond girl – probably Naomi Zeigler – standing in Ali's yard. *One of these things doesn't belong*, said A's accompanying note. *Figure it out quickly ... or else.*

A had also tipped off Emily that Jenna and Jason DiLaurentis were arguing at Jenna's window. Emily had seen the fight with her own eyes, though she had no idea what it could've been about. Why would A show her these things? Why would A say that Jenna didn't belong? Was A simply pointing out that Jenna and Ali were closer than everyone thought? Jenna and Ali *had* co-conspired in getting rid of Toby for good; perhaps Ali had confided in Jenna that she'd planned to run away. Perhaps Jenna had even helped her.

Emily and Lucy walked down the front steps and across the field to Mary's parents' house. A buggy was parked in the gravel lot, and there were an old-fashioned seesaw and tire swing near the front porch, crusted over with snow. Before they started up the porch, Lucy gave Emily a sidelong glance. 'Thanks for everything, by the way. You've been a huge help.'

'No problem,' Emily said.

Lucy leaned against the porch railing, looking like she wasn't finished. Her throat bobbed as she swallowed, and her eyes looked even greener in the dying, slanted light. 'Why are you really here?'

Emily's heart shot to her throat. There was a clattering sound from inside the house. 'W-what do you mean?' she stammered. Had Lucy found her out?

'I've been trying to figure it out. What did you do?'

'Do?'

'You were obviously sent here because we're a more traditional community.' Lucy smoothed her long wool

134

coat under her butt and sat down on the wooden porch steps. 'This is to get back on a virtuous path again, right? I'm guessing something happened to you. If you need to unburden yourself, you can tell me. I won't say anything.'

Despite the air being bitingly cold, Emily's palms began to sweat. Isaac's bedroom appeared in her mind. She winced at the thought of them naked under Isaac's covers, giggling. It seemed like so, so long ago, almost like it happened to a different person. All her life, she'd figured her first time having sex would be special and meaningful, something she'd treasure for the rest of her life. Instead, it had been an awful mistake.

'It was this thing with a guy,' she admitted.

'I thought it might be something like that.' Lucy picked at a splintered plank on the steps. 'Do you want to talk about it?'

Emily watched Lucy's face. She seemed genuinely sincere, not prying or judgmental. She sank down on the porch next to her. 'I thought we were in love. It was so great at first. But then ...'

'What happened?' Lucy asked.

'It just didn't work.' Tears came to Emily's eyes. 'He didn't really know me at all. I didn't know him, either.'

'Did your parents disapprove?' Lucy goaded, blinking her long lashes.

Emily sniffed sarcastically. 'No, actually, *his* parents didn't approve.' She didn't even have to lie about that part.

Lucy bit one of her small, crescent-shaped fingernails. The door to the house opened, and an older, stern-faced woman stuck her head out, scowled at them, and then

135

disappeared back into the house. A lemony smell of cleaning solution wafted out. Inside, the women were chattering in Pennsylvania Dutch, which sounded a lot like German.

'I'm kind of in a situation like that too,' Lucy whispered.

Emily cocked her head, intrigued. Something crystallized in her mind. 'Is it the guy I saw running out of your house the other day?'

Lucy slid her gaze to the right. Two older Amish women walked up the steps and into the house, smiling politely at the two of them. After they passed, Emily touched Lucy's arm. 'I won't say anything. I promise.'

'He lives in Hershey,' Lucy said in almost a whisper. 'I met him when I was buying fabric for my mom. My parents would kill me if they knew I was still talking to him.'

'Why?'

'Because he's *English*,' Lucy said in an *uh-duh* voice. *English* was the Amish term for regular, modern-living people. 'And anyway, they already lost one daughter. They can't lose me, too.'

Emily watched Lucy's face, trying to figure out what she meant. Lucy's eyes were fixed on the iced-over pond across the street. A couple of ducks were nestled at the bank, quacking irritably. When she turned back to Emily, her lips were trembling. 'You asked me yesterday where my sister Leah was. She went away during *rumspringa*.'

Emily nodded. According to the Amish Wikipedia entries she'd read, *rumspringa* was a time when Amish teenagers could leave their homes and experience things Emily took for granted, like wearing normal clothes,

136

working, and driving cars. After a while, they could either choose to return to the Amish faith or leave it forever. She was pretty sure if they chose not to be Amish, they could never see their families again.

'And ... well, she never came back,' Lucy admitted. 'One day, she was writing my parents letters, telling them what she was doing. The next ... nothing. No correspondence. No word of her. She was just ... gone.'

Emily pressed her hands into the hard, worn slats on the porch. 'What happened to her?'

Lucy scrunched up her shoulders. 'I don't know. She had this boyfriend, this guy who was part of our community. They had dated for years, since they were both about thirteen, but I always thought there was something weird about him. He just seemed ... well, he certainly wasn't worthy of her. I was so happy when he decided to leave the community forever after *rumspringa*. But he wanted Leah to come with him too – he begged her, in fact. But she had always said no.' Lucy flicked a piece of dried mud off her black boots. 'My parents figured Leah died in an accident, or maybe of natural causes. But I always wondered ...' She trailed off, shaking her head. 'They used to fight. Sometimes it got pretty intense.'

A gust of wind pulled a strand of dark hair from Lucy's bun. Emily shivered.

'We got the police involved. They searched for her but came up with nothing. They told us that people ran away all the time, and that there was nothing we could do. We even got a private investigator – we thought that she maybe just ran away and wanted nothing to do with us. Even that would've been fine – at least it meant she was alive. For a long time, we were sure Leah was out there, but one day my parents just gave up. They said they needed closure. I was the only one who still hoped.'

'I understand,' Emily whispered. 'I've lost someone too. But people come back. Amazing things happen.'

Lucy turned away, gazing across the field at a big, cylindrical grain silo. 'It's been almost four years since she left. Maybe my parents are right. Maybe Leah's really gone.'

'You can't give up!' Emily cried. 'It hasn't been that long!'

A farm dog with patchy brown fur and no collar trotted up to the porch, sniffed Lucy's hand, and then settled by her feet. 'I guess anything's possible,' Lucy mused. 'But maybe I'm just being silly. There's time to keep hope alive and a time to let go.' She gestured down the road to the little cemetery behind the church. 'We have a gravestone for her there. We had a funeral and everything. I haven't gone in there since, though.'

Tears began to spill down her cheeks. Lucy's chin wobbled, and a small squeak emerged from the back of her throat. Leaning over her thighs, she took deep, shuddering breaths. The farm dog stared at Lucy worriedly. Emily placed her hand on Lucy's back. 'It's okay.'

Lucy nodded. 'It's so hard.' She lifted her head. The tip of her nose was bright red. She gave Emily a sad, wry smile. 'Pastor Adam is always bugging me to talk about this to someone. This is the first time I've admitted aloud that Leah could be dead. I haven't wanted to believe it.'

There was a huge lump in Emily's throat. She didn't want Lucy to believe it either – she wanted Lucy to have the same kind of hope that Emily did about Ali. But because Emily didn't know Leah personally, because she wasn't *Ali*, Emily could be more realistic about what might have happened. People who disappear don't usually come home. Lucy's parents were probably right that Leah was dead.

A single bright star appeared on the horizon. Ever since Emily was little, she'd wish on the first evening star, recite the 'Star Light, Star Bright' rhyme, and make a wish. After Ali vanished, all of Emily's wishes on the star were about bringing Ali back safe and sound. But if Emily looked at her own life as objectively as she could look at Lucy's family, what would she come to realize about what had happened to Ali? Was she just being silly too? Maybe the doctors were right – maybe the girl in the woods had simply been a figment of her imagination. And maybe Wilden wasn't lying, either – maybe there really *was* a DNA report at the police station that matched Ali's. Maybe Emily had just become so fanatical about Ali being alive that she'd twisted around all the facts to meet her needs, to prove that Ali was still out there. And now she'd come all the way to Amish Country to pursue a lead that probably didn't even exist. A few minutes ago, she'd even entertained the idea that sweet, innocent Jenna Cavanaugh could've helped smuggle Ali out of Rosewood. Maybe she needed to let go too, just like Lucy and her family did about Leah. Maybe it would be the only way she'd be able to move on with her life.

From inside the house, there was a bonging, clanging sound of a pot hitting the floor. Then there were more crashes as dishes shattered. A woman squealed, sounding a little like a cow. Emily sneaked a peek at Lucy, trying not to laugh. One corner of Lucy's lip curled up. Emily covered her mouth and let out a snort. Suddenly, both girls exploded into giggles. The same stern woman stuck her head out the door and glared at them again. That just made them laugh harder.

Emily reached over and touched Lucy's hand, overcome with warmth and gratitude. In a parallel, Amish universe, she and Lucy would probably be good friends. 'Thank you,' Emily said.

Lucy looked surprised. 'What for?'

But Lucy obviously didn't get it. A might have sent Emily to Amish Country to find Ali, but what Emily had found instead was peace.

15
Facebook Friends

Spencer and Andrew sat on the couch in the Hastingses' finished basement, blissfully snuggling and flipping through the TV channels. Things had returned to normal with Andrew – *better* than normal, their fight of last week long forgotten. They'd sent each other flirty Twitters during study hall, and when Andrew had arrived at her house, he'd presented her with a J. Crew gift box. Inside was a brand-new, winter white cashmere V-neck, an exact match to Spencer's favorite sweater, which had been ruined in the fire. Spencer had made a passing reference to the sweater on the phone with Andrew Monday. Andrew had even guessed her correct size.

She lingered on CNN, which had switched from a stock market report to a breaking news story about something that wasn't really breaking news at all. *Waiting for Proof*, the caption said. There was an interior shot of Steam, Rosewood Day's espresso bar. This footage must have been taken only a few hours earlier, because the chalkboard said WEDNESDAY SPECIAL: HAZELNUT ICE CREAM

SMOOTHIE. Crowds of students in navy blue blazers stood in line for lattes and hot chocolate. Kristen Cullen was talking to James Freed. Jenna Cavanaugh lingered hauntingly in the doorway, her service dog panting. In the corner, Spencer spied Hanna's stepsister-to-be, Kate Randall, flanked by Naomi Zeigler and Riley Wolfe. Hanna wasn't with them; Spencer had heard Hanna had abruptly left for Singapore. Emily was gone, too, on a trip to Boston. It seemed odd that Emily was staying out of the limelight – she'd been so adamant that the police look for Ali – but it was also good.

'The DNA results for the body that was found in the DiLaurentises' backyard are due in any day now,' said a voice-over. 'Let's get the reaction of Alison's old classmates.'

Spencer flipped channels fast. The last thing she wanted to hear was some random girl who hadn't known Ali pontificate about what a *tragedy* this was. Andrew squeezed her hand comfortingly and shook his head.

On the next station, Aria's face popped into view. Reporters chased her as she ran from her dad's Civic into Rosewood Day. 'Ms. Montgomery! Did someone set the fire to cover up a vital clue?' screamed a voice. Aria kept going, not answering them. A headline popped up on the screen. *What Is This Little Liar Hiding?*

'Whoa.' Andrew's face was red. 'They seriously need to stop this.'

Spencer massaged her temples. At least Aria wasn't spouting that they'd seen Ali. But then she thought about the texts she'd received from Aria earlier that day, suggesting that Ali's spirit was trying to tell them something important about the night she died. Spencer didn't believe in any of that nonsense, but her words reminded Spencer of something Ian had said the day he broke house arrest. *What if I told you there's something you don't know?* he'd whispered to her as she sat on her back porch. *There's a secret that's going to turn your life upside down.* Ian had been wrong in thinking that Jason and Wilden were involved in Ali's murder, but she still believed there was something going on out there that none of them understood.

The alarm on Andrew's diving watch beeped and he stood. 'The Valentine's Day dance committee calls.' He groaned. He leaned over and pecked her on the cheek, then squeezed her limp hand. 'You okay?'

Spencer didn't make eye contact. 'I think so.'

He cocked his head, waiting. 'Are you sure?'

Spencer opened and closed her fists. It was pointless trying to hide it; Andrew had an uncanny knack for knowing when something was bothering her. 'I found out some really crazy stuff about my parents,' she blurted. 'My mom kept this really big secret from me about how she and my dad met. Which makes me wonder if she's covering up other stuff too.' *Like why we can't talk about the night Ali died ever again*, she almost added.

Andrew wrinkled his nose. 'Why don't you just talk to her about it?'

Spencer picked an imaginary piece of lint off her lilac cashmere sweater. 'Because it seems off-limits.'

Andrew sat back down. 'Look. The last time you suspected something about your family, you snuck around behind their backs trying to figure out the truth ... and you just got burned in the end. Whatever it is, just be open about it. Otherwise you might end up assuming the wrong thing.'

Spencer nodded. Andrew kissed her, slipped on his old, battered wingtips, slid into his wool duffel coat, and went out the door. She watched him walk down the path, then sighed. Maybe he was right. Sneaking around wouldn't do her any good.

She was on the second riser of the stairs when she heard whispering in the kitchen. Curious, she paused, pricking up her ears to listen.

'You have to keep this quiet,' her mother hissed. 'It's very important. Can you do that this time?'

'*Yes*,' Melissa answered defensively.

And then they banged their way through the back door. Spencer stood still, her ears ringing with the silence. If Melissa was on the outs with their mother, why were they sharing secrets? She thought again about what her mom had told her yesterday – the secret even Melissa didn't know. Spencer still couldn't wrap her mind around the idea that her mother had been a student at Yale Law.

As she listened to the garage door rumble up and the Mercedes pull out of the garage, she suddenly needed tangible proof.

Spinning around, Spencer walked into her dad's dark, cigar-stinky office. The last time she'd been in here, she'd burned his entire computer hard drive to a CD and found the bank account that got her into the whole Olivia mess. Scanning her dad's bookshelves now, which contained law volumes, first-edition Hemingways, and Lucite plaques congratulating him for winning such-and-such a court

144

battle, she noticed a red book tucked away in an upper corner. YALE LAW YEARBOOK, the spine said.

Quietly, she dragged her dad's Aeron desk chair to the bookshelf, climbed on the wobbling seat, and grabbed the book with the tips of her fingers. As she cracked it open, the smell of mildewed paper wafted out. An old photo fluttered out too, sliding across the freshly waxed wood floor. She bent down and picked it up. It was a small, square Polaroid of a pregnant blond woman in front of a pretty brick building. The woman's face was blurry. It wasn't Spencer's mom, but there was something familiar about her. She flipped the photo over. Written on the back was the date June 2, almost seventeen years ago. Could this be Olivia, Spencer's surrogate? Spencer was born in April, but maybe Olivia hadn't lost the baby weight right away?

Spencer slipped the photo back into the yearbook and leafed through the portraits of first-year law students. She found her father right away. He looked almost identical to how he looked today, except his face was a little less weathered and his hair was thicker and longer, almost feathery. Taking a deep breath, she flipped forward to the M's for Macadam, her mother's maiden name. And there she was, with the same lake-straight, chin-length blond hair and broad, dazzling smile. There was a faded yellow ring from a coffee cup above her picture, as if Spencer's dad had propped the book open to this page, staring long-ingly at her mother's picture for hours.

It really was true – her mom had been a student at Yale.

Aimlessly, Spencer flipped through more pages. The first-year students were smiling so enthusiastically, having no idea how hard law school was going to be. Then, something in her brain caught. She did a double take at one of the student's names, then examined his picture. A young man with light-colored hair and an eerily familiar hooked, oversize nose stared back at her. Ali had always said that if she'd inherited that nose, she would have gone straight to a plastic surgeon and gotten it fixed.

Spots swam in front of Spencer's eyes. This had to be another hallucination. She checked the student's name again. And once more after that. *Kenneth DiLaurentis*. It was Ali's father.

Beep.

The book fell from her hands. Her cell phone vibrated from inside her cardigan pocket. Spencer stared out the windows of her father's office, suddenly feeling like someone was watching her. Had she just heard a giggle? Was that a person darting behind the fence? Her heart pounded as she opened her phone.

Think that's crazy? Now take another spin through your dad's hard drive … starting with J. You won't believe what you find. – A

16
It's The Queen Bee's Knees

Hanna and Iris sat at a round table in the Preserve at Addison-Stevens' cafe, with steaming lattes, homemade organic yogurt, and fresh fruit cups in front of them. They definitely had the best table in the place – not only was it the farthest one from the nurses' station, but it also gave them a prime view out the window of the hot groundskeeper, who was vigorously shoveling snow off the drive in a tight, long-sleeved thermal tee.

Iris nudged Hanna. 'Omigod. Tara's going to eat a pooberry!'

Hanna swiveled her head. Tara, who was sitting with Alexis and Ruby at the same table they'd sat at when Hanna had joined them for dinner two nights ago, had just popped a blueberry into her mouth. '*Ewwww,*' Hanna and Iris exclaimed in unison. For whatever reason, blueberries here were called *poo*berries. It was a huge faux pas to eat them.

Tara stopped and smiled hopefully at them. 'Hi, Hanna! What's ew?'

'You.' Iris smirked.

Tara's smile evaporated. A bloom of red crept into her chubby cheeks. Her eyes moved to Hanna, an acrid, vengeful look on her face. Hanna turned away haughtily, pretending she didn't notice. Then Iris stood up and tossed her yogurt in the trash. 'C'mon, Han. I have something to show you.' She grabbed Hanna's arm.

'Where are you going?' Tara whined, but both girls ignored her.

Iris snorted as they exited the cafeteria and walked down the long corridor toward the patient rooms. 'Did you see her shoes? She claims they're Tory Burch, but they look more like Payless.'

Hanna snickered and then felt a tiny twinge of guilt – Tara had been the first girl to speak to her. But whatever. It wasn't Hanna's fault Tara was so clueless.

And besides, hanging out with Iris had made Hanna's stay at the Preserve at Addison-Stevens – or the Preserve, as everyone here called it – *fabulous*. She'd shown Hanna the gym and the spa, and last night, they'd stolen cleansers, toners, and milk masks from a spa treatment room and given each other facials. Hanna had awoken this morning atop 1,000-thread-count sheets, well rested for the first time in what seemed like years, and her legs already looked thinner from the organic fruits and veggies she'd been eating.

Hanna and Iris had bonded instantly, spending hours in their shared bedroom talking. Iris had admitted point-blank that she was at the Preserve for an eating disorder – 'the *only* acceptable reason to be here,' she added. Hanna had quickly said that she was here for eating issues, too –

148

which was kind of the truth. The first time Iris was sent to the Preserve for treatment was when she was in seventh grade, she said. She'd gone a whole week without eating. She'd gotten out just in time for summer vacation – right around when Ali went missing, Hanna couldn't help but note to herself – but Iris's mom forced her back in by the beginning of October when her weight dropped low again. The Preserve wasn't the only hospital Iris had been to, but she said she liked it here the best.

Just knowing Iris had eating issues made Hanna less self-conscious about her own. Safe in their room, she didn't struggle to hide the food journal she'd kept since the summer after seventh grade, a record of all the calories she ate in a day. Nor did she freak out when Iris caught her struggling into her jeans from eighth grade, which she'd brought along for the express purpose to gauge whether she was gaining or losing weight. As it turned out, Iris had an old pair of skinny jeans in her closet too.

Whatever A intended by sending Hanna here, it was having the opposite effect. Which had led Hanna to a new theory: Maybe A was on Hanna's side. Maybe A had sent her here to get her away from the chaos of Rosewood, to keep her safe from whoever had set that fire.

Now Hanna followed Iris down the saffron yellow hall to a small door marked EMERGENCY EXIT. Iris wiggled her eyebrows, put her finger to her lips, then punched numbers into a small keypad located just to the left of the knob. The bolt released and the door opened. At the top of a set of metal stairs was a small, cozy room, just big enough for two comfy chairs. Graffiti covered the four walls, amazing murals of people's faces, big, spindly trees,

149

a couple of cartoonish owls, and tons of scribbled messages and names. There was also a big stack of contraband *People* and *Us Weekly* magazines on the windowsill.

'Wow,' Hanna breathed.

'This is my secret hiding spot,' Iris said, throwing her arms open as if to say *taa-daah!* 'I'm the only one here right now who knows the combo to get in. Most of the staff don't even know it, and those who do just let me do whatever I want.' She held up a copy of *People*. Angelina Jolie was on the cover, as usual. 'I've got someone who sneaks these in for me. I'm totally addicted. I've got a bunch in the drawer of my nightstand, too. You can read them, as long as you keep quiet about it.'

'Absolutely,' Hanna said, grinning. 'Thanks.'

Iris gestured at the drawings on the walls. 'They're all by former patients. Isn't it awesome?'

Hanna nodded, though she also felt eerie shivers as she looked at all the names. *Eileen. Stef. Jenny.* Why had they been here? What had they suffered from – an eating disorder or ADD, the milder reasons for coming to the Preserve, or something much scarier? Ali's brother, Jason, had apparently spent time in a hospital like this back in high school. His name had been all over that ledger Emily found in the office at the Radley party.

It was weird that Ali had never shared that secret with any of them. There was only one memory Hanna could recall where Ali might have hinted at Jason's mental problems. At the beginning of seventh grade, Hanna and Ali were hanging out alone on a Sunday afternoon, trying to pick out their outfits for the next day. As Ali was slipping

150

out of a pair of Citizens corduroys, the phone rang. Ali picked it up and was silent. Her mouth got very small, and her face paled a shade. Hanna heard screechy, spooky laughter through the receiver. 'For the last time, stop it, loser!' Ali screamed, and hung up.

'Who was that?' Hanna whispered.

'Just my stupid brother,' Ali mumbled into her chest.

And then she dropped it. But now, Hanna was pretty sure Jason had been calling from the Radley – the log-books Emily found said he checked in for a few hours on the weekends. Maybe he'd called Ali from there to scare her. *Jerk*.

Iris settled on one of the chairs, and Hanna plopped down on the other. Silently, they both stared at the doodles and names. *Helena. Becky. Lindsay*. 'I wonder where they all are now,' Hanna said softly.

'Who knows,' Iris answered, finger-combing her white-blond hair. 'Though I heard a rumor about this one patient who was supposed to check in for, like, two weeks, but her parents forgot about her. She still lives here ... in the *basement*.'

Hanna snorted. 'That's so not true.'

'Yeah, probably not. But you never know.'

Iris reached under the cushion and pulled out a small disposable camera wrapped in green paper. 'I smuggled this in from the outside, too. Want to get a picture of us together?'

Hanna hesitated – the last thing she wanted was proof that she'd been in a mental hospital. 'It's not like you'll be able to get it developed,' she said warily.

'I want to send the camera to my dad.' Iris lowered her

151

eyes. 'Not that he opens my letters.' Her bottom lip started to tremble. 'We used to be really close, but then he took this high-stress job as the dean of medicine at some stupid hospital. He has no time for me anymore. And now that I'm here ...' She shrugged. 'I don't exist for him.'

'My dad's the same,' Hanna gasped, amazed they had this in common, too. 'I used to talk to him about everything, but then he moved away and got this new girlfriend, Isabel. Now they're living in my house – with Isabel's perfect daughter, Kate.' She curled her toes. 'Kate can do absolutely nothing wrong. My dad's totally obsessed with her.'

'I can't believe your dad would like someone better than you.' Iris sounded appalled.

'Thanks,' Hanna said gratefully, staring out the little attic window at the empty tennis courts behind the facility. For a long time, she'd reasoned that her dad no longer loved her as much because she wasn't pretty and perfect. But Iris *was* perfect ... and her dad still treated her like shit. Maybe daughters weren't the problem – maybe fathers were.

Fueled with fury, she plucked the camera from Iris's hand and held it outstretched between the two of them. 'Let's give all the sucky dads in the world the finger.'

'Totally,' Iris said, and at the count of three, both of them squished their faces close and raised their middle fingers. Hanna pressed the button.

'Awesome,' Iris said, advancing the film and slipping the camera back into her bag.

Hanna slid down the arm so that she and Iris shared the chair. They were both skinny enough to fit. The room smelled a little like cinnamon and sun-baked wood. 'How'd you find out about this place, anyway?'

'Courtney gave me the code,' Iris said, kicking off her navy studded Maloles ballet flats.

Hanna picked at her thumbnail. The only slightly annoying thing about Iris was that she talked nonstop about her old roommate, Courtney, who apparently used to be the grand dame of the Preserve. In the past day, Iris had told twelve separate stories about this Courtney bitch – not that Hanna had been counting or anything.

'So when did Courtney leave?' Hanna asked as non-chalantly as she could.

One corner of Iris's mouth turned down. 'November, I think? I can't remember.' She reached into the metal cup and pulled out a blue Magic Marker.

'So what happened to her? Is she normal now?'

Iris uncapped the marker and began doodling on the wall. 'Who knows? I haven't talked to her since she left.'

Hanna felt a dart of triumph. 'Why not?'

Iris shrugged, absently scribbling. 'She lied about why she was in here. She said it was because of mild depression, but it turned out she had way bigger issues. I only found out afterward. She was as messed up as all the other patients here.'

The wind creaked against the windowpanes. Hanna faked a cough, hiding her guilty expression. It wasn't like she'd been particularly forthcoming with Iris about why she was in here, either – she hadn't told her a thing about Ali, A, or Mona.

Iris pulled the Magic Marker away, revealing what she'd drawn on the wall. It was an old-fashioned wishing

153

well, complete with an A-frame roof and a crank. Hanna blinked hard, stunned. Little prickles danced up her arms. The wishing well was eerily familiar ... and definitely not a coincidence.

'Why did you draw that?' she whispered.

Iris paused for a moment, looking caught. She nervously twisted the cap back on the marker. Hanna's heart raced faster and faster. Finally, Iris pointed at Hanna's purse. 'Your bag was open on the bureau today. I didn't mean to peek inside, but that shirt thing was sitting right on top. What is it, anyway?'

Hanna stared at her purse and let out a breath. Of *course* – she'd been carrying around Ali's Time Capsule flag like it was the Hope diamond, never letting it out of her sight.

She touched the fabric with her fingertips. Sure enough, the drawing of the wishing well was on top, clearly visible. Next to it was a strange symbol Hanna couldn't decipher – it looked like a letter in a circle with a slash through it, like a No Parking sign. Instead of the letter *P*, there was a smudged *I* ... or a *J*. Maybe for Jason. No Jason Allowed. A shiver rippled through her. Every time she looked at Ali's flag, it felt like Ali's presence was close, watching. For a moment, she almost thought she could detect a faint whiff of Ali's favorite vanilla soap.

Hanna felt Iris's eyes on her, waiting for an answer. *Don't tell her*, a voice in her head said. *If you tell her the truth, she'll think you're a wacko.* 'It's for this game we do at school,' she heard herself say nonchalantly. 'I'm keeping it for my friend, Alison.' She zipped up her bag and squished it under the seat.

Iris checked her Movado watch and groaned. 'Shit. I have therapy now. *So* boring.' She uncrossed her legs and stood.

Hanna stood too. Both girls clomped down the stairs, through the secret door, and parted ways. Hanna's nerves still felt jangled from the wishing well drawing. She felt like she needed to pop a Valium and lie down. If only she could call Mike: She longed to hear his voice, even his lascivious remarks. The no-phone-calls rule they had in this place blew.

She was unlocking the door to her bedroom when someone behind her coughed. Tara was jiggling up and down, running her tongue disgustingly over her braces.

'Oh.' Hanna's heart sank. 'Hi.'

Tara placed her hands on her meaty hips. 'So you and Iris are roommates?' she lisped.

'Yeah,' Hanna said in a *duh* voice. Tara had been with Hanna when Iris introduced herself. And both their names were written on the door in shiny gold ink.

'So you know about her, right?'

Hanna turned the lock and heard the bolt release. 'What's there to know?'

Tara pushed her hands in the pockets of her terry-cloth hoodie. 'Iris is certifiably insane. That's why she's here. So don't do anything to piss her off. I'm telling you this as a friend.'

Hanna studied Tara for a moment. Her skin felt hot, then cold. She whipped the door open. 'Tara, we're *not* friends.' She slammed the door in Tara's face.

Once inside, she shook the tension out of her hands. 'Your funeral,' she heard Tara say through the door. She watched Tara through the peephole as she walked away. Suddenly, Hanna realized why she'd been repulsed by Tara from the very start. Tara had the same stubby round body, hideous braces, and dull brown hair as Hanna did before her makeover in eighth grade. It was like looking at her former self, back when she was miserable and unpopular and lost. Before she was beautiful. Before she was *someone*.

Hanna sat down on the bed and pressed her fingers to her temples. If Tara was anything like the old Hanna inside, it was obvious why she'd said that about Iris – and why Hanna shouldn't believe a word of it. Tara was insanely, voraciously jealous – just like Hanna had been of Ali. Staring at her frazzled reflection in the mirror across the room, she conjured up the old catchphrase Ali used to use all the time, the one Hanna had adopted herself after Ali disappeared. *I'm Hanna, and I'm fabulous.* Her days of being like Tara were long gone.

17

Just Another Kegger At The Kahns'

By the time Aria and Mike pulled up to the Kahns' monstrosity of a house on Thursday night, there were already tons of cars parked in the driveway and on the lawn. Music thumped from inside the house, and Aria heard a splash from the hot tub out back.

'Sweet,' Mike said, leaping out the passenger door. In a blink, he had run halfway around the side of the house toward the backyard. Aria glowered. So much for an escort.

Aria got out of the car and joined a knot of thin, pretty girls from the Quaker prep school making their way to Noel's door. Each girl was blonder than the last. They were wearing matching fur-trimmed hats that probably cost more than Aria's entire outfit. Aria felt shabby and weird next to them in her deep green mohair sweater dress, gray suede boots, and leg warmers. The girls jostled on the porch, each trying desperately to be the first one through the door, bumping into Aria as if she wasn't even there.

Just as Aria was about to turn and run back to her car, Noel flung open the door, dressed in a plain black T-shirt and black swim trunks. 'You're here!' he whooped to Aria and only Aria, ignoring the other girls. 'Are you ready for the hot tub?'

'I don't know,' Aria answered shyly. At the last minute, she'd thrown a bikini in her bag, but she hadn't decided whether she'd wear it. She still didn't even know what she was doing here. This wasn't exactly her group.

Noel scowled. 'It's a hot tub *party*. You're going in.'

Aria giggled, trying to relax. But then Mason Byers grabbed Noel's arm and asked where the bottle opener was. Naomi Zeigler waltzed over and said that a skanky drunk girl was throwing up in the powder room. Aria sighed, deflated. It was a Typical Kahn party – what did she expect? That just because she and Noel had shared something special yesterday, he'd cancel the kegger and instead host a sophisticated wine-and-cheese event?

As if sensing her annoyance, Noel glanced over his shoulder at Aria and held up a single finger. *Be back in a sec*, he mouthed. Aria wandered past the double staircase and the legendary marble lions that Mr Kahn had allegedly procured from an Egyptian pharaoh's tomb. To her right was the living room, stuffed full of authentic O'Keeffes and Jasper Johnses. She walked into the gigantic stainless-steel kitchen. Kids were everywhere. Devon Arliss was mixing drinks in a blender. Kate Randall was parading around the room in a skimpy Missoni bikini. Jenna Cavanaugh was leaning against the window, whispering in Emily's ex-girlfriend's ear.

Aria stopped, backtracking. Jenna *Cavanaugh*? No one

had bothered to tell Jenna that her service dog was lapping up a puddle of beer on the floor, or that someone had fastened a black lacy bra around the dog's neck, its padded cups hanging down like a bow tie.

Suddenly Aria was desperate to know what Jenna and Jason had been fighting about in her house last week, when Emily had seen them through the window. Aria had been Ali's best friend, but Jenna seemed to know much more about Ali's family than Aria did – including Ali's alleged 'sibling problems' with Jason. Aria nudged through the crowd, but then more kids filed into the kitchen, blocking her way. By the time Aria could see the window again, Jenna and Maya had disappeared.

A bunch of guys on the Rosewood Day swim team came up behind Aria and grabbed some beer from the cooler under the table. Aria felt a tug on her arm. When she turned, she saw a bleached-blond girl with flawless skin and big boobs staring at her. She was one of the Quaker school girls Aria had stood next to on the front porch.

'You're Aria Montgomery, right?' the girl said. Aria nodded, and the girl gave her a knowing smirk. 'Pretty Little Liar,' she chanted.

A skinny brunette in a fuchsia silk dress sidled up too. 'Have you seen Alison today?' she teased. 'Do you see her right now? Is she standing right next to you?' She wiggled her fingers in front of her face spookily.

Aria took a step back, bumping into the round kitchen table.

The jeers continued. '*I see dead people*,' Mason Byers said in falsetto, leaning against the counter near the pot rack.

159

'She just likes the attention,' Naomi Zeigler scoffed from the sliding glass door. Beyond that was the Kahns' patio. Steam rose from the hot tub. Aria caught sight of Mike way at the edge of the lawn, horsing around with James Freed.

'She probably just wants to be on the news,' Riley Wolfe added, perched on a stool near the veggies and dip.

'That's not true!' Aria protested.

More kids entered the room, staring Aria down: Their eyes were derisive and hateful. Aria looked right and left, eager to escape, but she was pinned against the kitchen table, barely able to move. Then someone grabbed her left wrist. 'C'mon,' Noel said. He pulled her through the crowd.

Kids parted immediately. 'Are you kicking her out?' a boy on the baseball team whose name Aria never remembered crowed.

'You should turn her in!' Seth Cardiff encouraged.

'No, he shouldn't, idiot,' Mason Byers's voice rose above the din. 'This party is a cop-free zone.'

Noel dragged Aria up to the second floor. 'I'm so sorry,' he said, nudging open a dark bedroom that had an enormous oil painting of Mrs Kahn on the wall. The room smelled overpoweringly like mothballs. 'You don't need to be in the middle of that.'

Aria sat down on the bed, tears streaming down her cheeks. What had she been thinking, coming here? Noel settled next to her, offering Aria a Kleenex and his gin and tonic. She shook her head. Downstairs, someone turned up the stereo. A girl shrieked. Noel rested his glass on his knee. Aria glanced at his sloped nose, his bushy eyebrows, his long eyelashes. It felt comforting, sitting here in the dark next to him.

'I'm *not* doing this for attention,' she blubbered.

Noel turned to her. 'I know. People are idiots. They have nothing better to do than gossip.'

She flopped back on the pillow. Noel settled next to her. Their fingers lightly touched. Aria felt her heart begin to pound. 'I have something to tell you,' Noel said.

'Oh?' Aria squeaked. Her throat suddenly felt dry.

It was a long time before Noel spoke again. Trembling with anticipation, Aria tried to calm down by watching the rotating ceiling fan above their heads. 'I found another medium,' Noel finally admitted.

All the air slowly drained from Aria's body. 'Oh.'

'And this one's supposedly really good. She, like, *becomes* the person you're trying to contact. All she needs is to be at the spot where the person died, and then ...' Noel waved his hands in the air, indicating a magical transformation. 'But we don't have to do it if you don't want to. Like I said, going to the cemetery and just talking also really helps too. It's peaceful.'

Aria laced her hands over her belly. 'But going to the cemetery isn't going to give me answers. It's not like Ali's going to talk back.'

'Okay.' Noel set his drink on the side table, pulled out his cell phone, and scrolled through his contacts. 'How about I call the medium and tell her we can meet tomorrow night? I could pick you up and we could drive to Ali's old backyard together.'

'Wait.' Aria sat up, the bedsprings squeaking. 'Ali's ... *backyard*?'

161

Noel nodded. 'We have to go where the person died. That's how it works.'

Aria's hands tingled and it felt like the temperature in the room had dropped at least ten degrees. The idea of standing over the half-dug hole where Ali had been found chilled Aria to the bone. Did she really want to speak to Ali's ghost *that* badly?

Yet a nagging feeling tugged at her. Deep down, she felt like Ali really *did* have something important to say, and it was Aria's responsibility to listen.

'Okay.' Aria gazed out the window at the fingernail-shaped moon above the trees. 'I'll do it.' She pulled her knees in so that she was sitting cross-legged. 'Thanks for helping me with this. And for getting me out of that mess downstairs. And ...' She took a deep breath. 'Thanks for being so nice to me in general.'

Noel gave her a crazy look. 'Why wouldn't I be nice to you?'

'Because ...' Aria trailed off. *Because you're a Typical Rosewood Boy*, she was about to say, but she stopped. She didn't really know what that meant anymore.

They were silent for what seemed like hours. Not able to stand the tension any longer, she leaned over and kissed him. His skin smelled like chlorine from the hot tub, and his mouth tasted like gin. Aria shut her eyes, forgetting momentarily where she was. When she opened them, Noel was there, smiling at her, like he'd been waiting for her to do that for years.

18
An Affair To Forget

Friday morning, Spencer sat at the kitchen table, slicing an apple over a bowl of steaming oatmeal. The yard workers had started early this morning, dragging more burnt timber out of the woods and loading it into a long green Dumpster. A police photographer was standing near the barn, taking pictures with a high-tech digital camera.

The phone rang. When Spencer picked up the kitchen extension, a woman's voice screeched in her ear. 'Is this Miss Hastings?'

'Uh,' Spencer stammered, caught off guard.

The woman spoke in rapid staccato. 'My name is Anna Nichols. I'm a reporter with MSNBC. Would you like to give a comment about what you saw in the woods last week?'

Spencer's muscles tensed. 'No. Please, just leave me alone.'

'Can you confirm an unverified report that you actually wanted to be the leader of the clique? Maybe your frustration with Ms. DiLaurentis got the best of you and you accidentally ... did something. It happens to all of us.'

Spencer squeezed the phone so hard that she accidentally hit a bunch of digits. They beeped in her ears. 'What are you implying?'

'Nothing, nothing!' The reporter paused to murmur something to someone on her end. Spencer slammed the phone down, shaking. She was so overcome, the only thing she could do for the next few minutes was stare at the blinking red numbers on the microwave across the room.

Why was she still getting phone calls? And why were the reporters digging around to see if *she* could have had anything to do with Ali's death? Ali was her best friend. And what about Ian? Didn't the cops still think he was guilty? Or the person who'd tried to roast them alive in the woods? How could the public not realize they were all victims in this, the same as Ali?

A door slammed, and Spencer shot up from her slumped position against the wall. She heard voices in the laundry room and stood very still, listening.

'It would be better if you didn't tell her,' Mrs Hastings was saying.

'But, Mom,' Melissa whispered back, 'I think she already *knows*.'

The door flung open, and Spencer shot back to the kitchen island, feigning obliviousness. Her mother paraded in from her morning walk, holding both the family's labradoodles on a split leash. Then Spencer heard the laundry room door bang and saw Melissa storming around the side of the house toward the driveway.

Mrs Hastings unhooked the dogs and set the leash on the island. 'Hi, Spence!' she said in a voice that was way too chipper, as if she was working hard to seem nonchalant and unbothered. 'Come see the purse I bought at the mall last night. Kate Spade's spring line is *gorgeous*.'

Spencer couldn't answer. Her limbs quivered, and her stomach felt sliced to ribbons. 'Mom?' she said shakily. 'What were you and Melissa whispering about?'

Mrs Hastings turned quickly to the coffeemaker and poured herself a cup. 'Oh, nothing important. Just stuff about Melissa's town house.'

The phone rang again, but Spencer made no motion to get it. Her mom glanced at the phone, then at Spencer, but didn't answer it either. After the answering machine picked up, she touched Spencer's shoulder. 'Are you okay?'

Tons of words felt choked in Spencer's throat. 'Thanks, Mom. I'm fine.'

'Are you sure you don't want to talk about it?' A worried line formed between Mrs Hastings's perfectly waxed brows.

Spencer turned away. There was so much she *wanted* to talk about with her mom, but all of it seemed taboo. Why had her parents never told her that her dad and Ali's dad went to Yale Law School together? Did it have something to do with why Mrs Hastings didn't like Ali? The whole time Ali's family lived here, the families maintained a cool distance, behaving like strangers. In fact, in third grade, when Spencer giddily announced that a girl her age had moved in next door and asked if she could go over there and meet her, Spencer's dad caught her arm and said, 'We should give them some space. Let them settle in.' Then, when Ali chose Spencer as her new BFF, her parents seemed ... well, not upset, exactly, but Mrs Hastings hadn't encouraged Spencer to invite Ali over for dinner, like she usually did with new friends. At the time, Spencer had thought her parents were just jealous – she thought everyone was jealous of Ali's attention, even adults. But apparently, Spencer's mom had thought her friendship with Ali was unhealthy.

Ali must not have known about their dads going to Yale Law together, either – if she had, she definitely would have brought it up. She did, though, make a lot of cutting remarks about Spencer's parents. *My parents think your parents are so showy. Do you guys seriously need another addition on your house?* And toward the end of their friendship, she asked Spencer a lot of questions about her father, her voice dripping with disdain. *Why does your dad wear those gay tight clothes when he goes on bike rides? Why does your dad still call his mother 'Nana'? Ew!*

'They'll never be invited to my parents' gazebo parties,' Ali had said just days before she disappeared. The way things had been going between them, Ali might as well have tacked on, *and neither will* you.

Spencer wanted to ask her mom why the families pretended not to know each other. *Think* that's *crazy?* A's note had said. *Now take another spin through your dad's hard drive ... starting with J.*

Her hands started to tremble. But what if A was bullshitting her? Things were finally going well with her mom. Andrew was right. Why rock the boat before she had all the information?

'I'll be back,' she murmured to her mom.

'Okay, but come back down so I can show you what I bought!' Mrs Hastings chirped.

The second floor smelled like Fantastik and lavender hand soap from the hall bathroom. Spencer pushed open the door to her bedroom and snapped the on switch to the brand-new MacBook Pro her parents had just bought her; her old computer had died the week before and Melissa's loaner had been destroyed in the fire. Then she inserted the CD that held her dad's entire hard drive – she'd secretly copied it to a disk when she was trying to find out whether or not she was adopted. The computer beeped and whirred.

Out the window, the morning sky was a dull gray. Spencer could just see the tip of the charred windmill and the dilapidated barn. She swung her gaze to the front of the house. The plumbing trucks were outside the Cavanaugh house again. A skinny blond guy wearing a dingy, faded jumpsuit ambled out the Cavanaughs' door and lit a cigarette. Jenna Cavanaugh was walking out of the house at the exact same time. The plumber watched Jenna as she and her guide dog slowly made their way to Mrs Cavanaugh's Lexus. As he reached to scratch his lip, Spencer noticed he had a gold front tooth.

Her computer beeped, and Spencer turned back to the screen. The CD had loaded. She clicked on the folder marked *Dad*. Sure enough, there was a folder called *J*. Inside were two untitled Word documents.

The chair creaked as she sat back. Did she really need to open these? Did she really need to know?

Downstairs, she heard the KitchenAid mixer start to

whir. A siren whooped. Spencer massaged her temples. But what if the secret had something to do with Ali?

The temptation too great, Spencer clicked on the first file. It opened quickly, and Spencer leaned forward, too anxious to take a full breath.

Dear Jessica, I'm sorry things got cut short at your house tonight. I can give you all the time you need, but I can't wait to be alone with you again.
Much love, Peter

Spencer felt sick. *Jessica?* Why was her dad writing to someone named Jessica, telling her that he wanted to *be* with her?

She clicked on the next document. It was another letter. *Dear Jessica*, it said again. *Per our discussion, I think I can help. Please take this. Xx, Peter*

Below was a screen grab of a bank wire transfer. A row of zeroes swam before Spencer's eyes. It was a huge sum, much more than had been in Spencer's college savings account. Then she spied the account names in the bottom corner of the document. The wire had come from a credit line belonging to Peter Hastings, and it had gone into an account called the Alison DiLaurentis Recovery Fund. The beneficiary collecting the funds was Jessica DiLaurentis.

Jessica DiLaurentis. Of *course*. Ali's mom.

Spencer stared at the screen for a long time. *Dear Jessica. Much Love. Xx.* All that money. The Alison DiLaurentis Recovery Fund. She cycled back to the first letter again. *I'm sorry things got cut short tonight. I can't wait to be alone with you again.* She right-clicked on the document to check when it was last modified. The date read: June 20, three and a half years ago.

'What the hell?' she whispered.

There was a lot about that sticky, awful summer that Spencer had tried her hardest to forget, but she would always, *always* remember June 20 for as long as she lived. It was the day seventh grade ended. The night of their seventh-grade sleepover.

The night Ali died.

19
Secrets Don't Stay Buried For Long

Lucy tucked the final corner of the top sheet under the bed mattress and stood up straight. 'Ready to go?' she asked.

'Yep,' Emily said sadly. It was Friday morning, and she was about to leave to catch her bus back to Rosewood. Lucy was walking Emily only to the highway, not the bus station. Though it was acceptable for Amish people to ride buses, Emily didn't want Lucy to know she was going to Philadelphia and not Ohio, where she said she was from. After everything Lucy had entrusted her with, Emily didn't want to admit that she wasn't really Amish. Then again, part of her wondered if Lucy had already guessed and just wasn't asking. Maybe it was better just not to broach the subject at all.

Emily took a final look around the house. She'd already said good-bye to Lucy's parents, who asked her countless times if she couldn't stay one more day for the wedding. She'd petted the cows and horses one last time, realizing she'd miss them. She'd miss other things about here, too – the quiet nights, the smell of freshly made cheese, the random moos from the cows. And everyone in this community smiled and said hello to her, even though she was a stranger. That didn't happen in Rosewood.

Emily and Lucy pushed out the door, shivering in the sudden, bracing cold. The smell of freshly baked loaves of bread was in the air, all for the wedding celebration that would take place tomorrow. It seemed like every Amish family in the community was preparing for the wedding. Men were brushing the horses for the procession. Women were hanging flowers on Mary's family's door, and obedient Amish children were clearing litter from the surrounding farmyard.

Lucy whistled under her breath, her arms swinging loosely at her sides. Since their conversation about Leah, Lucy had seemed much lighter, like a huge camping backpack had been lifted off her shoulders. Emily, on the other hand, felt leaden and weak, as if the hope that Ali was alive had kept her energetic all this time.

They passed the church, a squat, nondescript building without any religious symbols on it whatsoever. A few horses were tied to posts, their snorting breath visible in the frosty air. The graveyard was in the back of the church, cordoned off by a wrought-iron gate. Then Lucy stopped, considering. 'Do you mind if we stop in there for a sec?' She fiddled nervously with her wool gloves. 'I want to see Leah, I think.'

Emily checked her watch. Her bus wasn't for another hour. 'Sure.'

The gate squeaked as Lucy pushed it open. Their shoes

swished against the dead, dry grass. Lined up were gray, simple graves for babies, old men, and an entire family named Stevenson. Emily squeezed her eyes shut, trying to let reality sink in. All of these people were dead ... and so was Ali.

Ali is dead. Emily tried to let it fill her body. She thought not about the horrible parts of Ali's death, like her heart beating for the last time, her lungs filling with their very last breath, her bones turning to dust. Instead, she thought about Ali's thrilling, decadent afterlife. It was probably filled with beautiful beaches, perfect, cloudless days, and shrimp cocktail and red velvet cake – Ali's favorite foods. Every guy there had a crush on her and every girl wanted to be her, even Princess Diana and Audrey Hepburn. She was still fabulous Alison DiLaurentis, ruling heaven just as she ruled earth.

'I'll miss you so much, Ali,' Emily mouthed quietly, the wind carrying the words away. She took a few deep breaths, waiting to see if she felt any different, any cleaner. But her heart still thrummed and her head continued to ache. It felt like a vital, special part of her had been ripped clean out.

She opened her eyes and saw Lucy staring at her from a few rows over. 'Everything okay?'

Emily struggled to nod, stepping around a few crooked headstones. Dry weeds jutted haphazardly around many of them. 'Is that Leah's grave?'

'Yes,' Lucy said, running her fingers along the top of the stone.

Emily walked over, and looked down. Leah's gravestone was gray marble, the inscription plain. *Leah Zook.*

Emily blinked at the dates on the stone. Leah had died June 19, almost four years ago. *Whoa.* Ali had gone missing the very next day, on June 20.

Then, Emily noticed an eight-pointed star above Leah's name. A spark ignited in her brain; she'd seen that pattern recently. 'What's that for?' She pointed at it.

Lucy's face clouded. 'My parents really wanted it on the headstone. It's the symbol of our community. But I didn't want it there. It reminds me *of him*.'

A crow landed on one of the headstones, flapping its inky wings. The wind gusted, making the cemetery gate hinges creak. 'Who's "him"?' Emily asked.

Lucy looked off in the distance at a lone, spindly tree in the middle of the field. 'Leah's boyfriend.'

'Th-the one she used to fight with?' Emily stammered. The crow lifted from the headstone and flapped away. 'The one you didn't like?'

Lucy nodded. 'When he left on *rumspringa*, he got a tattoo of that on his arm.'

Emily stared hard at the headstone, a horrible thought congealing in her mind. She looked again at the date on Leah's headstone. *June 19.* The day before Ali went missing, the very same year.

All at once, a memory unfurled before her, exact and clear, of a man sitting in a hospital room, his sleeves rolled up to his elbows, the overhead lights bright and hot. There was that star tattoo, black and obvious on the inside of his wrist. There *was* a connection here. There *was* a reason A had sent Emily to Lancaster. Because someone had been here before her. Someone she *knew*.

She raised her eyes to Lucy and gripped her shoulders.

173

'What was your sister's boyfriend's name?' she asked urgently.

Lucy took a deep breath, as if mustering up the strength to say a name she hadn't dared in a long, long time. 'His name was Darren Wilden.'

20
Minefields, Indeed

Hanna stood at the bathroom mirror, slathering on another coat of Bliss lip gloss and fluffing her auburn hair with a round brush. After a moment, Iris breezed in beside her, shooting Hanna a smile. 'Hey, bitch,' she said.

'What up, ho?' Hanna said in return. It had become their morning routine.

Even though they'd stayed up almost all night, writing love letters to Mike and Oliver, Iris's boyfriend from home, and picking apart stars' bodies in the pages of *People*, neither of them looked too much the worse for wear. As usual, Iris's pale blond hair hung in flawless waves down her back. Hanna's eyelashes looked extra long thanks to the Dior mascara she'd borrowed from Iris's bottomless makeup stash. Just because it was Group Therapy Friday didn't mean they had to look like pathetic slobs.

As they exited their room, Tara, Ruby, and Alexis followed, obviously spying. 'Hey, Hanna, can I talk to you for a sec?' Tara simpered.

Iris whipped around. 'She doesn't want to talk to you.'

'Can't Hanna speak for herself?' Tara demanded. 'Or have you brainwashed her, too?'

They had reached the window seats that looked out onto the gardens behind the facility. A few pink-patterned boxes of Kleenex sat next to the window seats; apparently, this was a prime spot for girls to sit and cry. Hanna sneered at Tara, who was obviously seething with jealousy and rejection and was trying to pit Hanna and Iris against each other. Not that Hanna believed a word of it. *Puh-lease.* 'We're trying to have a private conversation,' Hanna snapped. 'No freaks allowed.'

'You can't get rid of us that easily,' Tara spat. 'We have GT today too.'

The GT room was just ahead through a large oak door. Hanna rolled her eyes and whirled around. Unfortunately, Tara was right – all the girls on the floor had GT this morning.

Hanna didn't understand GT at all. Private, one-on-one therapy she could handle – she'd met with her therapist, Dr Foster, again yesterday, but all they'd talked about were the facials the Preserve offered, how she'd started dating Mike Montgomery just before she checked in, and the benefits of her insta-friendship with Iris. She hadn't mentioned Mona or A once, and there was no way she was going to spill any of her secrets to Tara and her gang of trolls.

Iris looked over, noticing Hanna's sullen expression. 'GT is okay,' she assured her. 'Just sit there and shrug. Or say you have your period and don't feel like talking.'

Dr Roderick – or 'Dr Felicia,' as she liked everyone to

176

call her – was the polished, chirpy, whirlwind of a woman in charge of GT. Now she poked her head out into the hall and grinned broadly. 'Come in, come in!' she singsonged.

The girls filed in. Cushy leather chairs and ottomans were arranged in a circle in the center of the room. A small fountain burbled away in the corner, and there was a large line of bottled waters and sodas on a mahogany sideboard. There were more boxes of Kleenex on the tables, and a big, mesh bin near the door held those foam fun noodles Hanna, Ali, and the others used to play with in Spencer's pool. A bunch of bongo drums, wooden flutes, and tambourines were stacked on shelves in the corner. Were they going to start a *band*?

After all the girls sat down, Dr Felicia shut the door and sat too. 'So,' she said, cracking open an enormous leather-bound day planner. 'Today, after we talk about how our weeks have gone, we're going to play Minefield.'

Everyone made varying grunts and groans. Hanna looked at Iris. 'What's that?'

'It's a trust exercise,' Iris explained, rolling her eyes. 'She scatters this stuff around the room, and it's supposed to represent bombs and landmines. One person is blindfolded, and her partner leads her around the mines so she doesn't get hurt.'

Hanna made a face. *This* was what her dad was paying a thousand dollars a day for?

Dr Felicia clapped her hands to get everyone's attention. 'Okay, let's talk about how we're doing. Who wants to start?'

No one spoke. Hanna scratched her leg, her mind on whether she would get a French manicure today or a hot oil hair treatment. A slender, dark-haired girl across the room named Paige chewed her fingernails.

Dr Felicia cupped her hands around her knees, sighing wearily. Then her gaze locked on Hanna. 'Hanna!' she chirped. 'Welcome to the group. Everyone, this is Hanna's first time here. Let's all make her feel safe and accepted.'

Hanna curled her toes inside her black Proenza Schouler ankle boots. 'Thanks,' she mumbled into her chest. The burbling fountain roared in her ears. It kind of made her have to pee.

'Do you like it here?' Dr Felicia's voice swooped up and down. She was one of those people who never blinked but always smiled. It made her seem like a deranged cheerleader on Ritalin.

'It's great,' Hanna said. 'Really, um, fun so far.'

The doctor frowned. 'Well, fun is good, but is there anything you'd like to discuss with the group?'

'Not really,' Hanna snapped.

Dr Felicia pursed her lips, looking disappointed.

'Hanna's my roommate, and she seems fine,' Iris jumped in. 'She and I talk tons – I think this place is doing wonders for her. I mean, at least she doesn't pull out her hair like Ruby.'

At that, everyone turned to Ruby, who indeed was grasping her hair in mid-yank. Hanna shot Iris a grateful smile, appreciative that she'd diverted Felicia's attention elsewhere.

But after Dr Felicia asked Ruby a few questions, she

turned back to Hanna. 'So, Hanna, would you like to tell us why you're here? You'd be amazed at how much talking helps.'

Hanna jiggled her foot. Maybe if she sat here silent for long enough, Felicia would move on to someone else. Then she heard someone across the room take a breath.

'Hanna has normal, run-of-the-mill problems,' Tara said in a high-pitched, scathing voice. 'She has eating issues, like every perfect girl does. Her daddy doesn't love her anymore, but she's trying not to think about it. And oh, she had a bitchy ex-best friend. Blah, blah, blah, nothing worth talking about.'

Satisfied, Tara leaned back, crossed her arms over her chest, and shot Hanna a look that said, *You asked for it*.

Iris sniffed. 'Wow, Tara, good for you. You spied on us. You have *ears*. And what ugly little rat ears they are.'

'Now,' Dr Felicia warned.

Hanna didn't want to give Tara the satisfaction either, but as she reviewed Tara's words, the blood drained from her face. Something Tara had just said was very, very wrong.

'H-how did you know about my best friend?' she stammered. Mona's face swam into her mind, her eyes fiery with rage as she gunned the engine of her SUV.

Tara blinked, caught off guard.

'It's obvious,' Iris jumped in acidly. 'She had her ear pressed to our door all night.'

Hanna's heart beat faster and faster. A salt truck roared by outside. The sound of its plow blade scraping against the pavement made her wince. She looked at Iris.

'But I never said anything about my bitch ex-best friend. Do *you* remember me saying anything about her?'

Iris scratched her chin. 'Well, no. But I was tired, so maybe I'd fallen asleep by then.'

Hanna ran her hand over her forehead. What the hell was happening? She'd taken an extra dose of Valium last night to help her sleep; had it made her blurt out stuff about Mona? Her mind felt like a dark, endless tunnel.

'Maybe you didn't want to talk about this friend, Hanna,' Dr Felicia rushed in. She rose to her feet and walked to the windows. 'But sometimes our minds and bodies have a way of pushing our problems out nevertheless.'

Hanna glared at her. 'I don't just blurt shit out. I don't have Tourette's. I'm not a *moron*.'

'You don't need to get worked up,' Dr Felicia said gently.

'I'm not getting worked up!' Hanna roared, her voice echoing off the walls.

Felicia backed off, her eyes round. A tense ripple swept through the other girls. Megan coughed, '*Psycho*,' into her hand. Pinpricks danced across Hanna's skin.

Dr Felicia returned to her chair and riffled her notebook pages. 'Well. Let's move on.' She turned a page in her notebook. 'Uh ... Gina. Have you spoken to your mom this week? How did that go?'

But as Dr Felicia asked the other girls about how their weeks had been, Hanna's mind wouldn't quiet down. It was like there was a tiny splinter in her brain that desperately needed to be dislodged. When she shut her eyes, she was in the Rosewood Day parking lot again, Mona's car barreling toward her. *No*, she shouted to herself. She couldn't go down this path, not here, not ever again. She forced her eyes open. The fun noodles in the corner blurred and wobbled. The girls' faces warped and stretched, like she was looking at them through a fun house mirror.

Unable to stand it any longer, Hanna pointed a shaking finger at Tara. 'You have to tell me how you know about Mona.'

Silence fell. Tara's pimply brow crinkled. 'Excuse me?'

'Did A tell you about her?' Hanna asked.

Tara shook her head slowly. 'A who?'

Dr Felicia stood up, crossed the room, and touched Hanna's arm. 'You seem confused, honey. Maybe you should go back to your room and rest.'

But Hanna didn't move. Tara matched her stare for a while, then rolled her eyes and shrugged. 'I have no idea who Mona is. I thought your bitchy best friend was Alison.'

Hanna's throat shunted closed. She sank back into her seat.

Iris perked up. 'Alison? Isn't that the girl whose flag you have? Why is she an *ex*-best friend?'

Hanna barely heard her. She stared at Tara. 'How do you know about Alison?' she whispered.

Begrudgingly, Tara reached into her grubby canvas bag. 'From this.' She tossed a copy of *People* Hanna had never seen before across the room. It skidded to a stop next to Hanna's chair. 'I was *going* to tell you about this before GT. But you were too *cool* to talk to me.'

Hanna snatched the magazine and opened to a marked page. Splashed out across the spread was the headline *A Week of Secrets and Lies*. Beneath it was a picture of Hanna, Spencer, Aria, and Emily, running from the fire in the woods. The caption said *The Pretty Little Liars*, followed by each of their names.

'Oh my God,' Hanna whispered.

Then she noticed a box and a graph in the bottom right-hand corner. DID THE PRETTY LITTLE LIARS KILL ALISON DILAURENTIS? They'd surveyed a hundred people in Times Square. Almost the whole pie – 92 percent – was purple for *yes*.

'I love your nickname, by the way,' Tara simpered, crossing her legs. 'Pretty Little Liars. *So* cute.'

Everyone crowded around Hanna's chair to read. She felt powerless to stop them. Ruby gasped. A patient named Julie clucked her tongue. And Iris – well, Iris looked horrified and disgusted. Everyone's opinions about Hanna were changing instantaneously. From now on, she would be *that girl*. The psycho everyone thought killed her best friend four years ago.

Dr Felicia snatched the magazine from Hanna's lap. 'Where did you get this?' she scolded Tara. 'You know magazines aren't allowed.'

Tara cowered, shy and sheepish now that she was in trouble. 'Iris always brags that she gets early editions of the magazine snuck in,' she mumbled, peeling away the wrapping on her water bottle. 'I just wanted to see a copy for myself.'

Iris rose to her feet, almost knocking over a chrome floor lamp next to her. She strode over to Tara. 'I had that issue in my bedroom, you bitch! I hadn't even read it yet! You went through my stuff!'

'Iris.' Dr Felicia clapped her hands, trying to regain control. A nurse peered through the little side pane in the GT door, probably trying to decide whether or not she should come to Dr Felicia's aid. 'Iris, you know your room is locked. No patient can get in.'

'It wasn't in her bedroom,' Tara cried. She pointed toward the hall. 'It was on the window seat near the lobby.'

'That's impossible!' Iris screamed, whirling around and facing Dr Felicia again. Her eyes yo-yoed from the magazine in Dr Felicia's fist to Hanna's stricken face. 'And *you*. You tried to come off as so cool, Hanna. But you're just as messed up as everyone else in here.'

'Pretty Little Liar,' a girl across the room teased.

A huge lump formed in Hanna's throat. Now all eyes were on her again. She wanted to get up and run out of the room, but it felt like her butt was stitched into the seat. 'I'm not a liar,' she said in a small voice.

Iris snorted, looking Hanna up and down disdainfully, as if Hanna had suddenly sprouted a rash of zits all over her face and arms. 'Whatever.'

'Girls, stop!' Dr Felicia pulled Iris by her sleeve. 'And, Iris and Tara, you both broke the rules and you're both in trouble.' She shoved *People* into her back pocket, then pulled Tara to her feet, grabbed Iris's arm, and marched both girls out the door. Before they left, Tara turned around and shot Hanna a smirk.

'Iris,' Hanna pleaded to Iris's receding back, 'it's not what you think!'

183

Iris turned in the doorway, staring at Hanna blankly, as if she were a stranger. 'Sorry, but I don't talk to freaks.' And then she whirled around and followed Felicia down the hall, leaving Hanna behind.

21
The Truth Hurts

A big Greyhound huffed in the parking lot of the Lancaster bus station, its final destination, Philadelphia, emblazoned above the windshield. Emily tentatively climbed aboard, breathing in the smell of new upholstery and heavy-duty bathroom cleaner. Even though she'd only spent a few days with Lucy and her family, the bus seemed jarringly modern, almost monstrous.

Emily had barely said a word to Lucy after Lucy admitted that Wilden had been her dead sister's old boyfriend. Lucy had repeatedly asked Emily what was wrong, but Emily said she was fine – just tired. What *could* she say? *I know your sister's old boyfriend. I think he really might have killed Leah. There's a hole in the back of someone's yard where he might have dumped her.*

Her brain had been on warp speed ever since, circling memory after memory of that horrible time. The day after Ali vanished, after their talk with Mrs DiLaurentis, Emily and her friends went in opposite directions. Emily had

185

passed right by the big hole where they'd eventually find the body.

The workers, she remembered, had been filling the hole with concrete that very day. All their cars were along the curb next to the DiLaurentises' lawn. There was one at the end that she'd studied for a second or two, wondering where she'd seen it before. It was an old black sedan, like something out of a sixties or seventies movie. It was the same car that screeched up to the Rosewood Day Lower School curb the day Ali bragged to everyone that she was going to find a piece of the Time Capsule flag. After his fight with Ian, Jason DiLaurentis had yanked open the passenger door to that car and slumped inside. It was the same car that chugged outside the DiLaurentis house the day Emily and the others tried to steal Ali's flag. And here it was in her memory again, looming at the DiLaurentises' house the day the concrete covered up that body for three long years. That car belonged to Darren Wilden.

The bus pulled away a few minutes later, the green fields of Lancaster disappearing behind them. There were only four other passengers, so Emily had a row to herself. Spying an outlet near her feet, she leaned down, plugged in her cell phone, and switched it on. The screen glowed with life.

Emily had to do something about what she'd learned, but what? If she called Spencer, Hanna, or Aria, they'd tell her she was crazy for thinking Ali was alive *and* for following A's instructions to go to Amish Country. She couldn't call her parents, either – they thought she was in Boston. And she couldn't call the police – Wilden *was* the police.

It was incredible that Wilden had really once been Amish. Emily knew very little about his life, only that he'd been a rebel at Rosewood Day but then had reinvented himself as a cop. It probably wouldn't take too much effort to find out when Wilden had left the community and started school at Rosewood Day, though, and when he spoke to Emily and the others in the hospital, he'd mentioned that he'd lived with his uncle in high school. According to Lucy, Wilden had convinced Leah, Lucy's sister, to leave the community as well. Maybe when she refused, he'd gotten angry ... and made plans to do away with her for good.

Wilden could have talked to Ali about her secret dreams to run away since he and Jason were friends. Wilden might have even promised Ali to help her run away for good, sneaking her out of Rosewood the night she went missing. He dumped a body into the hole in the DiLaurentises' backyard, making it look like Ali had been killed. But the body in that hole didn't belong to Ali. It belonged to the girl who broke Wilden's heart.

Horribly, it all fit. It explained why Leah had never been found. It explained why Ali showed up in the woods last Saturday and why Wilden was dissuading the police force from investigating the possibility that Ali was alive – if they realized it wasn't her body in that hole, they'd have to figure out whose body it *was*. It was why Wilden didn't believe in A and didn't buy that Ian knew a secret about what happened that night. A had been right all along – there *had* been a secret. But it wasn't about Ali's death. It was about who had been killed in Ali's *place*.

Emily stared at the graffiti someone had drawn on the

187

wall of the bus under the window. MIMI LUVS CHRISTOPHER. TINA HAS A FAT ASS. There was even a sketch of two fat butt cheeks next to it. Ali was out there, somewhere, just as she'd always known. But where had she been all this time? It seemed implausible that a seventh grader could survive on her own. Or perhaps she'd known someone who'd taken her in. Why hadn't she contacted Emily to let her know she was okay? Or maybe she hadn't *wanted* to contact anyone. Maybe she'd decided to forget her entire life in Rosewood, even her four best friends.

Emily's phone beeped, signaling three unread texts. She scrolled through her inbox. Two were from her sister Caroline; both subject lines read *People Survey*. Aria had sent a text too; its subject line said *We need to talk*.

An old woman at the front of the bus coughed. The bus rolled past a farm, and the cabin temporarily smelled like manure. Emily moved the cursor from text to text, trying to decide which to read first. Just then, her phone pinged again, this time with a text from an unknown number. Her pulse raced. This *had* to be from A. And for once, Emily couldn't wait to know what A had to say. She pressed read immediately.

It was a photo text. The picture was of a bunch of blurry papers fanned out on a table. The top document was titled ALISON DILAURENTIS DISAPPEARANCE: TIMELINE. The paper below it said INTERVIEW, JESSICA DILAURENTIS, JUNE 21, 10:30 P.M. Another paper had a crest of something called the Preserve at Addison-Stevens, with the last name 'DiLaurentis' shown. A red stamp on each of the papers said PROPERTY OF ROSEWOOD POLICE DEPARTMENT. EVIDENCE. DO NOT REMOVE.

Emily gasped.

Then, she noticed a final piece of paper peeking out from underneath the others. Emily squinted until her eyes hurt. DNA REPORT, it said. But Emily couldn't read the results.

'No,' Emily moaned, feeling like she was going to explode. Then, as the bus went over a bone-jarring bump, she noticed an accompanying note with the photo.

Wanna see for yourself? The evidence room is in the back of the Rosewood police station. I'll leave a door open. – A

22
Ali Returns ... Sort Of

Friday after school, Noel picked Aria up at Byron's house. As she got in the car, he leaned over and gave her a little kiss on the cheek. Despite the butterflies eating away at Aria's stomach lining, she felt a thrill run down her spine.

They drove through the winding streets of various neighborhoods, passing the old farmhouses and the township playground that still had a couple of discarded Christmas trees at the far end of the parking lot. Neither Aria nor Noel spoke, though the silence felt comfortable instead of awkward. Aria was grateful not to have to scramble for small talk.

Aria's phone rang just as they were turning onto Ali's old street. *Private caller*, said the screen. Aria answered. 'Ms. Montgomery?' chirped a voice. 'This is Bethany Richards from *Us Weekly*!'

'Sorry, not interested,' Aria said quickly, cursing herself for answering.

She was about to hang up the phone when the reporter

breathed in sharply. 'I just wanted to know if you had a response to the *People* article.'

'What *People* article?' Aria snapped. Noel glanced at her worriedly.

'The one with the poll that says ninety-two percent of people surveyed think you and your friends killed Alison DiLaurentis!' The reporter sounded giddy.

'*What?*' Aria gasped. 'It's not true!' Then she stabbed end and dropped her phone into her bag. Noel gazed at her, an anxious look on his face. 'There's an article in *People* that says *we* killed Ali,' she whispered.

Noel's eyebrows knit together in a V. 'Jesus.'

Aria pressed her head to the window, staring vacantly at a passing green sign for the Hollis Arboretum. How on earth could people believe such a crazy thing? Just because of their stupid nickname? Because they hadn't wanted to answer any of the press's rude, prying questions?

They pulled up to Ali's old cul-de-sac. Aria could smell the singed remains from the fire even through the rolled-up windows. The trees were twisted and black, like decomposed limbs, and the Hastingses' windmill was now a pulpy, incinerated carcass. But the worst thing was the Hastingses' barn. Half of it had collapsed, nothing more than a bunch of dark, ruined planks on the ground. The old porch glider, once painted antique white, was now a dirty, rusted color, hanging creakily by one hinge. It swayed gently, as if a ghost were lazily swinging back and forth.

Noel drew his bottom lip into his mouth, eyeing the barn. 'It's like the House of Usher.'

Aria gawked at him, amazed. Noel shrugged. 'You

know. The Poe story where the crazy guy buries his sister in that old, ruined, scary house? And for a while he feels really unsettled and even *crazier*, and it's because it turns out she's not really dead?'

'I can't believe you know that story,' Aria said, pleased.

Noel looked hurt. 'I'm in AP English, same as you. I do *read* from time to time.'

'I didn't mean it like that,' Aria said quickly, although she wondered if she kind of did.

They parked in front of the DiLaurentises' house and got out. The new owners, the St. Germains, had moved back in after the Ali media circus had died down, but they didn't look to be home, which was a relief. Even better, there wasn't a single news van parked at the curb. Then Aria spied Spencer at her mailbox, a stack of envelopes in her hand. Spencer saw Aria at the exact same time. Her eyes shifted from Aria to Noel, looking a little confused. 'What are you guys doing here?' she blurted.

'Hey.' Aria walked over, skirting around a large, round hedge. Her nerves jumped and crackled. 'Did you hear that people think *we* killed Ali?'

Spencer made a sour face. 'Yeah.'

'We need some real answers.' Aria gestured toward Ali's old backyard, which was still haphazardly surrounded by yellow police tape. 'I know you think the Ali ghost thing is crazy, but a medium is going to perform a séance where she died. Do you want to watch?'

Spencer took a step away. '*No!*'

'But what if she actually contacts Ali? Don't you want to know what really happened?'

Spencer straightened the envelopes in her hands until

they all faced the same direction. 'That stuff isn't real, Aria. And you shouldn't be hanging around that hole. The press will have a field day!'

A gust of wind whipped across Aria's face, and she drew her coat tighter around her. 'We're not doing anything wrong. We'll just be *standing* there.'

Spencer slammed the door to the mailbox hard and turned away. 'Well, count me out.'

'Fine,' Aria said indignantly, whirling around. As she stormed back to Noel, she peeked over her shoulder. Spencer was still standing by her mailbox, looking conflicted and sad. Aria wished Spencer would let her guard down and believe in what couldn't be explained. This was *Ali* they were talking about. But after a moment, Spencer threw her shoulders back and headed for the front door.

Noel was waiting by the Ali shrine on the curb. As usual, it was crowded with flowers and candles and impersonal notes that said things like *We'll Miss You* and *Rest in Peace*. 'Should we go back there?' he asked.

Aria nodded numbly, pressing her wool scarf to her nose – the burnt smell from the fire was making her eyes water. Silently, they walked across the stiff, frosty yard to the back of Ali's property. Even though it was only a little past 4 P.M., the sky was already growing dark. It was strangely foggy, and thick mist swirled around Ali's old back deck. A crow cawed from deep inside the woods.

Crack. Aria jumped in fright. When she turned, a woman was suddenly right behind her, breathing down her neck. She had flyaway salt-and-pepper hair, bulging eyes, and sallow, papery skin. Her teeth were yellowish and rotting, and her fingernails were at least an inch long.

She looked like a corpse who'd just climbed out of a coffin.

'I'm Esmeralda,' the woman said in a thin, low voice.

Aria was too terrified to speak. Noel stepped forward. 'This is Aria.' The woman touched Aria's hand. Her fingers were ice-cold and nothing but bones.

Esmeralda glanced toward the taped-off hole. 'Come. She's been waiting to talk to you.'

The lump in Aria's throat tripled in size. They shuffled closer to the hole. The air felt cooler there. The wind had died down to an eerie standstill, and the mist was even thicker. It was like the hole was in the eye of a storm, a portal to a different dimension. *This can't be happening*, she thought, trying to stay calm. *Ali isn't here. It isn't possible. I'm just getting caught up in the moment.*

'Now …' Esmeralda took Aria's hand and led her to the edge of the hole. 'Look down. We need to reach her together.'

Aria began to tremble. She'd never looked into the half-dug hole before. When she glanced helplessly at Noel, who was a few paces behind them, he nodded faintly, nudging his chin toward the hole. Taking a deep breath, she craned her neck and looked down. Her heart hammered. Her skin felt cold. The inside of the hole was dark and filled with clumps of dirt and cracked pieces of cement. A couple of pieces of police tape had fallen to the bottom, about nine feet down. Though Ali's body had long since been removed, Aria could see a matted-down indentation where something heavy had lain for a long, long time.

She shut her eyes. Ali had been down there for years,

covered up by cement, slowly deteriorating into the soil. Her skin had fallen off her bones. Her beautiful face had rotted. In life, Ali was captivating, someone you couldn't help but stare at, but in death, she'd been silent, invisible. For years, she'd hid in her own backyard. She'd taken with her the secret of what had really happened.

Aria reached for Noel's hand. He quickly curled his fingers around hers and squeezed.

Esmeralda remained at the edge of the hole for a long time, inhaling deep, guttural breaths, rolling her neck around, rocking back and forth on her heels. Then she started to writhe. It seemed like something was infiltrating her body, slipping in through her skin and getting comfortable. Aria's breath caught in her throat. Noel didn't move, awestruck. When Aria's gaze broke from Esmeralda for a moment, she noticed a light on in Spencer's bedroom window next door. Spencer was standing at the window, staring at them.

Finally, Esmeralda raised her head. Astonishingly, she somehow appeared younger, and there was a whisper of a smirk on her face. 'Hey,' Esmeralda said in a completely different voice.

Aria gasped. Noel flinched too. It was *Ali's* voice.

'So you wanted to talk to me?' Esmeralda-as-Ali said, sounding bored. 'You only get one question, so make it good.'

A dog howled in the distance. A door slammed across the street, and when Aria turned, she thought she saw Jenna Cavanaugh gliding past the bay window in her living room. And Aria even thought she could smell a hint of vanilla soap wafting out from the bottom of the hole.

Could Ali be right here, staring at her through this woman's eyes? And what was Aria supposed to ask her? There were so many secrets Ali had kept from them – about her tryst with Ian, the problems with her brother, the truth about blinding Jenna, and the possibility that Ali wasn't as happy as everyone thought. But really, one question stood out cleanly from the others.

'Who killed you?' she finally asked in a quiet, quaking whisper.

Esmeralda wrinkled her nose, like this was the stupidest question in the world. 'Are you sure you want to know?'

Aria leaned forward. '*Yes.*'

The medium lowered her head. 'I'm afraid to say it out loud,' she blurted, still in Ali's voice. 'I'll have to write it down.'

'Okay,' Aria said quickly.

'And then you have to leave,' Esmeralda-as-Ali said. 'I don't want you here anymore.'

'Sure,' Aria wheezed. 'Anything.'

Esmeralda reached into her purse and pulled out a small, leather-bound notebook and a ballpoint pen. Scribbling quickly, she folded the note and handed it to Aria. '*Now go,*' she growled.

Aria backed away from the hole, nearly tripping as she went. She didn't even feel her legs as she sprinted to Noel's car. Noel was right behind her, pulling her to him and holding her close. For a moment, they both were too overwhelmed to speak. Aria stared at the Ali Shrine again. A single candle flame illuminated Ali's school picture from seventh grade. Ali's wide, toothy smile and unblinking eyes suddenly made her look possessed.

She thought about the story Noel had mentioned – 'The Fall of the House of Usher.' Just like the sister in the story who had been entombed in that old house, Ali's body had been trapped under the concrete for three long years. Were souls released from their earthly vessels as soon as a person died … or much later? Had Ali's soul escaped that hole just after Ali took her last breath … or only after the workers excavated her rotted corpse from the ground?

The slip of paper Esmeralda had given her was still in Aria's palm. She began to slowly unfold it. 'Do you need a minute alone?' Noel asked softly.

Aria swallowed hard. 'It's okay.' She needed him here. She was too afraid to look at the note by herself.

The paper crinkled as she spread it out. The letters were round and bubbly – *Ali's* handwriting. Slowly, Aria read the words. There were only three, and they chilled her to her very core:

Ali killed Ali.

23
All In The Family

About an hour later, Spencer sat at her desk in her bedroom, staring out the big bay window. The back porch lights threw an eerie glow over the ruined barn and the twisted, hideous forest. All the snow had melted, leaving a film of muck over the ground. A bunch of tree surgeons had hacked away at the brambles with chain saws, leaving a big pile of dead timber on the lawn. A cleanup crew had ransacked the barn today, depositing the remaining furniture near the patio. The round rug where Spencer and the others had sat the night Ali hypnotized them was propped against the steps of the deck. It had once been white, but it was now burnt-marshmallow brown.

Aria and Noel were no longer gathered around the hole. Spencer had watched them from the window; the whole thing with the medium had taken only about ten minutes. Though she was curious about what Aria had discovered with Madame Psychic Friend, she felt too stubborn to ask. The medium looked suspiciously like the woman who hung out on the Hollis College green, claiming she could speak to trees. Spencer hoped the press wouldn't get wind of what Aria was doing – it would just make them look crazier.

'Hey, Spence.'

She jumped. Her father stood in her doorway, still in a dark pin-striped suit from work.

'Want to look at windmill Web sites with me?' he asked. Her parents had decided to replace the fire-damaged windmill with a new one that would help to power the house.

'Um …' Spencer felt a twinge of regret. When had her dad last asked her to take part in a family decision?

Yet she couldn't even look at him. The letter she'd found on his hard drive scrolled through her mind like the CNN news ticker. *Dear Jessica, I'm sorry things got cut short … I can't wait to be alone with you again. Xx, Peter.* It wasn't hard to draw awful conclusions. She kept imagining her father and Mrs DiLaurentis sitting on the beige wraparound sofa in Ali's living room – the very same couch Spencer, Ali, and the others sat on when they watched *American Idol* – nuzzling noses in the same way some PDA-obsessed couples did in the hallways of Rosewood Day.

'I have homework,' she lied, the grilled chicken salad she'd had for lunch churning in her stomach.

Her dad looked disappointed. 'Okay, maybe later then.' He turned and padded down the stairs.

Spencer let out a pent-up breath. She *needed* to talk to someone about this. The secret was too weighty and over-whelming to handle alone. She pulled out her phone and dialed Melissa's number. It rang and rang.

'It's Spencer,' she said shakily after the voice mail beep. 'I need to talk to you about something with Mom and Dad. Call me back.'

She pressed the end button with despair. *Where's Mom?* Melissa had bleated to their dad the night Ali went missing. *We need to find her.* According to their father's letter to Ali's mom, the two of them had met up that same night. What if Spencer's mom caught them together and *that* was why she never wanted to talk about that night again?

The realization hit her again. Her dad ... and Ali's mom. She shuddered. It was unthinkable.

The woods were eerily still. A flutter to her right caught her eye, and she turned. There was a flash of yellow at Ali's old bedroom window. Then a light flipped on. Maya, the girl who lived there now, crossed the room and plopped down on the bed.

Spencer's phone buzzed, and she let out a bleat of surprise. But instead of a return call from Melissa, an IM had appeared on her screen. *Is this Spencer?*

She stared at the sender's screen name in disbelief. *USCMidfielderRoxx.* It was *Ian.*

Before Spencer could decide what to do, another message flashed on Spencer's screen. *I got your IM name from Melissa. Is it okay that I'm IMing you?*

Spencer's head felt scrambled. So Ian and Melissa *had* been in contact.

I'm not sure I want to talk to you, she rapidly typed. *You were wrong about Jason and Wilden. And then someone tried to kill us.*

He wrote back immediately. *I feel terrible that that happened. But everything I told you is true. Wilden and Jason hated me. They were coming to mess with me that night. Maybe they didn't hurt Ali ... but they ARE hiding something.*

Spencer let out a low groan. *How do I know YOU didn't kill Ali and are now trying to set us up to take the fall? The police hate us now. All of Rosewood does.*

I'm so sorry about that, Spencer, Ian wrote. *But I didn't kill Ali, I swear. You have to believe me.*

The curtains in Maya's window fluttered again. Spencer squeezed her phone with her fingers. She couldn't put Ian at the scene the moment Ali disappeared anymore. And neither could Melissa.

Then something occurred to her. Ian had been with Melissa the night Ali vanished – and the night Melissa and their dad fought. He might know something about what happened.

I have a question about something else, she typed quickly. *Do you remember Melissa fighting with my dad the night Ali died? She met him at the door and was yelling at him about something. Did she say anything to you about it?*

The cursor flashed. Spencer drummed her fingers on her Tiffany desk blotter, impatient. Twenty long seconds passed before Ian responded. *I think this is something you should talk about with your parents.*

Spencer bit down hard on her lip. *I can't,* she hammered on the keyboard. *If you know something say it.*

There was another long pause. A couple of crows fluttered out from the burnt woods, settling on a far-off telephone pole. Spencer's gaze wandered over to the ruined, crumbled barn, to the taped-off hole in the

DiLaurentises' backyard. Her nerves felt snappy and raw. In one sweeping glance, she could see everywhere Ali traveled in her last few hours alive.

Finally, a new message appeared. *Melissa and I were sleeping in the den,* Ian wrote. *I remember her getting up that night and talking to your dad. When she came back, she was really upset. She said she was pretty sure your dad was having an affair with Ali's mom. She also said that your mom had just found out. 'I'm afraid she's going to do something stupid,' she said.*

Something stupid like what? Spencer shot back, her heart pounding.

I don't know.

'God,' Spencer said out loud. Where had her mom caught them? Were Mrs DiLaurentis and her father in the DiLaurentises' kitchen, tempting fate in plain sight?

Spencer pressed her fingers to her temple. The day after Ali disappeared, Ali's mom had sat the girls down and asked if Ali told them about overhearing something in the house – she thought she saw Ali in the doorway. What if Ali caught their parents too? Maybe Ali entered her house through the back door, padded down the corridor to the kitchen, and came upon them ... together. If Spencer walked in on a scene like that, she knew just what she'd do – turn around and march right back out again.

Maybe that was what Ali did too. And then whatever happened to her ... happened.

Spencer's phone pinged again. *And, Spence, I hate to tell you this – but I already knew about the affair before she told me. I saw your dad and Ali's mom together two weeks before that night. I accidentally told Ali about it,*

202

too. *I didn't mean to, but she knew I was keeping some-thing from her. She forced it out of me.*

Spencer held the phone at arm's length. *Ali* knew? 'Jesus,' she whispered.

Another IM popped up. *I never told you why Jason was coming to mess with me that night Ali went missing. I hoped I wouldn't have to. But it's because I told Ali about the affair. She took it really hard, and Jason thought I'd told her just to be cruel. He and Wilden hated me for a lot of things, but that was the final straw.*

Before Spencer had a chance to process what he said, more words appeared. *And there's something else I always thought was weird. Have you noticed how similar you, Melissa, and Ali all look? Maybe that's why I liked all of you.*

Spencer frowned, feeling dizzy. Ian's implication trick-led into her brain and began to fester. It *was* weird how Ali had looked absolutely nothing like her dad. She hadn't inherited his flyaway, frizzy hair or his beakish, hooked nose. Then again, Ali hadn't inherited her mother's long, pointy nose, either, like Jason had, but instead had been blessed with a petite button one with a tiny bit of an upturn at the tip. It looked a lot like Spencer's father's nose, come to think of it. And, even scarier, like her own.

She thought about what her parents had told her in the hospital: that although Olivia had carried Spencer, she was the product of her dad and her mom. If what Ian sug-gested was true, it would mean that Spencer and Ali were ... related. *Sisters.*

And then Spencer remembered something else.

She jumped to her feet and wheeled around, gazing unfocusedly into her room. Then she ran down to her dad's office. Thankfully, it was empty. She pulled the Yale yearbook off the wall and held it upside down. The blurry Polaroid photo fell to the Oriental rug. Spencer picked it up and stared at it.

The lines were blurry, but the heart-shaped face and corn-silk blond hair were unmistakable. Spencer should have known immediately. The picture wasn't of Olivia. It was of Jessica DiLaurentis – a very pregnant Jessica DiLaurentis.

Shaking, Spencer turned it over and looked at the date that was written on the back. June 2, almost seventeen years ago. It was a few weeks before Ali was born.

She clutched her stomach, holding in a nauseated heave. If her mother had known about the affair, it explained why she hated Ali. It had probably driven her crazy, knowing that the physical embodiment of her failed marriage was living next door to them – and worse, that she was the girl who everyone loved. The girl who got whoever and whatever she wanted.

In fact, if Spencer's mother's suspicions were confirmed on that spooky night that seventh grade ended, she might have been pushed right over the edge. It could have made her do something unthinkable and unplanned, something she needed to desperately cover up.

Let's never talk about that night again, her mother had said. And the day after the seventh-grade sleepover, just after Mrs DiLaurentis got done questioning the girls, Spencer came upon her mother sitting at the kitchen table, so distracted she didn't even hear Spencer call her name.

Because she was so guilt-addled, maybe. So horrified at what she'd just done to her daughters' half sister.

'Oh my God,' Spencer croaked. '*No.*'

'No what?'

Spencer spun around fast. Her mother stood in the doorway of the office, dressed in a black silk dress and silver Givenchy heels.

A thin squeak escaped from the back of Spencer's throat. Then her mother's eyes moved from the Yale yearbook that was sitting open on the desk to the Polaroid photo in Spencer's hand. Spencer immediately shoved it in her pocket, but a cloudy look came over her mother's face. Swiftly, she crossed the room and touched Spencer's arm. Her hands were ice-cold. When Spencer looked into her mother's narrowed eyes, she felt a flicker of fear.

'Get your coat, Spence,' Mrs Hastings said, her voice eerily calm. 'We're going for a ride.'

24
Another Breakthrough At The Preserve

Hanna opened her eyes and found herself in a small hospital room. The walls were pea green. Next to her was a big bouquet of flowers and near the door was a smiley-faced GET WELL SOON balloon with accordion arms and legs. Oddly, it was the same balloon her father had given her after Mona hit Hanna with her SUV. And come to think of it, the walls of that room had been this same greenish color, too. When she tilted her neck to the right, she saw a pale silver clutch sitting on the pillow next to her. When had she last used *that*? And then she remembered: the night of Mona's Sweet Seventeen party. The night of her accident.

She gasped and jolted up, noticing for the first time the clunky cast on her arm. Had she traveled back in time? Or had she never left the room in the first place? Had the past few months been nothing but a horrible nightmare? Then a familiar figure loomed over her.

'Hi, Hanna,' Ali lilted. She looked taller and older, her face more angular, her hair a slightly darker blond. There was a smudge of soot on her cheek, as if she'd just emerged from the fiery woods.

Hanna blinked. 'Am I dead?'

Ali giggled. 'No, silly.' Then she cocked her head, listening for something in the distance. 'I have to go soon. But listen, okay? She knows more than you think.'

'What?' Hanna cried, struggling to sit up.

An entranced look came over Ali's face. 'We were best friends once,' she said. 'But you can't trust her.'

'Who? Tara?' she blurted, perplexed.

Ali sighed. 'She wants to hurt you.'

Hanna struggled to pull her arms out from under the sheets. 'What do you mean? Who wants to hurt me?'

'She wants to hurt you like she already hurt me.' Tears rolled down Ali's cheeks, first salty and clear, then thick and bloody. One plopped square in the middle of Hanna's cheek. It felt hot and sizzling, like acid seeping through her skin.

Hanna shot up, breathing hard. She felt her cheek, but it no longer stung. The walls around her were pale blue. Moonlight streamed through the big picture window. There were no flowers on her nightstand or balloons in the corner. The bed next to her was empty, the sheets pulled tight. The little shoe-a-day calendar on Iris's side of the room was still turned to Friday. Hanna must have fallen asleep.

Iris hadn't yet returned to their shared bedroom after the dreadful GT incident. Hanna wondered if she was still in another part of the facility, enduring her punishment for sneaking magazines in. Hanna had been too ashamed to go to the cafe for lunch, not wanting to give Tara the satisfaction that she'd taken away Hanna's only friend. The only people she'd seen were Betsy, the nurse who administered meds; Dr Foster, who apologized to Hanna for her peers' behavior; and George, one of the janitors who had come to clean out Iris's *People* magazines, tossing them into a big gray Dumpster.

It was so silent in the room that Hanna could hear the tinny, high-pitched ringing of the fluorescent bulb in her bedside lamp. Her dream had felt so real, like Ali had just been there. *She knows more than you think*, Ali said. *She wants to hurt you like she already hurt me.* She had to be talking about Tara and what she did in GT. For an ugly, chubby loser, Tara was much shrewder than Hanna thought.

A key turned in the lock and the door creaked open. 'Oh.' Iris's face soured when she saw Hanna. 'Hi.'

'Where have you been?' Hanna gasped, sitting up fast. 'Are you okay?'

'I'm golden,' Iris said blandly. She walked over to the mirror and began to inspect her pores.

'I didn't know I was going to get you in trouble,' Hanna gushed. 'I'm so sorry Felicia took away your magazines.'

Iris's eyes met Hanna's in the mirror. Her face was etched with disappointment. 'It's not about the magazines, Hanna. I told you everything about *me*, but I had to find out everything about you from some stupid magazine. *Tara* knew before I did.'

Hanna swung her legs over the bed. 'I'm sorry.'

Iris crossed her arms over her chest. 'Sorry doesn't cut it. I thought you were normal. And you're not.'

Hanna pressed her thumbs into her eye sockets. 'So

208

some shit happened to me,' she blurted. 'You heard some of it in group.' She launched into an explanation about the night Ali went missing, her makeover, A, and how Mona had tried to kill her. 'Everyone around me is crazy, but I'm normal, I swear.' Hanna dropped her hands in her lap and looked at Iris's eyes in the mirror. 'I wanted to tell you, but I just don't know who to trust anymore.'

Iris stood very still for a few long moments, her back still turned. The vanilla-scented Glade plug-in in the corner outlet let out a *sfft*. It reminded Hanna eerily of Ali. Finally, Iris whirled around. 'God, Hanna.' She exhaled. 'That sounds *awful*.'

'It was,' Hanna admitted.

And then the tears came fast and hot. It felt like every shred of tension and fear she'd been holding in for months erupted from her. For so long, she'd thought if she pretended she was over Mona and Ali and A, it all would eventually fade away. But it *wasn't* fading. She was so angry at Mona it physically hurt. She was angry at Ali for being so nasty to Mona that she'd turned into vicious, heartless A. And she was furious at herself for falling for Mona's friendship – and Ali's.

'If I hadn't been friends with Ali, none of this would've happened,' Hanna wailed, crying so hard now that her chest heaved uncontrollably. 'I wish she'd never been in my life. I wish I never *knew* her.'

'Shhhh.' Iris petted Hanna's hair. 'You don't mean that.'

But Hanna *did* mean it. All Ali gave Hanna was a few months of bliss and then many years of pain. 'Would it have been the worst thing if I had stayed an ugly, chubby loser?' Hanna asked. At least then she wouldn't have hurt people. At least people wouldn't have hurt *her*. 'Maybe I deserved what Mona did to me. Maybe Ali deserved what someone did to her, too.'

Iris sat back, flinching as if Hanna had pinched her. Hanna realized too late how her words probably sounded. But then Iris stood and straightened her skirt. 'The staff is making us watch *Ella Enchanted* in the theater room.' She rolled her eyes and made a face. 'I'll tell them you're sick if you want me to. Maybe you need some time alone. I understand if you don't want to see Tara and the others right now.'

Hanna was about to nod, but then her stomach let out a gurgle. She squared her shoulders. It was true – she *didn't* want to face Tara and the other patients, now that they knew the truth. But all of a sudden, she didn't really care. Everyone here was screwed up. They were no better than she was.

'I'll be there,' she decided.

Iris smiled. 'Take your time.' The door clonked shut on her way out.

Hanna felt her pulse begin to slow. She dabbed her eyes with more Kleenexes, slid her feet into her Ugg slippers, and walked to the mirror. Fixing her puffy eyes was going to take a lot of makeup. Then, she noticed Iris's black patent leather Chanel purse on the bureau, the corner of a magazine poking out. Hanna pulled at it, hardly believing what she saw.

It was the newest issue of *People*. The one with the story about Hanna inside.

Alarm bolted through her. Hadn't the nurses taken this

away? Frantically, Hanna leafed to the page where the story about her began. *A Week of Secrets and Lies*. Her eyes scanned the text. There were details about their friendship with Alison. Their dealings with Mona-as-A. Seeing Ian Thomas's body, narrowly escaping the fire. There was the box that said 92 percent of the country thought Hanna and the others killed Ali. And then Hanna noticed another sidebar. *And where's Hanna Marin?* said bold type. *You'll never believe it!* Next to it was a picture of the front of the Preserve.

Hanna's blood went ice-cold.

There was a list of drugs Hanna was taking, the sleeping pills and the Valium. There was an itinerary of how she spent her days, down to what she ate for breakfast, how long she ran on the treadmill, and how often she wrote in her leather-bound food journal. Below the article was a blurry picture of Hanna in leggings and a T-shirt, sticking her tongue out at the camera, the graffiti on the walls of the secret attic room behind her. Hanna's raised middle finger had been cropped out, as had the other girl in the picture. 'Oh my God,' Hanna whispered.

She stared at the magazine, nausea burbling up in her stomach. In group, Hanna had blamed Tara. But something didn't fit. Even if Tara had somehow found Iris's disposable camera, some of these details were too specific. They were things only someone who spent every waking moment with Hanna could know.

Just before Hanna hurled the magazine across the room, she saw something else in the photo. Behind her head, right next to Iris's sketch of the wishing well, was another drawing in the exact same style and the same

211

color ink. It was of a girl with a heart-shaped face, Cupid-bow lips, and wide, big blue eyes. Hanna brought the magazine closer to her face, staring at it until her eyes crossed. It was the spitting image of a girl Hanna knew very, very well. A girl she thought she'd seen in the woods the week before.

And suddenly, Ali's voice lilted in her ear. *She wants to hurt you just like she already hurt me.*

Ali hadn't been talking about Tara at all; she'd been talking about *Iris*.

25
Aria Says Good-Bye

An hour after her meeting with Esmeralda, Aria parked at the gates of St. Basil's cemetery. The majestic mausoleums and headstones were dappled with silver moonlight. A couple of tall, old-fashioned lanterns lit the brick pathway. There was a gentle breeze shaking the bare willow trees. Aria knew every step to Ali's grave, but that wouldn't make the journey there any easier.

Ali killed Ali. It was shocking ... and unbelievable ... and filled Aria with penetrating, unbelievable guilt. Someone murdering Ali was one thing, truly tragic. But Ali killing herself? It could have been prevented. Ali could have sought help.

And still, Aria was skeptical that Ali could have done such a thing. She'd seemed so happy, so *carefree*. But the day Mrs DiLaurentis questioned them about Ali's whereabouts, after Aria and her friends parted ways, she'd started down the DiLaurentises' driveway and noticed the lid to one of their garbage cans had blown off. Bending down to put it back on the can, she spied an empty bottle for pills nestled atop the trash bags. The prescription was for Ali, but the medication's name had been rubbed off. At the time, Aria hadn't thought much of it, but now she reexamined the memory more closely. What if the pills were to treat depression or anxiety? What if Ali took a whole handful of them on the night of the seventh-grade sleepover, too overcome to go on? She could have climbed into that hole on purpose, folded her hands over her chest, and waited for the drugs to take effect. But there was no way to prove it – Ali's body had been so decomposed by the time the workers found her that there was no way to test for a drug overdose.

R U avoiding me? Ali had texted Aria in those last few weeks she was alive. *I want 2 talk.* But Aria had ignored almost every one of them – there was only so much teasing about Byron's affair she could take. What if Ali had needed to talk about something else? How had Aria missed something so huge?

Even though she'd only seen Noel an hour ago, she pulled out her phone and called him. He answered right away. 'I'm at the cemetery,' she said. Then she paused, figuring Noel would know why.

'It'll be okay,' Noel said. 'It'll make you feel better, I promise.'

Aria picked up the crinkly wrapping around the bouquet of flowers she'd picked up at the grocery store just minutes ago. She wasn't sure what she was going to say to Ali here – or what answers she'd get. But at this point, she was willing to try anything to feel better. She swallowed hard, pressing the phone to her ear. 'Ali might have been reaching out to me about something, but I ignored her. This is all my fault.'

214

'It's not,' Noel soothed. The other end crackled with static. 'I think that about my brother sometimes, too … but you can't. It's nothing I could've prevented, and it's nothing you could've stopped, either. And it wasn't like you were Ali's only friend. She could've reached out to Spencer or Hanna or her parents. But she didn't.'

'I'll talk to you later, okay?' Aria said, her voice thick with tears. Then she hung up, grabbed the flowers, opened the passenger door, and started up the walk. The grass was wet and squishy under her feet. Within minutes, she was climbing the hill and approaching Ali's headstone. Someone had set up fresh flowers at the headstone's base and taped a picture of Ali to the stone itself.

'*Aria?*'

She jumped. A shiver went down her back. Jason DiLaurentis was standing a few feet away under a big sycamore tree. She braced herself, ready for him to get angry, but he just stood there, his eyes darting back and forth. He wore a heavy black jacket with a thick, padded hood, black pants, and black gloves. For a wild second Aria wondered if he was going to rob a bank.

'H-hey,' she finally sputtered. 'I just … wanted to talk to Ali. Is that okay?'

Jason shrugged. 'Sure.' He began to walk down the hill, giving her space. 'Wait,' Aria called. Jason stopped, leaned his hand against a tree, and peered at her.

Aria considered her words. One short week ago, when they were dating, Jason had encouraged her to discuss Ali with him – he said everyone else seemed too uncomfortable to even utter her name in his presence. She brushed her hands on her jeans. 'We've found out a lot about Ali

215

that we didn't know,' she finally said. 'A lot that's really painful. I'm sure it's been hard on you, too.'

Jason kicked his toe into a loose clump of soil. 'Yeah.'

'And sometimes you just don't know what's going on inside of people,' Aria added, thinking about how Ali had happily pirouetted across the lawn the evening seventh grade ended, seemingly overjoyed to see her best friends. 'People always seem so perfect on the surface,' she added. 'But ... it's not always the case. Everyone hides things.'

Jason's toe kicked up more dirt.

'But it's not your fault,' Aria went on. 'It's not any of our faults.'

And all of a sudden, she really believed that. If Ali really had committed suicide, and if she'd known she was going to do it ahead of time, Aria still might not have been able to do anything to stop her. It broke her heart that she hadn't sensed it coming, and it sucked that she didn't know *why* Ali had done it ... but maybe she just had to accept it, grieve, and move on.

Jason opened his mouth as if to speak, but a shrill ring pierced the air. He reached into his pocket and pulled out his phone. 'I should get this,' he said, glancing at the screen, his tone apologetic. Aria gave him a wave as he turned and walked down the hill into the shadows.

Then she faced Ali's headstone. *Alison Lauren DiLaurentis*. Nothing else. Had Ali known the night of the sleepover would be her last on earth, or had it been a spur-of-the-moment, *I can't take it anymore* thing? The very last time Aria saw Ali alive, Ali had been about to hypnotize them, but Spencer had jumped up and tried to open the blinds. *It's too dark in here*, Spencer said. *It has*

216

to be dark, Ali argued, whipping the blinds shut. *That's how it works.*

Then, when Ali turned, Aria got a peek at her face. She hadn't seemed manipulative and domineering, but fragile and scared. Seconds later, Spencer told Ali to leave ... and Ali did. She backed down, something she'd never done before, like her spunk and resolve had evaporated.

Aria knelt down in the grass, touching the cool marble of Ali's headstone. Hot tears rushed to her eyes. 'Ali, I'm sorry,' she whispered. 'Whatever was going on, I'm sorry.'

A jet roared overhead. The fragrant bouquet of roses next to Ali's grave made Aria's nose itch. 'I'm sorry,' she repeated. 'I'm so, so sorry.'

'Aria?' a high-pitched voice called.

Aria jumped. There was a blinding light in her face. Her hands shook, and for a moment, she was sure it was Ali. But then the light shifted. A woman cop in dark-framed glasses and a Rosewood PD ski cap knelt down. 'Aria Montgomery?'

'Y-yes?' Aria stammered.

The cop touched Aria's arm. 'You need to come with me.'

'Why?' Aria laughed nervously, pulling her arm away.

The walkie-talkie on the cop's belt bleeped. 'It would be best if you spoke to the boys downtown.'

'What's going on? I didn't do anything.'

The cop curled her lips into a smile that didn't reach her eyes. 'What are you so sorry about, Aria?' She glanced at Ali's grave, obviously having heard everything Aria had just said. 'Is it because you've been hiding evidence from us?'

217

Aria shook her head, not understanding. 'Evidence?'

The cop gave her a knowing, condescending look. 'A certain ring.'

Aria's throat instantly went dry. She clutched her yak-fur bag to her chest. Ian's ring was still nestled in the inner pocket. She'd been so busy trying to contact Ali, she hadn't thought about it in days. 'I didn't do anything wrong!'

'Mm-hmm,' the cop murmured, neither interested nor impressed. She unclipped a pair of handcuffs from her belt and glanced at Jason, who was standing just a few feet away. 'Thanks for your call, telling us she was here.'

Aria's mouth fell open. She whipped around and stared at Jason too. '*You* told them I was here?' she exclaimed. 'Why?'

Jason shook his head, his eyes wide. 'What? I didn't—'

'Mr DiLaurentis told the officer at the station everything he knew,' the cop interrupted. 'He's just doing his civic duty, Miss Montgomery.' She wrested Aria's bag from her hands, then placed her cuffs over Aria's wrists. 'Don't be angry at him for what *you* did. What all of you did.'

The reality of what the cop was saying slowly sank in. Could she really mean what Aria thought she meant? She whipped around to Jason. 'You're making this up!'

'Aria, you don't understand,' Jason protested. 'I didn't—'

'Come on,' the cop blustered. Aria's arms were now roughly bent behind her back. She could see Jason's lips moving but couldn't make out the words.

'And since when do the police take advice from psychos?' she exploded to the cop. 'Don't you know Jason's been in and out of mental hospitals for years?'

The cop cocked her head, seemingly perplexed. Jason made a gurgling sound. 'Aria ...' His voice cracked. '*No. You've got it all wrong.*'

Aria paused. Jason sounded aghast. 'What do you mean?' she asked sharply.

The cop grabbed her arm. 'Come on, Miss Montgomery. Let's go.'

But Aria's gaze was still on Jason. 'What do I have wrong?' Jason stared, his lips parted. 'Tell me!' she pleaded. '*What do I have wrong?*' But Jason just stood there, watching as the cop pulled Aria down the hill to the flashing cruiser.

26
The Evidence Doesn't Lie

The trip from Lancaster to Rosewood was supposed to take two hours at the most, but Emily had made the mistake of getting on a bus that stopped at a couple of authentic Pennsylvania Dutch farms on the way back. It had then deposited her in Philadelphia, meaning she'd had to get on *another* bus to Rosewood, which sat in the station for an additional forty-five minutes before then getting stuck in jammed traffic on the Schuylkill Expressway. By the time the Greyhound sighed into Rosewood, Emily had bit every fingernail to the quick and had torn a giant hole in the vinyl bus seat. It was almost 6 P.M., and a cold, ugly sleet had begun to fall. The bus opened its doors, and Emily scampered down the steps.

The town was quiet and dead. The traffic lights changed from red to green, but no cars passed through. Ferra's Cheesesteaks still had an OPEN sign in the window, but there wasn't a single customer inside. The smell of roasted coffee beans wafted from the Unicorn Cafe, but the place was locked up tight.

Emily started to run, skidding down the shiny sidewalk, careful not to slip in her pathetically thin, tractionless Amish boots. The police station was only a few blocks away. There were lights on in the main building, where Emily and the others had gone when they'd figured out Mona Vanderwaal was Old A. The back of the complex, where New A had told her to go, had no windows, making it impossible to tell whether it was occupied. Emily spied a big metal door propped open by a coffee cup and gasped. A had left the door open, as promised.

A long hallway stretched in front of her. The floors smelled like industrial-strength cleaner, and an exit sign glowed at the far end of the corridor. The only sound was a faint, annoying buzz from the overhead fluorescent light, and Emily could hear every breath she took.

She ran her fingers along the edges of the walls as she walked, stopping at each office door to read the names on the plaques. FILING. MAINTENANCE. EMPLOYEES ONLY. Four offices down, her heart leapt. EVIDENCE.

Emily peered through the little window in the metal door. The room was long and dark, with a mess of shelves, folders, file boxes, and metal filing cabinets. She thought of the papers in that photo A had texted. The interview with Ali's mom. The timeline of when Ali went missing. The weird paper from the Preserve at Something-or-other, which sounded like a swanky housing development. And, last but not least, the DNA report, surely saying the body in the hole wasn't Ali's, but Leah's.

Suddenly, a hand clapped on her shoulder. 'What do you think you're doing?'

Emily jumped away from the door and whirled around.

A Rosewood cop held her roughly by the upper arm, his eyes aflame. The EXIT sign above him cast eerie red shadows along his cheeks. 'I ...' she stammered.

His brow furrowed. 'You're not supposed to be down here!' Then he stared at her harder. Recognition flickered across his face. 'I *know* you,' he said.

Emily tried to back away from him, but he held her tight. His jaw dropped. 'You're one of the girls who thought she saw Alison DiLaurentis.' The corners of his lips curled into a smile and he pressed his face close to hers. His breath smelled like onion rings. 'We've been looking for you.'

A streak of fear shot through Emily's stomach. 'It's Darren Wilden you should be looking for! The body in that hole isn't Alison DiLaurentis – it's a girl named Leah Zook! Wilden murdered her and dumped her there! He's guilty.'

But the cop just laughed and, to Emily's horror, began to handcuff her hands behind her back. 'Sweetheart,' he said as he led her down the hall, 'the only guilty one here is you.'

27
That's Amore!

Mrs Hastings refused to tell Spencer where they were going, only that it was a surprise. The large, turreted houses on their street swept by, followed by the rambling Springton Farm and then the upscale Gray Horse Inn. Spencer took her money out of her wallet and rearranged her bills by serial number. Her mom had always been a quiet driver, fiercely concentrating on the roads and traffic, but something was different today, and it had Spencer on edge.

They drove for almost a half hour. The sky was pitch-black, all of the stars twinkling brightly, everyone's porch lights blazing. When Spencer closed her eyes, she saw that awful night Ali went missing. Last week, her foggy memory had conjured an image of Ali standing at the edge of the woods with Jason. But that vision shifted again, and the person she thought was Jason morphed into someone smaller, slighter, more feminine.

When had her mother finally come back to the house? Had she confronted Mr Hastings about what he'd done –

and revealed what she'd done? Maybe that was why he'd wired an exorbitant sum of money into the Alison DiLaurentis Recovery Fund. Surely a family that gave so much cash to the fund to help find Ali couldn't be responsible for her murder.

Spencer's cell phone beeped, and she jumped. Swallowing hard, she reached for her phone in her bag. *One new text message*, the screen said.

> Your sister is counting on you to make this right, Spence. Or else the blood will be on your hands too. – A

'Who's that?' Spencer's mom eased on the brakes for a red light. She unglued her eyes from the SUV stopped in front of her and glanced over at Spencer.

Spencer clapped her hand over her cell phone's screen. 'No one.' The light turned green, and Spencer squeezed her eyes shut again.

Your sister. Spencer had spent a lot of time resenting Ali, but that all felt wiped away now. She and Ali had shared the same dad, the same blood. She'd lost more than a friend that summer – she'd lost a family member.

Her mother veered off the main road and pulled the Mercedes into Otto, Rosewood's oldest and nicest Italian restaurant. Golden light shone from inside the building's grotto dining room, and Spencer could almost smell garlic and olive oil and red wine. 'We're going out to dinner?' she said shakily.

'Not just dinner,' her mom said, pursing her lips. 'Come on.'

The parking lot was clogged with cars. At the far end, Spencer saw two Rosewood police cars. Just beyond that, blond twins climbed out of a black SUV. They looked about thirteen and both were dressed in puffy jackets, wooly white hats, and the matching sweatpants that said KENSINGTON PREP FIELD HOCKEY in collegiate-style letters down the legs. Spencer and Ali sometimes used to wear their field hockey sweats on the same day, too. She wondered if anyone had ever glanced at them and thought they were twins. Spencer's breath caught in her throat.

'Mom,' she said, her voice cracking.

Her mother turned. 'Yes?'

Say something, a voice in Spencer's head screamed. But her mouth felt welded shut.

'There she is!' Two figures were illuminated by floodlights across the parking lot, waving wildly at them. Mr Hastings had changed from his work clothes into a blue polo shirt and khakis. Next to him, Melissa smiled primly, wearing a blue tulip-skirt dress and clutching a satin purse under her elbow. 'Sorry I didn't call you back,' her sister said as Spencer approached. 'I was afraid if we talked, I'd ruin the surprise!'

'Surprise?' Spencer bleated weakly, distracted. She glanced at the police cars in the lot again. *Say something*, a voice in her head screamed. *Your sister is counting on you*.

Mrs Hastings started toward the door. 'Well? Should we go in?'

'Absolutely,' Mr Hastings agreed.

'Wait!' Spencer cried.

Everyone stopped and turned. Her mother's hair looked

225

glossy under the lot's fluorescent floodlights. Her dad's cheeks were red from the cold. They were both smiling expectantly at her. And suddenly, Spencer realized her mother had no idea what Spencer was about to say. She hadn't seen the photo of Mrs DiLaurentis that Spencer was holding. She hadn't known what Spencer and Ian had been IMing about just seconds before that. For the first time ever, Spencer felt sorry for her parents. She wished she could throw a blanket over them and protect them from this. She wished she'd never found this out in the first place.

But she had.

'Why did you guys do it?' she said quietly.

Mrs Hastings took a step forward, one of her high heels making a solid *clunk* against the stone walkway. 'Why did we do what?'

Spencer noticed then that cops were sitting inside the cars. She lowered her voice, directing her words at her mom. 'I know what happened the night Ali died. You found out about dad and Mrs DiLaurentis's affair – you saw them at Ali's house. And you found out how Ali was my … was Dad's—'

Mrs Hastings head jerked back like she'd been slapped. '*What?*'

'*Spencer!*' Mr Hastings cried, appalled. 'What the hell?'

The words were spilling out now. She barely even noticed that the wind had picked up and was biting into her skin. 'Did it start when you were in law school together, Dad? Is this why you never told us that Mr DiLaurentis was a student at Yale the same time you were – because something between you and Jessica had happened then, too? Is that why you never spoke to Ali's family?'

Another car pulled into the lot. Her father didn't respond. He just stood in the middle of the parking lot, bobbing ever so slightly back and forth like a buoy. Melissa dropped her clutch and bent quickly to retrieve it. Her mouth was open and her eyes looked glassy.

Spencer turned to her mother. 'How could you have hurt her? She was my *sister*. And, Dad, how could you cover it up when she was your daughter?'

The bones in Mrs Hastings's face seemed to turn to ash. She blinked slowly, as if she'd just woken up.

She turned to her husband. 'You and ... *Jessica*?'

Spencer's father opened his mouth to speak, but only a few unintelligible syllables came out.

'I knew it,' Mrs Hastings whispered. Her voice was eerily calm and steady. A muscle in her neck twitched. 'I asked you a million times, but you always said it wasn't true.'

And then she lunged for Mr Hastings and started pummeling him with her Gucci purse. 'And you used to go over to her house? How many times did you do that? What the hell is wrong with you?'

It felt like all the air had drained from the parking lot. Spencer's ears buzzed, and she processed the scene as if in slow motion. Everything was unfolding all wrong. Her mom was acting like she didn't know. She thought back to Ian's IMs. Was it possible that her mother hadn't known *any* of this, that this was the first she'd heard of it ... ever?

Her mother finally stopped hitting her dad. He wheeled back, gasping. Beads of sweat dripped down his face.

227

'Just admit it. For once, just tell me the truth,' she gasped.

The next few seconds stretched out forever. 'Yes,' her father finally admitted, his head hung low.

Melissa shrieked. Mrs Hastings let out a shrill wail. Her dad paced nervously.

Spencer closed her eyes for a long minute. When she opened them again, Melissa had disappeared. Mrs Hastings turned to her husband again. 'How long did this go on?' she demanded. Ropy veins stood out at her temples. 'And was she *yours*?'

Mr Hastings's shoulders shook. A thin, guttural sound escaped from his lips. He covered his face with his hands. 'I didn't know about the kids until later.'

Mrs Hastings backed up, her teeth bared and her fists clenched. 'When I come home tonight, I want you gone,' she roared.

'Veronica—'

'Go!'

After a pregnant pause, her father did as she asked. A moment later, his Jaguar revved to life and he gunned his way out of the parking lot, leaving his family behind.

'Mom.' Spencer reached for her mom's shoulder.

'Leave me alone,' her mother snapped, collapsing against the stone wall just outside the restaurant. Happy Italian accordion music tinkled out through the outdoor speakers. Inside the restaurant, someone let out a high-pitched laugh.

'I thought you knew,' Spencer said desperately. 'I thought you found out about this the night Ali went missing. You seemed so distracted the next day, like you'd done something awful. I thought this was why we couldn't ever talk about that night.'

Her mother whirled around, her eyes wild, her lipstick smudged. 'You honestly think I could have *killed* that girl?' she hissed. 'Am I really that much of a monster to you?'

'No!' Spencer squeaked in a tiny voice. 'I just—'

'You just *nothing*,' her mother growled, shaking a finger at her so violently, Spencer took a couple of frightened steps back into the flower beds. 'You know why I told you we should never talk about that night, Spencer? Because your best friend went *missing*. Because Ali's disappearance has taken over your life and you need to move on. Not because I *murdered* her!'

'I'm sorry!' Spencer wailed. 'It was just that … I mean, Melissa couldn't find you that night and she seemed so—'

'I was out with friends,' her mother boomed. 'Late. And the only reason I even remember that is because the police asked me about it nearly fifty times over the next few days!'

There was a cough behind them. Melissa was crumpled next to a small topiary. Spencer grabbed her arm. 'Why did you tell Dad over and over that you needed to find Mom?'

Melissa shook her head, baffled. 'What?'

'You guys were at the door that night and you kept saying, "We need to find Mom. We need to find Mom."'

Melissa gaped at Spencer helplessly. Then, her eyes doubled in size, the memory coming to her. 'You mean when I asked Dad about needing a ride to the airport to catch my flight to Prague?' she said weakly. 'I knew I'd be too

229

hungover, but Dad basically told me tough luck. I should've thought about that before getting drunk.' She blinked at Spencer in bewilderment.

A family with a young girl got out of a minivan. The husband and wife were holding hands, smiling at each other. The girl stared curiously at Spencer, her thumb in her mouth, before following her parents inside the restaurant.

'But ...' Spencer felt dizzy. The smell of olive oil floating from the restaurant was suddenly overpoweringly putrid. She searched her sister's stricken face. 'You weren't fighting with Dad because Mom found out about the affair? You didn't run back to Ian and say, "My dad is having an affair with Mrs DiLaurentis, and I think my mom went and did something horrible"?'

'*Ian?*' Melissa interrupted, her eyebrows shooting up. 'I never said that. When did he tell you that?'

Spencer ground to a halt. 'Today. He said he's been IMing you, too.'

'What?' Melissa exploded.

Spencer clutched the sides of her head, feeling disoriented. Ian, Melissa, and her mother's words mixed together in a hazy swirl, twisting and blending until she had no idea what was the truth.

Was Spencer even IMing Ian at all? She'd been IMing *someone* who claimed he was Ian, but did she really know for sure?

'But what about what you and Mom have been whispering about all week?' Spencer begged, desperate to make sense of the situation, to justify what she'd just done.

'We were planning a special dinner for you.' Her mom

looked up, the fight suddenly draining from her voice. Melissa uttered a sigh of disgust and walked away. 'Andrew and Kristen Cullen are in there. We were going to take you all to the new production of *The Importance of Being Earnest* at the Walnut Street Theater.'

Goose bumps rose on Spencer's arms. Her stomach roiled. Her family had been trying to show how much they loved her, and look what she'd done.

Tears began to cascade down Spencer's cheeks. Of course her mother hadn't killed Alison. Her mother hadn't even *known* about the affair. Whoever had IMed her had lied.

A shadow fell over her. When she turned, she saw a gray-haired, stern-looking Rosewood cop. His gun gleamed in his belt.

'Miss Hastings,' the cop said, shaking his head solemnly. 'You're going to have to come with me.'

'W-what?' Spencer shrieked. 'Why?'

'It would be better if you did this quietly,' the cop murmured. Wordlessly, he stepped in front of her, nudging her mother out of the way. He pinned Spencer's hands behind her back, and she felt cold, hard metal on her wrists.

'No!' Spencer cried. It was happening so quickly. She looked over her shoulder. Her mother just stood there, mascara running down her cheeks, her mouth a small O. 'Why are you doing this?' she begged the officer.

'Communicating with a criminal on the lam is a serious crime,' he said. 'Conspiracy after the fact. And we have the IMs to prove it.'

'IMs?' Spencer repeated, her heart sinking into her gut. The IMs from Ian. Had one of the cops overheard what she just said to her family? Had Melissa run to the police and told on her?

'You don't understand!' she pleaded. 'I wasn't conspiring with anyone! I don't even think those IMs are from Ian!'

But the cop wasn't paying any attention. He opened the door to the backseat, placed a hand on Spencer's head, and shoved her inside. He slammed his own door shut, then pulled out of the lot, sirens blaring, lights flashing, heading straight to the Rosewood police station.

28
Now Who's The Crazy One?

Hanna skidded down the Preserve hall past the cafeteria, arriving at the entrance to Iris's secret lair. 'Let me in, Iris,' she snarled. She pressed her ear to the door, but there weren't any sounds from upstairs.

Hanna had been looking for Iris for the past hour, but Iris seemed to have vanished. She wasn't in the theater watching *Ella Enchanted* with the other patients. She wasn't in the dining room, the gym, or the spa. Aggravated, Hanna leaned against the locked door. There were a few doodles on the jamb. At the top left corner was the name *Courtney*, Iris's old roommate. Next to Courtney's name was a winking smiley face. Hanna was dying to get back inside the attic and see the drawing of Ali – she had no idea how she'd missed it when she was up there.

Hanna was sure Iris knew Ali, she just didn't know how. From Jason, perhaps? Iris had said she'd stayed at different facilities besides this one; perhaps she'd been at the Radley, where Jason had been treated. She could have met Ali when she came to visit her brother, instantly striking up a friendship that turned to jealousy. The day after Ali went missing, Ali's mom grilled them with questions they couldn't answer. *Did Ali ever talk about anyone teasing her?* Certainly no one from Rosewood would tease Ali … but someone from a mental hospital might. When Hanna and Ali had been trying on clothes in her closet and Ali had gotten that prank call, maybe it had been Iris moaning on the other end, not Jason. Perhaps Iris was furious that Ali was able to come and go from the hospital, whereas she was condemned inside. Or maybe Iris was simply jealous that Ali was *Ali*.

She's psychotic, Tara had warned Hanna in the hall a few days ago. *Don't cross her*. Hanna should have listened.

And maybe … just maybe … Iris had killed Ali. Iris had told Hanna that she'd been out of the hospital at the exact same time Ali had vanished. Hanna thought of that letter with the slash through it on Ali's Time Capsule flag – it might have been a *J*, but it also could've been an *I*. For *Iris*. Had A sent Hanna to the Preserve so she'd learn about Iris … or was Iris A, leading Hanna right into her trap?

She wants to hurt you, Ali had said.

Hanna jogged down the hall, her Tory Burch flip-flops smacking against the soles of her feet. As she rounded the corner, a nurse stopped her. 'No running, honey.'

Hanna paused, out of breath. 'Have you seen Iris?'

The nurse shook her head. 'No, but she's probably watching the movie with the other girls. Why don't you go in too? There's popcorn!'

Hanna wanted to smack the cheerful grin off her face. 'We need to find Iris. It's serious.'

The nurse's smile wilted a little. There was a flicker of

fear behind her eyes, as if Hanna was a homicidal maniac. Then Hanna spied a red phone on the wall.

'Can I use that?' Hanna begged. She could call the Rosewood PD and tell them everything.

'Sorry, sweetie, but that phone is switched off until four P.M. on Sunday. You know the rules.' The nurse gently took Hanna's elbow and began guiding her back toward the patient rooms. 'Why don't you get some rest? Betsy can bring you an aromatherapy eye mask.'

Hanna wrenched away. 'I. Need. To. Find. Iris. She's a *killer*. She wants to hurt me, too!'

'Honey ...' The nurse's gaze flickered to the red emergency button on the wall. Staff could press it to summon help with a patient disturbance.

'Hanna?'

Hanna spun around. Iris stood about ten paces away, leaning casually against the water bubbler. Her blond hair gleamed, her teeth so white they almost looked blue.

'Who *are* you?' Hanna whispered, walking toward her.

Iris pursed her ultra-red lips. 'What do you mean? I'm Iris. And I'm fabulous.'

A bolt of electricity slashed through Hanna's chest as Iris parroted Ali's old mantra. 'Who *are* you?' she repeated, louder.

The nurse swept forward and stepped between them. 'Hanna, honey, you seem really excited. Let's just calm down.'

But Hanna didn't listen. She stared into Iris's wide, glowing eyes. 'How do you know Alison?' she cried. 'Were you in the hospital with her brother? Did you *kill* her? Are you A?'

235

'Alison?' Iris chirped. 'That friend of yours who was murdered? The one you told me you wanted dead? The one you thought got what she deserved?'

Hanna backed up, keenly aware that the nurse was still standing right behind her. A few stunned seconds crept by. 'I was just ... talking. It's not *true*. And I told you that in confidence. When I thought we were *friends*.'

Iris threw her head back in cruel laughter. 'Friends!' she hooted, as if it was the punch line to a joke.

Her laughter made Hanna's hands quiver. This was all painfully familiar. Ali laughed just like this when she teased Hanna about overeating. Mona laughed like this when Hanna's too-small Sweet Seventeen court dress ripped and split its seams on the dance floor. Hanna was everyone's punch line. The girl everyone loved to ruin.

'*Tell me how you knew Alison*,' Hanna growled.

'Who?' Iris teased.

'Tell me how you knew her!'

Iris giggled. 'I have no idea who you're talking about.'

Something inside Hanna stirred, struggled, and then broke free. Just as Hanna lunged for Iris, a loud *boom* sounded behind them. A bunch of nurses and guards burst through a side door, and two strong arms grabbed Hanna from behind. 'Get her out of here,' yelled a voice. Someone dragged Hanna into the hallway and pressed her up against the far wall. Searing pain shot through her shoulder.

Hanna kicked her bare legs, fighting to get free. 'Let go of me! What's going on?'

A security guard swam into view. 'That's enough,' he snarled. There was a click, and then Hanna felt hard metal handcuffs close around her wrists.

236

'I'm not the one you want!' Hanna screamed frantically. 'It's Iris! She's a killer!'

'Hanna,' the nurse scolded sharply.

'Why isn't anyone listening to me?'

The guards began to push her down the hall. Every other patient in the ward was standing outside the theater room, gaping at the commotion. Tara looked thrilled. Alexis had her knuckles in her mouth. Ruby looked Hanna up and down, giggling.

Hanna twisted around and stared at Iris. 'How do you know Alison?' But Iris just gave a mysterious smile.

The guards marched Hanna through a door and down an unfamiliar hallway. The vinyl floors were dingy, and the overhead fluorescent lights snapped and buzzed. There was a strange smell in the air, too, kind of like something in the walls was decaying.

A tall figure in a police uniform came into view at the end of the hall. He calmly watched as the guards dragged Hanna to him. As they got closer, Hanna realized it was the Rosewood chief of police. Her heart lifted. *Finally*, someone who would listen to her!

'Hello, Miss Marin,' the chief said.

Hanna breathed a sigh of relief. 'I was just going to call you,' she blurted. 'Thank God you came. Ali's killer is *here*. I can lead you right to her.'

The chief chuckled reproachfully, looking almost amused. 'Lead me right to her? That's a good one, Ms. Marin.' He leaned down until his face was parallel with hers. His skin glowed red under the neon EXIT sign. 'Considering that you're under arrest.'

237

29
Master Of Puppets

When they reached the Rosewood police station, the cop undid Aria's cuffs and showed her into a dark interrogation room. 'We'll be back for you later.'

Aria stumbled inside, her hip banging against the sharp edge of a wooden table. Slowly, her eyes adjusted. The room was small and windowless and reeked of sweat. Four chairs surrounded the table. Aria dropped into one of them and started to cry silently.

The door squeaked, and someone else staggered into the room. It was a girl with long, auburn hair and thin legs. She wore a pair of black yoga pants, a long-sleeved striped T-shirt, and gold flats. Aria shot to her feet.

'*Hanna?*' she cried.

Hanna slowly raised her head. 'Oh,' she said in a numb, subdued voice. 'Hi.' Her eyes were glazed over. There was a small cut near her mouth. Her eyes darted to and fro.

'What are you *doing* here?' Aria gasped.

Hanna's lips parted slowly. A sarcastic smile flickered across her face. 'Same reason you are. Apparently we were part of some conspiracy to kill Ali. We helped Ian escape and obstructed justice.'

Aria clutched the sides of her head. Could this really be happening? How could the cops believe such a thing?

Before she could answer, the door opened again. Two more people were thrust inside. Spencer wore a green sheath and tall black heels, while Emily had on a prairie dress, thin leather shoes, and a small white skullcap. Aria gaped at them in astonishment. They stared back. For a moment, everyone was speechless.

'They think we did it,' Emily whispered, walking to the table. 'They think we killed Ali.'

'The cops found out about Ian's IMs,' Spencer admitted. 'I talked to him online earlier today. And they thought ... well, they thought we were conspiring together. But, guys ... I'm not sure it *is* Ian we were talking to. I think it's A.'

'But you swore it was Ian!' Aria spouted.

'I thought it was,' Spencer said defensively. 'But now I'm not sure.' She pointed at Aria. 'The cops said they know about Ian's ring. Did you give it to them?'

'No!' Aria cried. 'But maybe I should have. They thought I was keeping this huge secret.'

'How could they have known about Ian's ring?' Hanna wondered aloud, her eyes fixed on a black stain on the linoleum floor.

'Jason DiLaurentis was at the cemetery,' Aria said. 'The cop said *he* told them, but Jason claimed he didn't. I don't know what to think. I have no idea how Jason could've known about the ring.' She thought of the other thing Jason said after Aria exposed that he'd been a mental

239

patient. *You've got it all wrong. What* did she have wrong?

'Maybe Wilden told him,' Hanna whispered. 'He could have heard us talking at the hospital. He *was* outside the room.'

Aria slumped in her chair and watched as a spider climbed industriously up the gray cinder-block wall. 'That doesn't even make any sense,' Spencer piped up. 'Wilden's a cop. He wouldn't tell Jason – he'd just handle it on his own.'

'And why would Wilden wait days to ambush me?' Aria added. 'Besides, I thought Wilden was on our side.'

Emily snorted. '*Right*.'

Aria glanced at Emily, really taking in her bizarre outfit. 'What on earth are you wearing?'

Emily bit her chapped lip. 'A sent me to an Amish commune and then told me to get the DNA report from the evidence room.' Her green eyes were wide. 'Some cop found me before I could get inside.'

Aria squeezed her eyes shut. No *wonder* the cops thought they were guilty. They probably figured Emily was tampering with evidence.

'But, guys, Wilden is *lying* about the DNA of the body in the hole,' Emily went on. 'It's not Ali – it's an Amish girl named Leah Zook.'

Spencer's mouth fell open. 'You *still* think Ali is alive?'

'I *saw* her,' Emily said, shrinking against the wall. 'I know it sounds crazy, but I did, Spencer. I can't let this go. I tried to tell the cops, but they wouldn't listen.'

Spencer snorted. 'Of *course* they didn't listen.'

Aria wrinkled her nose. 'Emily, it was definitely Ali in

240

that hole. Ali killed herself. That's what A helped *me* to figure out.'

Spencer whirled around and stared at Aria. 'Is this what the psychic told you?'

'It might be true,' Aria protested. 'It's as good a theory as anything else.'

'No, a crazy girl named Iris killed Ali,' Hanna inserted loudly, trying to smooth her tangles. 'A sent me right to her.'

Then everyone looked at Spencer, waiting to see what her theory was. There were goose bumps on Spencer's arms. 'A told me my mom killed Ali because ... well, because my dad had an affair with Ali's mom. Ali's my sister.'

'*What?*' Aria gasped. Emily just stared. Hanna looked disgusted, like she might throw up into the dented metal trash can in the corner.

'But my mom didn't do it,' Spencer explained. 'She didn't even know about the affair. I probably ruined my parents' marriage. A was just ... messing with me. I think A messed with all of us.'

Everyone stiffened. The realization hit Aria like a heavy boxing glove to her temple. A *had* messed with all of them. A was behind all of this. Jason hadn't told the cops about Ian's ring – A had. Maybe A had even planted it in the woods so Aria would find it. A had sent Emily to look for the DNA report in the evidence room, only to report her to the on-duty cop. A told the police about Ian's IMs, too, making it look like they'd conspired with him.

A had been toying with them all along, pulling all the

241

strings. And now they were in jail for a murder they didn't commit.

Aria gazed around at the others. By the stunned looks on their faces, it seemed like they'd just come to the same conclusion. 'A's our worst *enemy*,' she whispered. She patted her pocket, reaching for her cell phone. Surely A had sent them a group text to show just how gullible and stupid they all were. *Gotcha!* it probably said. Or, *Who's laughing now!*

But then Aria remembered – the cops had confiscated all their phones. If A had sent them a message, they wouldn't get it.

30
Free At Last

About thirty minutes later, there was a knock on the holding-cell doors. All the girls jumped. Emily's heart catapulted to her throat. This was it. They were going to be interrogated ... and then they were going to jail.

A woman police officer peered into the room. There were purple circles under her eyes and a coffee stain on the chest of her uniform shirt. 'Get your things, girls. You're being released.'

Everyone fell silent, stunned. Then Emily collapsed with relief. '*Really?*'

'Did you find A?' Aria asked.

'What happened?' Hanna said at the same time.

The cop's expression was stony. 'All charges against you are dropped.' But there was an uncomfortable look on her face, like there was something else she wanted to say. 'Let's just say circumstances have changed.'

Emily followed the others out of the room, working the words over in her mind. *Circumstances have changed?* That could mean only one thing. Her heart leapt.

'That body in the hole wasn't Ali's, right?' she cried. 'You found her!' So they *had* been listening when she told them that Wilden was a murderer!

Spencer nudged Emily's ribs. 'Would you shut *up* about that?'

'No,' Emily snapped. A might have sent them to jail, but Emily's theory was still right. She knew it at the bottom of her heart. She turned back to the cop, who was walking briskly down the hall. 'Is Ali okay? Is she safe?'

'You girls are going home,' the cop answered. Her keys jingled on her belt. 'That's all I can tell you.'

They received their personal items from another officer at the front desk. Emily immediately checked her phone, thinking that perhaps Ali had texted, but there were no new messages. Not even a derisive note from A, laughing that Emily had walked right into the trap.

The female cop hit a buzzer, and double doors opened to the parking lot. It was crammed with police cars and news vans. Emily hadn't seen so much commotion since the fire in the woods.

'Emily,' a voice said.

Darren Wilden ran at them from across the dark parking lot, his quilted police jacket flapping open. 'Good. They let you out. I'm sorry about this.'

Emily recoiled, her heart jumping to her throat. Why was Wilden *here*? Shouldn't he be arrested?

'What's going on?' Aria demanded, stopping near an empty patrol car. 'Why did they suddenly set us free?'

Wilden guided them away from the crowd, not answering. 'Just be glad you're out of this mess. We're getting guys to escort you home.'

Emily planted her feet. 'I know what you did,' she said in a low voice. 'And I'm going to make sure everyone else knows it too.'

Wilden swiveled around, staring at her. His walkie-talkie made a noise, but he ignored it. Finally, he sighed. 'What you think you know isn't true, Emily. I know you went to Lancaster. And I know what you were led to believe. But I didn't hurt Leah. I'd never do that.'

The blood drained from Emily's head. 'What? How do you know where I was?'

Wilden stared at the glowing parking space lines in the lot. 'You guys were right about your new A. I should have listened.'

Aria stomped her foot. 'Oh, *now* you believe us? Why couldn't you have listened last week, maybe before we were almost fried alive in a forest fire?'

'And before A sent me to the Preserve at Addison-Stevens!' Hanna wailed. 'I was locked up with crazy people!'

Emily shot up. *The Preserve at Addison-Stevens*. That name was in Ali's evidence file. It was a *mental hospital*?

'I'm sorry I didn't believe you guys,' Wilden was saying, striding past a chain-link fence. Behind it were unused police vehicles and a large white school bus. 'It was a mistake. But we know everything now. We have all the notes he sent you.'

The girls stopped dead. 'He?' Spencer squeaked.

'Who is *he*?' Hanna whispered. 'Ian?'

Just then, another police car wailed into the lot. Policemen ran over and started to pull someone out of the backseat. There were shouts, and then a kicking leg, then

245

a flash of teeth. The cops finally managed to get whoever it was out of the car and began marching him toward the station. When there was a break in action, Emily saw a tall, lanky man with greasy blond hair and a moustache. Her stomach curdled.

There was a worried crinkle between Spencer's eyes. 'Why does he look familiar?' she murmured.

'I don't know,' Emily whispered, her mind frantically searching.

Members of the press rushed to the cops and started snapping pictures. 'How long have you been planning this, Mr Ford?' they screamed. 'What made you do it?' And finally, rising above the rest, 'Why did you kill Alison?'

Aria grabbed Emily's hand hard. Emily's knees went weak. '*What* did they say?'

'He killed Alison,' Spencer murmured. 'That guy killed Alison.'

'But who *is* he?' Hanna blurted.

'Come on,' Wilden said gruffly, shoving them away. 'You shouldn't see this.'

None of the girls could move. The man's untied shoelace dragged along the pavement as the cops shoved him toward the station. His head was hung low, exposing a bald patch. Emily raked her nails up the side of her arms. Ali was ... *dead*? What about Leah? What about the girl Emily had seen in the woods?

The reporters kept screaming, their voices blurring incoherently. Then one reporter shouted louder than the others. 'And what about the body that was just found? Are you responsible for that murder, too?'

Hanna turned to Wilden. 'Another murder?'

'Oh my God.' Emily's insides turned to mush.

'Girls,' Wilden said sternly. 'Come on.'

By now, Ali's alleged killer was at the front steps, only twenty or so feet away from Emily. He noticed Emily and smiled lewdly, revealing a gold front tooth.

Electricity crackled in Emily's veins. She *knew* that smile. Nearly four years ago, workers began pouring concrete into the hole in the DiLaurentises' backyard the day after Ali went missing. Wilden had been there ... but so had a lot of other guys, too. After Mrs DiLaurentis interrogated them, Emily cut through Ali's backyard to the woods. One of the workers turned and leered at her. He'd been tall and lanky, and when he smiled, he'd had that same horrible gold front tooth.

Emily turned to Spencer, aghast. 'That guy was one of the workers who filled in the gazebo hole the day after Ali went missing. I remember him.'

Spencer was very pale. 'I saw him a few days ago. On my *street*.'

31
The Very Good And The Very Evil

Four junior Rosewood cops arrived to escort Spencer and the others home. Spencer climbed into the back of the cruiser that would drive her back, choking on the smell of fake car leather, vomit, and sweat. A dark-haired cop slid into the front seat, started the engine, and pulled to the exit.

Out the window, the press was clamoring at the police station door, eager for another glimpse of the killer. Spencer stared hard at the windows in front of the police station. All the blinds were shut tight. Could that guy really have done it? He was such a stranger, an outsider. It seemed so out of the blue.

She wrapped her fingers around the metal cage separating the front seat from the back. 'Who else did that guy kill?' she called. The cop didn't answer. 'How did you find out he killed Ali?' she tried. He merely turned up his CB radio. Frustrated, Spencer kicked the back of his seat hard. 'Are you deaf?'

The cop gave her a chilling glare in the rearview mirror. 'My orders are to bring you home. That's all.'

Spencer let out a small whimper. She wasn't exactly sure she *wanted to* go home. What kind of state would her house be in right now? Was her dad still there? Had he fled to be with Mrs DiLaurentis?

It was all so surreal and unthinkable. Spencer was certain that within minutes, she'd wake up in her bed, discovering it was just a dream. But another minute passed. And another, and she was still here, living her worst nightmare.

All of a sudden, she realized something. When her mother begged her dad to admit the truth, he'd blurted, *I didn't know about the kids until later*. He'd said *kids*, not *kid*. Was that a mistake ... or a slip? Was *Jason* her father's child – and Spencer's half brother – too?

They passed downtown Rosewood, a quaint, brick-paved shopping district full of chic furniture stores, antique shops, and homemade-ice cream parlors. Spencer plunged her hand into her gold Kate Spade satchel and found her Sidekick at the bottom. Amazingly, there were no new texts from A. She called her house. The phone rang and rang, but there was no answer. Then, she typed CNN's Web address on the keypad. Officer Tight Lips might not tell her anything, but the news would.

Sure enough, the top story was about how there had been a new arrest in the Alison DiLaurentis murder case. *Pretty Little Liars Exonerated*, the subhead added. Spencer quickly clicked on a live video feed. A dark-haired reporter was standing in front of the Ali shrine, the collection of photos, candles, flowers, and stuffed animals on the curb of the DiLaurentises' old house. Police lights blinked behind her. Her eyes were red-rimmed, as if she'd been crying.

'The saga of Alison DiLaurentis's murder has finally ended,' the reporter announced gravely. 'A man has just been arrested for Alison's murder on the basis of overwhelming evidence.'

A blurry black-and-white photo of the greasy blond man flashed on the screen. He was lurking in a convenience store parking lot, drinking a can of beer. His name was Billy Ford. Like Emily suspected, he'd been part of the crew that had dug the hole for the DiLaurentises' gazebo almost four years ago. Investigators now thought he'd stalked her.

Spencer shut her eyes, gripped with guilt. *Thank God the workers aren't here*, Ali had said when they passed the half-dug hole on the night of their seventh-grade sleepover. *They keep harassing me.* At the time, Spencer had thought Ali was bragging: *Ha ha, even older guys think I'm hot.* Meanwhile ...

'After another body was found earlier this evening,' the reporter was saying, 'police received a tip that the deaths might be connected. Their investigation led them to Mr Ford, and they found photos of Ms. DiLaurentis on a laptop in his truck. Also on the laptop were pictures of the foursome now known as the Pretty Little Liars – Spencer Hastings, Aria Montgomery, Hanna Marin, and Emily Fields.'

Spencer bit down hard on her fist.

'Also found in the car were records of correspondence in the form of text messages, photo messages, and IMs under the handle USCMidfielderRoxx,' the reporter continued.

Spencer pressed her forehead against the cool window

glass, watching the trees blur past. USCMidfielderRoxx was Ian's IM.

The shadowy memory from the night Ali was murdered flooded her mind. After Spencer and Ali had gotten in a fight outside the barn, Ali ran off into the thicket. There had been a signature giggle, rustling sounds, and then Spencer had seen two distinct shapes. Ali ... and someone else.

I saw two blonds in the woods, Ian had told Spencer when he'd accosted her on her porch, pleading that he was innocent. Spencer stared at the photo of the man on her cell phone's tiny screen. Billy had blond hair. And he was New A, sending each of them texts that blamed Jason, Wilden, and even Spencer's mom. But how did he know so much about all of them? Who *was* he? Why did he care?

Her cell screen flashed white. *New text message.* Spencer grappled with the keyboard and pressed read. It was from Andrew Campbell, Spencer's boyfriend. *I heard about jail ... and that you were released. Are you okay? Are you home? Do you know what's happening on your street?*

Spencer sat back in the seat, the streetlights whizzing past outside the window. What did he mean, on her *street?*

Another text popped in her inbox. This one was from Aria. *What's going on? Your road is blocked off. There are police cars everywhere.*

A horrible idea began to form. The radio had said there was another murder.

The police car made a wide left turn onto her street. At least ten vehicles were jackknifed across the road, blue

251

lights flashing. Neighbors stood on their yards, their faces slack. Police officers moved in and out of the shadows. They were right in front of Spencer's house.

Melissa.

'Oh my God,' Spencer cried. She pulled at the door and leapt out of the car.

'Hey!' her driver growled. 'You're not allowed out until we're in your driveway!'

But Spencer didn't listen. She sprinted toward the flashing lights, her limbs aching. Her house was ahead. She passed through the front gate and up the long drive. All sound disappeared. Shapes blurred in front of her. She could taste bile at the back of her throat. Then she saw a figure on the front porch, her body in silhouette. She shaded her hand over her forehead, squinting in the bright porch light. Her knees buckled. A relieved wail gurgled from her throat. She sank to the grass.

Melissa ran toward her and engulfed her in a hug. 'Oh, Spence, it's so awful.'

Spencer trembled. The sirens rang in her ears. A couple of neighborhood dogs howled along, disoriented and scared.

'It's so terrible,' Melissa sobbed on Spencer's shoulder. 'That poor girl.'

Spencer stepped back. The air was frigid and sharp. The smell of the fire was still pungent and suffocating. 'What girl?'

Melissa's jaw twitched. She grabbed Spencer's hand. 'Oh, Spence. You don't *know*?'

Then she gestured toward the sidewalk. The police weren't surrounding their house but the Cavanaughs' across the street. Yellow police tape covered the Cavanaughs' entire backyard. Mrs Cavanaugh stood in the driveway, screaming in agony. A German shepherd in a blue vest stood next to her, sniffing the ground. A small shrine had already begun at the curb, rife with pictures and candles and flowers. When Spencer saw the name written in pale green chalk on the pavement, she lurched back.

'No.' Spencer looked at Melissa imploringly, hoping this was a dream. 'No!'

And then she understood. A few days ago, she'd gazed out her bedroom window and seen a greasy-haired man dressed in a plumber's jumpsuit lope up the Cavanaughs' driveway. He'd given a beautiful girl a predatory look, revealing a gleaming gold front tooth. But the girl hadn't seen his look. She hadn't known to be afraid. She couldn't see anything … ever.

Spencer turned to Melissa in horror. '*Jenna?*'

Melissa nodded, tears spilling down her cheeks. 'They found her in a trench in her backyard, where plumbers were replacing one of the burst pipes,' she said. 'He killed her just like he killed Ali.'

What Happens Next…

Poor poor Jenna Cavanaugh. I'd feel bad, but what's done is done. *Finito*. Over. Stick a fork in her, she's dead. Does that make me sound heartless? Oh well!

Of course, the Pretty Little Liars are going to take this one hard. Aria will wish she'd asked Jenna about Ali's pesky sibling problems. Emily will cry because, well, Emily always cries. Hanna will wear a little black dress that makes her look skinny to the funeral. And Spencer . . . well, she'll just be glad her sister is alive.

So where do we go from here? A body has been found. DNA has been collected. An arrest has been made, a mug shot taken. But is it *my* mug shot? Am I the big, bad Billy Ford . . . or someone else entirely? Well, you'll just have to stay tuned because I'm keeping that my last little secret.

For now, anyway.

Kisses,

– A

Acknowledgments

Heartless was another tricky book to get right, but I had lots of help. My brilliant editors at Alloy: Lanie Davis, Sara Shandler, Josh Bank, and Les Morgenstein, pulled through as usual – whatever would I do without any of them? And Farrin Jacobs and Kari Sutherland at Harper had amazing edits and suggestions that turned a decent second draft into a stellar third one. Seriously, Team PLL is the best editorial team I could ever ask for.

Thanks also to Andy McNicol and Anais Borja at William Morris for being such dedicated PLL cheerleaders. Love to my husband, Joel, a source of so much happiness, and to my parents, Shep and Mindy, for the fantastic book party they threw me in June – complete with specialty drinks and late-night dancing (well, more like shuffling). Many thanks to Libby Mosier and daughters Alison and Cat for putting together an awesome Pretty Little Liars party in St. Davids, PA – with tough trivia and a nail-biter of a scavenger hunt. Kisses to all of my readers, too, for all your letters, Twitters, Facebook posts, YouTube adaptations of crucial PLL scenes, and various other ways of saying how much you love the series. You guys are the best.

And finally, this book is dedicated to my grandmother, Gloria Shepard, who has been a voracious reader of Pretty Little Liars from the start, and my late uncle, the always-cheerful, always-inspirational Tommy Shepard, the biggest fan of all things Michael Jackson and *Star Wars* I've ever met. Many hugs.

The mystery continues in . . .

Pretty Little Liars

WANTED

1
A Broken Home

Spencer Hastings rubbed her sleep-crusted eyes and put a Kashi waffle in the toaster. Her family's kitchen smelled of freshly brewed coffee, pastries, and lemon-scented household cleaner. The two labradoodles, Rufus and Beatrice, circled her legs, their tails wagging.

The tiny LCD TV in the corner was tuned to the news. A female reporter in a blue Burberry barn jacket was standing with the Rosewood chief of police and a gray-haired man in a black suit. The caption said *The Rosewood Murders*.

'My client has been wrongfully accused,' the man in the suit proclaimed. He was William 'Billy' Ford's publicly appointed lawyer and it was the first time he'd spoken to the press since Billy's arrest. 'He's absolutely innocent. He was framed.'

'Right,' Spencer spat. Her hand shook unsteadily as she poured coffee into a blue Rosewood Day Prep mug. There was no doubt in Spencer's mind that Billy had killed her best friend, Alison DiLaurentis, nearly four years ago. And now he'd murdered Jenna Cavanaugh, a blind girl in Spencer's grade, and probably Ian Thomas – Melissa's ex-boyfriend, Ali's secret crush, *and* her first accused killer. Cops found a bloody T-shirt that belonged to Ian in Billy's car and they were now searching for his body, though they hadn't come up with any leads.

Outside, a garbage truck grumbled around the cul-de-sac where Spencer lived. A split second later, the same exact sound growled through the speakers of the TV. Spencer walked to the living room and parted the curtains at the front window. Sure enough, a news van was parked at the curb. A cameraman swiveled from one person to the other, and another guy holding a giant microphone braced against the blustery wind. Spencer could see the reporter's mouth moving through the window and hear her voice through the TV speaker.

Across the street, the Cavanaughs' backyard was wrapped in yellow police tape. A cop car had been parked in their driveway ever since Jenna's murder. Jenna's guide dog, a burly German shepherd, peered out the bay window in the living room. He'd remained there day and night for the past two weeks, as if patiently waiting for Jenna to return.

The police had found Jenna's limp, lifeless body in a ditch behind her house. According to reports, Jenna's parents arrived home on Saturday evening to an empty house. Mr. and Mrs. Cavanaugh heard frantic and persistent barks from the back of their property. Jenna's guide dog was tied to a tree ... but Jenna was gone. When they released the dog, he sprinted straight to the hole plumbers had dug a few days ago to repair a burst water pipe. But there was more inside that hole than the newly fitted pipe. It was as if the murderer *wanted* Jenna to be found.

An anonymous tip led the police to Billy Ford. The cops also charged him with killing Alison DiLaurentis. It made sense – Billy had been a part of the construction crew installing a gazebo for the DiLaurentises the same weekend Ali disappeared. Ali had complained about the lascivious looks the workers gave her. At the time, Spencer had thought Ali was bragging. Now she knew what actually happened. The toaster popped and Spencer padded back to the kitchen. The news had cut back to the studio, where a brunette anchor wearing big hoop earrings sat at a long desk. 'Police recovered a series of incriminating images on Mr. Ford's laptop that helped lead to his arrest,' the anchor said in a grave voice. 'These photos show how closely Mr. Ford was stalking Ms. DiLaurentis, Ms. Cavanaugh, and four other girls known as the Pretty Little Liars.'

A montage of old photos of Jenna and Ali appeared, many of the shots looking like they'd been stealthily snapped from a hiding spot behind a tree or inside a car. Then came images of Spencer, Aria, Emily, and Hanna. Some of the pictures were from seventh grade, when Ali was still alive, but others were more recent – there was one of the four girls in dark dresses and heels at Ian's trial, waiting for Ian to show up. There was another shot of them gathered by the Rosewood Day swings clad in wool coats, hats, and mittens, probably discussing New A. Spencer winced.

'There are also messages on Mr. Ford's computer that

match the threatening notes sent to Alison's former best friends,' the reporter went on. An image of Darren Wilden coming out of a confessional and a bunch of familiar e-mails and IM conversations whizzed past. Each note was signed with a crisp, singular letter *A*. Spencer and her friends hadn't gotten a single message since Billy had been arrested.

Spencer took a gulp of coffee, barely noticing the hot liquid sliding down her throat. It was so bizarre that Billy Ford – a man she didn't know at all – was behind everything that had happened. Spencer had no idea *why* he'd done those things.

'Mr. Ford has a long history of violence,' the reporter went on. Spencer peered over her coffee mug. A YouTube video showed a fuzzy image of Billy and a guy in a Phillies cap fighting in a Wawa parking lot. Even after the guy fell to the ground, Billy kept on kicking him. Spencer put her hand to her mouth, picturing Billy doing the same thing to Ali.

'And these images, found in Mr. Ford's car, have never been seen before.'

A blurry Polaroid photo materialized. Spencer leaned forward, her eyes widening. It was a shot of the inside of a barn – her *family's* barn, which had been ruined in the fire Billy set several weeks ago, presumably to destroy evidence tying him to Ali's and Ian's murders. In the picture, four girls sat on the round rug in the center of the room, their heads bowed. A fifth girl stood above them, her arms in the air. The next photo was of the same scene, except the standing girl had moved a few inches to the left. In the following shot, one of the girls who had been sitting had stood up and moved toward the window. Spencer recognized the girl's dirty blond hair and rolled-up field hockey skirt. She gasped. She was looking at her younger self. These photos were from the night Ali went missing. Billy had been standing outside the barn, watching them.

And they'd never known.

Someone let out a small, dry cough behind her. Spencer whirled around. Mrs. Hastings sat at the kitchen table, staring blankly into a mug of Earl Grey tea. She was wearing a pair of gray Lululemon yoga pants with a tiny hole in the knee, dirty white socks, and an oversize Ralph Lauren polo. Her hair was stringy, and there were toast crumbs on her left cheek. Normally, Spencer's mom didn't even let the family dogs see her unless she looked absolutely pristine.

'Mom?' Spencer said tentatively, wondering if her mother had seen the Polaroids, too. Mrs. Hastings turned her head slowly, as though she were moving underwater. 'Hi, Spence,' she said tonelessly. Then she turned back to her tea, staring miserably at the bag steeping at the bottom of the cup.

Spencer bit off the tip of her French-manicured pinkie. On top of everything else, her mom was acting like a zombie ... and it was all her fault. If only she hadn't blurted out the horrible secret Billy-as-A had told her about her family: that her dad had had an affair with Ali's mother, and that Ali was Spencer's half sister. If only Billy hadn't convinced Spencer that her mom knew about the affair and killed Ali to punish her husband. Spencer had confronted her mother, only to discover that her mother hadn't known – or done – anything. After that, Mrs. Hastings kicked Spencer's dad out of the house, and then more or less gave up on life entirely.

The familiar *click-click-click* of heels on the mahogany hall floors rang through the air. Spencer's sister, Melissa, blustered into the room, surrounded by a cloud of Miss Dior. She wore a pale blue Kate Spade sweater dress and gray kitten heels, and her dark blond hair was pulled back in a gray headband. There was a silver clipboard under her arm and a Montblanc pen behind her right ear.

'Hey, Mom!' Melissa called brightly, giving her a kiss on the forehead. Then she appraised Spencer, setting her mouth in a straight line. 'Hey, Spence,' she said coolly.

Spencer slumped into the nearest chair. The benevolent, I'm-glad-you're-alive feelings she and her sister had shared the night Jenna was murdered had lasted exactly twenty-four hours. Now, things were back to status quo, with Melissa blaming Spencer for their family's ruin, snubbing Spencer every chance she got, and taking on all the home responsibilities like the prissy brownnoser she'd always been.

Melissa lifted the clipboard. 'I'm going to Fresh Fields for groceries. Want anything special?' She spoke to Mrs. Hastings in an overly loud voice, as if she were ninety years old and deaf.

'Oh, I don't know,' Mrs. Hastings said morosely. She stared into her open palms as if they contained great wisdom. 'It doesn't really matter, does it? We eat the food, and then it's gone, and then we're hungry again.' At that, she stood up, sighed loudly, and shuffled up the stairs to her bedroom.

Melissa's lip twitched. The clipboard knocked against her hip. She glanced over at Spencer, her eyes narrowing. *Look what you've done*, her expression screamed.

Spencer stared out the long line of windows that faced the backyard. Sheets of pale blue ice glistened on the back walkway. Pointed icicles hung from the singed trees. The family's old barn was a heap of black wood and ash, ruined from the fire. The windmill was still in pieces, the word *LIAR* scrawled on the base.

Tears rushed to Spencer's eyes. Whenever she looked at her backyard, she had to resist the urge to run upstairs, curl up under her bed, and shut the door. Things had been great between Spencer and her parents before she exposed the affair – for once. But Spencer now felt the same way she did when she first tasted homemade cappuccino ice cream from the Creamery in Hollis – after just one lick, she had to eat the whole cone. After a taste of what a decent, loving family was like, she couldn't go back to dysfunction and neglect.

The television continued to blare, a picture of Ali filling the screen. Melissa paused to listen for a moment as the reporter walked through the timeline of the murder.

Spencer bit down on her lip. She and Melissa hadn't discussed the fact that Ali was their half sister. Now that Spencer knew that she and Ali were related, it changed everything. For a long time, Spencer had kind of hated Ali – she'd controlled her every move, stockpiled her every secret. But none of that mattered now. Spencer just wished she could go back in time to save Ali from Billy that horrible night.

The station cut to a studio shot of pundits sitting

around a high, bistro-style table, discussing Billy's fate. 'You can't trust anyone anymore,' exclaimed an olive-skinned woman in a cherry-red power suit. 'No child is safe.'

'Now, wait a second.' A black man with a goatee waved his hands to stop them. 'Maybe we should give Mr. Ford a chance. A man is innocent until proven guilty, right?'

Melissa scooped up her black patent leather Gucci hobo bag from the island. 'I don't know why they're wasting their time discussing this,' she spat acidly. 'He deserves to rot in hell.'

Spencer gave her sister an uneasy look. That was another strange development in the Hastings household – Melissa had become unequivocally, almost fanatically confident that Billy was the murderer. Every time the news brought up an inconsistency in the case, Melissa grew enraged.

'He'll go to jail,' Spencer said reassuringly. 'Everyone knows he did it.'

'Good.' Melissa turned away, plucked the Mercedes car keys out of the ceramic bowl by the phone, buttoned the checkered Marc Jacobs jacket she'd bought at Saks the week before – apparently she wasn't too distraught over their broken home to shop – and slammed the door.

As the pundits continued to squabble, Spencer walked to the front window and watched as her sister backed out of the driveway. There was a disquieting smile on Melissa's lips that sent a shiver up Spencer's backbone.

For some reason, Melissa almost looked . . . *relieved.*

2
The Secrets Now Buried

Aria Montgomery and her boyfriend, Noel Kahn, huddled close as they walked from the Rosewood Day student parking lot to the lobby entrance. A rush of warm air greeted them as they swept inside the school, but when Aria noticed the display near the auditorium, her blood froze. On a long table across the room was a large photo of Jenna Cavanaugh.

Jenna's porcelain skin shone. Her naturally red lips revealed a hint of a smile. She wore big wraparound Gucci sunglasses that concealed her damaged eyes. *We'll miss you, Jenna*, said gold foil letters above the image. Next to it were smaller pictures, flowers, and other memorabilia and gifts. Someone had added a package of Marlboro Ultra Light cigarettes to the memorial, even though Jenna wasn't the kind of girl who would smoke.

Aria let out a small groan. She'd heard that the school might erect a shrine in Jenna's honor, but something about it seemed so ... *tacky*.

'Shit,' Noel whispered. 'We shouldn't have come in this door.'

Aria's eyes filled with tears. One minute, Jenna was alive – Aria had seen her at a party at Noel's house, laughing with Maya St. Germain. Then, practically the next minute … well, what happened next was too horrible to think about. Aria knew she should be relieved that at least Jenna's killer had been caught, Ali's murder had been solved, and the threatening notes from A had stopped, but what had happened couldn't be undone – an innocent girl was still dead.

Aria couldn't help but wonder if she and her friends could have done more to prevent Jenna's death. When Billy-as-A had been communicating with them, he'd sent Emily a photo of Jenna and Ali when they were younger. He'd then directed Emily to Jenna's house when Jenna and Jason DiLaurentis were fighting. He was obviously giving them a hint about his next victim. Jenna had also recently lingered on Aria's front lawn, looking as though she needed to tell Aria something. When Aria called out to her, Jenna had paled and quickly walked away. Did she sense Billy was going to hurt her? Should Aria have known something was wrong?

A sophomore girl placed a single red rose on the memorial. Aria closed her eyes. She didn't need any more reminders of all that Billy had done. Just that morning she'd seen a report about a set of Polaroids he'd taken of their end-of-seventh-grade sleepover. It was hard to believe Billy had been so close. As she'd chewed on her quinoa breakfast flakes, she'd parsed her memory of that night over and over, trying to recall anything more. Had she heard any strange noises on the porch or suspicious breathing at the window? Had she felt angry eyes glaring at her through the glass? But she couldn't remember a thing.

Aria leaned against the wall at the far end of the lobby. A bunch of boys on the crew team were crowded around an iPhone, laughing about an app that made a toilet-flushing noise. Sean Ackard and Kirsten Cullen were comparing answers to that day's trig assignment. Jennifer Thatcher and Jennings Silver were making out near the Jenna shrine. Jennifer's hip bumped against the table, knocking over a small photo of Jenna in a shiny gold frame.

A knot tightened in Aria's chest. She marched across the room and straightened the picture. Jennifer and Jennings broke apart, looking guilty.

'Have some respect,' Aria snapped at them anyway. Noel touched Aria's arm. 'Come on,' he said gently. 'Let's get out of here.'

He pulled her out of the lobby and around the corner. Kids were at their lockers, hanging up their coats and pulling out books. In a far corner, Shark Tones, Rosewood Day's a cappella group, was rehearsing a version of 'I Heard It Through The Grapevine' for an upcoming concert. Aria's brother, Mike, and Mason Byers were in a shoving match near the water fountains.

Aria approached her locker and spun the dial. 'It's like no one even remembers what happened,' she murmured.

'Maybe it's their way of dealing,' Noel suggested. He rested his arm on Aria's. 'Let's do something to get your mind off this.'

Aria wriggled out of the houndstooth coat that she'd bought at a thrift store in Philly and hung it on a hook in her locker. 'What do you have in mind?'

'Anything you want.'

Aria gave him a grateful hug. Noel smelled like spearmint gum and the licorice-scented tree that hung from the rearview mirror of his Cadillac Escalade.

'I wouldn't mind going to Clio tonight,' Aria suggested. Clio was a new, quaint café that had opened in downtown Rosewood. The hot chocolates were served in mugs the size of a baseball hat.

'Done,' Noel answered. But then he winced and squeezed his eyes shut. 'Wait. I can't tonight. I have my support group.'

Aria nodded. Noel had lost an older brother to suicide and now attended grief support meetings. After Aria and her old friends had seen Ali's spirit the night Spencer's woods burned down, Aria contacted a medium who told her that *Ali killed Ali*, leading Aria to briefly wonder if Ali had committed suicide, too. 'Is it helping?' she asked.

'I think so. Wait –' Noel snapped his fingers at something across the hall. 'Why don't we go to that?' He was pointing to a hot-pink poster. It had black silhouettes of dancing kids all over it, like the once-ubiquitous iPod ads. But instead of holding Nanos and Touches, they were holding small white hearts, FIND LOVE AT THE VALENTINE'S DAY DANCE THIS SATURDAY, the poster proclaimed in sparkly red letters.

'What do you say?' There was a sweetly vulnerable look on Noel's face. 'Want to go with me?'

'Oh!' Aria blurted. Truthfully, she'd wanted to go to the

Valentine's Day dance ever since Teagan Scott, a cute freshman, asked Ali in seventh grade. Aria and the others had helped Ali get ready like she was Cinderella going off to the ball. Hanna was in charge of curling Ali's hair, Emily helped Ali into her ballerina-skirt dress, and Aria had the honor of clipping the diamond pendant Mrs. DiLaurentis had let Ali borrow for the night around her neck. Afterward, Ali bragged about her beautiful wrist corsage, the awesome music the DJ played, and how the dance photographer followed her around the entire time, telling her she was the most beautiful girl in the room. *As usual.*

Aria gazed bashfully at Noel. 'Maybe that would be fun.'

'It'll definitely be fun,' Noel corrected her. 'I promise.' His piercing blue eyes softened. 'And you know, the people at the Y are starting another group for general grief. Maybe you should go.'

'Oh, I don't know,' Aria said noncommittally, moving out of the way as Gemma Curran tried to shove her violin case into the adjacent locker. 'I'm not really into the group therapy thing.'

'Just think about it,' Noel advised.

Then he leaned over, pecked Aria on the cheek, and left. Aria watched him disappear into the stairwell. Grief counseling wasn't the answer – she and her old friends had met with a grief counselor named Marion in January in an attempt to put Ali behind them, but it had only made them more obsessed.

The truth was, some niggling inconsistencies and unanswered questions about the case remained, things Aria still couldn't help thinking about. Like exactly how Billy knew so much about her and her friends – down to Spencer's family's dark secrets. Or what Jason DiLaurentis had said to Aria in the cemetery, after she accused him of being a psychiatric patient: *You've got it all wrong*. Only, *what* did Aria have wrong? Jason had obviously been an outpatient at the Radley, a mental hospital now turned classy hotel. Emily had seen his name all through the hospital's log-books.

Aria slammed her locker shut. As she started down the hall, she heard a far-off giggle – *just like* the one she'd been hearing ever since she started receiving notes from A. She looked around, her heart slamming against her rib cage. The halls were thinning out, everyone scuttling off to homeroom. No one was paying any attention to her.

With trembling hands, Aria reached into her yak-fur bag and pulled out her cell phone. She clicked on the envelope icon, but there were no new text messages. No new clues from A.

She sighed. Of course there wasn't a new note from A – Billy had been arrested. And all of A's clues had been mis-leads. The case was solved. The pieces that didn't make sense weren't worth thinking about anymore. Aria dropped her phone back into her bag and wiped the sweat from her palms on her blazer. *A is gone*, she told herself. Maybe if she repeated it enough, she'd actually begin to believe it.

Sara Shepard graduated from New York University and has an MFA from Brooklyn College. She currently lives in Tuscon, Arizona, with her husband. Sara's Pretty Little Liar novels were inspired by her upbringing in Philadelphia's Main Line.